D1562481

TANGO DOWN:
CHINA SEA

TANGO DOWN:
CHINA SEA

J. LEN SCIUTO

gatekeeper press™
Columbus, Ohio

TANGO DOWN:
China Sea

Published by **Gatekeeper Press**
2167 Stringtown Rd, Suite 109
Columbus, OH 43123-2989
www.GatekeeperPress.com

Library of Congress Control Number: 2021949824

ISBN (hardcover): 9781662922305
ISBN (paperback): 9781662922312
eISBN: 9781662922329

This book is dedicated to the men and women of the United States Navy Submarine Force, past, present, and future, and the sacrifices they and their families make to preserve world peace and defend and protect the American way of life.

It is also dedicated to the crews of the USS Bang (SS-385) from 1943 until 1973, when she was officially decommissioned and removed from active service.

I also wish to acknowledge and thank a group of family and friends who supported me in the writing of this book. Special thanks go to my friend and fellow shipmate, Harry Ross, a submarine qualified sonar technician, who provided me with advice and whose knowledge and experiences provided me with advice and support, which were integral in this book's creation.

Contents

The Cyberterrorist   5

Under Attack   9

Staying Alive   13

Coming Aboard   17

Getting Acquainted   23

The Navigation Team   31

One Addition   37

Meet, Greet, and Under Way   41

The Maneuvering Watch   47

Silent Running and Routine   51

Counseling and Kudos   57

The Warrants   65

The Cable Layer   69

The Diversion   71

Entering the China Sea   77

Carte Blanche   83

Hide and Go Seek   85

Leaving, Finding, and Hiding   93

A Tale of Woe   101

Aloha Tarpon   111

Being Cheated   115

The Reactor Officer   119

Fatal Interdiction	125	The Briefing	199
Foul Play	127	DC Bound	205
Sonar Contact	131	Accountability	219
The Wolves' Blockade	135	Supportive Evidence	223
Failure to Report	139	Requiring Substantiation	243
Run and Hide	143	Volunteering?	249
Deja Vu All Over Again	149	Mix and Match	251
How Deep Can We Go?	155	Truth Seeking	257
Listening In	161	Admiral's Briefing	265
Surrender: No Way	165	Confrontation	271
The Secret Weapon	169	Cards on the Table	279
Seek and Destroy	173	A Special Request	283
Condition Red	181	Truth or Consequences	287
Two for None	185	Reckoning Day	297
International Waters	193	Diplomatic Changes	303
Pearl Harbor	199	Policy and Security	307
The Reminiscent Letter	203	China Sea Again	311

The Cyberterrorist

Supercomputing Center of the China Academy of Sciences (SCCAS), Urumqi, China, early 2019

Zhang Wei finally and successfully cloned a random contractor's access to the US military's research weapons computer system. Unfortunately, it would only be valid for twenty-four hours. Sitting at his desk, he watched his computer screen as the letters, numbers, and symbols moved across the illuminated empty cipher box. The monotony of watching the light gray computer screen was annoying him, as it always did when nothing was happening. Shaking his head, he grabbed his hat and coat, and went outside to smoke a cigarette.

The unusually harsh and cold winter storm obscured his vision. Pulling the fur-lined flaps over his ears and lighting his cigarette, he cursed the bleak weather. The cigarette tasted good in the cold night air. After wiping away the continuing snowfall, he looked at the computer screen through the window. Suddenly, the screen blinked and turned from gray to white as two of the empty boxes of the cipher filled with a letter and a symbol. He crushed out the cigarette and quickly went back to his desk.

As he realized he was close to getting the secure password that opened the US military's classified weapons computer system, Zhang felt excited about future possibilities. He thought about a promotion and better wages as the computer continued searching for the remnant code characters. The digital clock on the wall read 2:30 a.m. He wrote an entry in his logbook identifying the beginning of his breaking of the US code. When the final code character completed the cipher, he documented it and notified his supervisor.

Sitting at Zhang's desk, Boqin Da viewed the screen. "Eagle Talons" was the only project that interested him. He highlighted the file and copied it to Zhang's computer. Patting Zhang on the back, he praised him for his hard work in hacking into the US system and getting the code. Boqin told Zhang that he was finished for the shift and suggested he take the rest of the night off and go home. Zhang bowed and thanked Boqin for allowing him to leave early.

Boqin phoned the director of the SCCAS and informed him that they now had the code and the file they were seeking. The director mentioned that Zhang was no longer useful with the clandestine job requirements being complete. They both agreed that Zhang was now a loose end of the project.

Boqin, now in the lounge, asked to talk to Cheng Fa in private. Cheng, who was playing Mahjong, excused himself. Both men walked to a quiet corner of the room. No words were spoken. Boqin, showing no emotion and looking into Cheng's eyes, put his hand on his holstered pistol. Cheng bowed.

An all-wheel-drive vehicle waited for Zhang at the front door. His friend, Cheng Fa, offered to drive him rather than have him wait for the shuttle. Zhang, smiling, thanked him and got in the vehicle. The two spoke of casual things as they drove through the Tian Shan mountains towards the city. Cheng stopped the car, telling Zhang that he heard an unusual noise coming from the engine. Both men examined the running engine after opening the engine compartment hood. Cheng, per Boqin's silent instructions, shot Zhang in the head. With a surprised look on his face, Zhang fell backwards and over the road embankment into the snow-covered abyss below.

The Chinese research and development of the newly acquired US Navy research project began in earnest and continued operating twenty-four-seven until a working prototype was produced and operational. The Chinese SCCAS planned, developed, and created a weapon that was still imaginary and experimental on the US drawing board. After successful testing, the weapon was installed on some of China's military arsenal. The US had no idea that their weapon came to fruition in Chinese hands.

Under Attack

"Captain, Sonar reports a group of Chinese warships fast approaching us from our stern. There are three destroyers, two subs, and a submersible that is unidentifiable. I don't know what it is."

At the same time, the destroyers' active sonar started searching for the SSN (nuclear submarine) Tarpon. Their speed increased, closing the distance. They detected and locked onto her.

Tarpon's sonar operator announced to Captain Duggan, "Depth charges in the water from the destroyers and there are two torpedoes from a submarine."

Duggan immediately ordered a change in course, depth, and speed, and had torpedo countermeasures released into the Tarpon's wake. He then turned to his executive officer (XO), Al Cadenhead, and said, "While we still have our floating radio wire antenna on the surface, get a message off to COMSUBPAC (Commander Submarines Forces, Pacific) that we are under attack from Chinese forces in the South China Sea. We have the sonar recordings on that new Chinese nuclear aircraft carrier. Add our latitude and longitude position as well. Sign it 'Duggan.'"

Cadenhead responded, "Roger that, Captain."

A couple of minutes later, the radio operator reported to the control room that the message was not sent due to the antenna being totally submerged.

The crew immediately went to their battle stations when they heard the general alarm. All hell was breaking loose. The boat pitched and rolled from the attack.

The depth charge second run was much closer. As the charges exploded near the boat, her pitching and rolling was more exaggerated, and she had a list to the starboard side of some twenty degrees. She returned to an upright position and on an even keel while managing to turn away from the onslaught. Fear replaced anger on the face of every man and woman as they quietly performed their duties. Reports of leaks, damage, and injuries came in from almost all compartments throughout the boat.

The Tarpon's sonar operator reported the sound of the counter-measures neutralizing the torpedoes. At the same time, the destroyers commenced another depth charge run. Sweat was added to the fear and anger on Duggan's face as he ordered a reverse in course and a change in depth. He thought, "I must find a way to get away from these attacks. But how?"

Simultaneously, the sonar operator could not identify a new low-pitch hum in the water. Then, there was a "pop." "Captain, it has to be a weapon of some sort. The computer doesn't know what it is and iden-tified it as an earth tremor. I don't know what it is either. That sound is brand new."

Another alarm sounded signifying there was a flooding casual-ty happening somewhere inside the boat. The on-watch reactor room operator announced water coming into the room through a breach in the hull and that the breach was getting larger. There was also a very loud hum as it increased in size. The room was vacated and sealed off as Duggan immediately ordered the emergency blow of all the ballast tanks as well as the negative and safety tanks, and the auxiliary tanks.

The destroyers' operators, hearing the escaping air from Tarpon, backed away from her and ceased the depth charging.

Cadenhead immediately ran aft to the reactor room and looked through the sight glass on the watertight door. The Tarpon hung momentarily and then experienced a downward angle by the stern. That angle continued to increase. He noticed that the reactor was still operating as the boat began losing its buoyancy. The angle momentarily helped keep the in-rushing sea away from the watertight door. Once inside, Cadenhead resealed and locked the door to prevent anyone else from entering. The downward angle on the boat was now fifty-four degrees and increasing as he waded over to the reactor control panel on the other side of the room.

The phone in the reactor room rang. It was Lieutenant Commander Kim Ziegler, the boat's lead reactor officer, standing outside the reactor room watertight door.

Ziegler yelled into the phone, "Let me in."

The XO shook his head no, replying, "I'm scramming the reactor, but I need your help."

The reactor officer shouted in the phone as the noise was now ear shattering, "No, don't do it. That's my job!"

Cadenhead yelled into the phone, "Tell me how. That's an order."

Moments later, he gave Ziegler a thumbs-up, indicating he was successful in following the reactor officer's instructions and shut down the reactor. The boat took a steeper angle with water rushing in at a much higher rate. Cadenhead disappeared as the water level rose above the sight glass in the watertight door.

Ziegler couldn't believe his eyes as the entire stern, aft of the reactor space, literally fell away from the rest of the boat. The view was nothing but air bubbles mixed with sea water and loose debris. As the stern dropped from sight, it took the lifeless body of the XO with it.

The flooding could not be stopped as the Tarpon, no longer able to control her depth, continued her descent, stern first, towards the bottom of the China Sea.

Staying Alive

No one moved as the Tarpon continued her slow downward death spiral towards the China Sea bottom. The inclinometer showed a downward stern angle of more than eighty degrees. The crew in the control room was silent, but the screaming and yelling continued throughout what was left of the boat. Many of the compartments were flooded.

Captain Duggan turned to the chief of the boat (COB) and ordered, "Pass the word across our 1MC (public address) system to be silent. Tell them to pray instead."

The COB made the sign of the cross on himself after he finished passing the captain's orders.

Duggan and all the crew in the room had their eyes glued to the depth gauge as it continued to click away and rotate into an ever-increasing number. Some were praying in silence while others, holding on to where they were, wiped the tears from their eyes. They all continued to try and clear their ears as the high-pressure air filled the remnant compartments of the boat to delay the eventual implosion.

Suddenly, at seven hundred feet, the Tarpon struck an unknown submerged object. The spiraling of the boat stopped. There was a very loud scraping noise as the boat slowly continued moving downward. Her stern struck another unknown object, and the boat became momentarily motionless. All the remaining crew, including Captain Duggan, stared at the depth gauge in utter disbelief.

Duggan immediately ordered, "Secure the air blow. Give me a reading on all air banks."

The COB acknowledged it and began taking the readings. At the same time, regular lighting throughout the boat shut down and the emergency lighting came on.

Duggan announced over the 1MC system, "Now hear this. All compartments report in with damage assessments. Also report the number of alive and injured personnel. Minimize your movements to prevent excessive breathing. That is all."

The incoming reports and information painted a bleak picture. The senior and only other officer in the control room besides Duggan was Ziegler. The total number of survivors from a crew of one hundred forty now totaled twenty-six.

Duggan turned to Ziegler and asked, "Where's Cadenhead? Where's the XO?"

With a quivering voice and tears in his eyes, Ziegler replied, "Dead, sir. He took my place in the reactor room. I am not sure how long we can last on our current air banks, but maybe just long enough until help arrives to get us out of here. We have enough food and water to last longer than the air. We'll need to ration both to remain alive as long as possible, sir."

The captain nodded and said nothing. He then patted Ziegler on the shoulder saying, "Thanks, Ziggy."

All was calm and quiet for almost an hour. Then it happened.

The boat started to slowly rotate to the right and stopped at forty-five degrees. Then the sliding down sideways began. The sliding stopped at seven hundred fifty feet. The boat, almost horizontal, had a final incline to the right of about twenty degrees.

After all the crying, yelling, and screaming stopped, Duggan asked for quiet and asked for another damage report. Nothing changed except the boat's angular position and depth.

Ziegler walked over to the captain, "What do you think, sir?"

Duggan answered him with a slight smile, "Providence may be interceding for us. We are now at seven hundred fifty feet. The bottom is well below us. I think we're sitting on a shelf or ledge. If we don't have any more events, there's a good chance someone will find us. Put someone on the UQC (underwater telephone) around the clock and start broadcasting our SOS only in our special frequency band."

With nothing changing and time slowly passing, the survivors began to show and feel an increase in fear, anxiety, tension, depression, and a sense of being forgotten and abandoned.

Coming Aboard

After paying the cab driver, Lieutenant Commander Rico Petrone dropped his bag and stood staring at the long black shape tied up on the north side of the pier. With his headquarters tour cut short, he was finally returning to submarines after serving as an admiral's aide in Washington, DC, for two years. Her long, smooth, and sleek round hull could not be seen beneath the water surface, but that did not matter, as her sail was a beautiful sight to Rico. Displaying an ear-to-ear grin, he stared at her with both excitement and apprehension about being assigned to this latest, high-tech submarine. He thought to himself, "I'm back where I belong."

SSN Cardinalfish was the first in a new class of hunter-killer submarines commissioned and placed into service at Pearl Harbor. The entire boat was a dull black. Only three items were visible on her sail: her hull numbers, the boat's commissioning pennant, and the stars and bars of the American flag that fluttered in the soft Hawaiian breeze.

Several trucks lined up on the pier next to the Cardinalfish. Many of the crew loaded groceries and supplies aboard while the weapons gang loaded torpedoes and Harpoon and Tomahawk missiles at another hatch. Something serious was up, as all the missiles and torpedoes were not the exercise type, but war shots. A civilian shipyard worker painted over the hull numbers on the port side of the sail and was preparing to paint over them on the starboard side.

His stomach tightened as he intently watched for a minute. He wondered if all this activity had anything to do with what he was investigating while temporarily assigned to Admiral Bennett's US Fleet Cyber Command at Fort Mead outside Washington, DC. Someone hacked into the US military experimental weapons computer system earlier in the year. Could it be the reason why he was suddenly assigned to this newest and latest high-tech submarine?

Right after Easter Sunday, a surveillance satellite, orbiting at three hundred ten miles above the earth, made multiple passes over China's SCCAS and detected unusual streams of intense solid green light emanating about a mile long. It was also later seen on the China Sea. What was its purpose? Might this be a new type of weapon and how did this kind of advanced technology suddenly develop in China, when they were well behind the US? Was this the reason the Cardinalfish was loading war shots? There were way too many questions and some of those he had to keep to himself.

Somewhere, something was amiss that required a Navy submarine. Releasing a deep breath and straightening his cap, he picked up his bag and walked down to the boat.

A topside watch wearing undress whites stood at parade rest at the ship side end of the gangway. Seeing that he was an officer, he came to attention and saluted, saying, "Good afternoon, sir."

Rico returned the salute and replied, "Good afternoon. Lieutenant Commander Petrone requests permission to come aboard."

The topside watch, completing his salute, answered, "Permission granted, sir. Come aboard."

Once aboard, Rico reached into a side pocket of the duffle bag and gave the watch a copy of his orders. The sailor said after reading the orders, "One moment please, sir. I need to notify the officer of the day (OOD) that you are here."

Noticing the two chevrons below a helm (ship's wheel) emblem on the man's left sleeve, Rico knew that this young man would be one of the quartermasters working for him in the navigation department.

A lieutenant came through the sail door and held out his hand. "Sir, my name is Lieutenant Watson. I am the weapons officer aboard the Cardinalfish. Please call me Burt, if you like, sir."

Shaking hands, Rico replied, "Call me Rico and I'm glad to be here. It took me two years to get another boat assignment, so when I say I'm glad to be here and not behind a desk, I really mean it."

Rico inquired, "What's up? You're loading war shots, the hull numbers are painted out, and you're taking on a lot of food and supplies."

Watson answered, "Sir, I am not at liberty to say since I don't know you and the security officer has not verified the level of your security clearance. You can ask the operations officer and he might tell you once you have checked aboard. The skipper and the XO are not aboard right now, but the ops boss is." Changing the subject, he asked, "I hope your trip from Washington, DC, was uneventful?"

Rico tilted his cap back a little and said, "The trip was long and tiresome. It took me two days to get here with little or no sleep."

Both men entered the sail and climbed down the two levels of ladders into the control room. Several men worked on the ship's gear while a couple of others conducted training for a few of the newer crew members.

As they entered "officer's country," Watson pointed to a closed door and said, "Sir, you share a room with the ops boss. His name is Lieutenant Commander Mike Samuels." Watson knocked on the door. There was no response.

Rico, entering the cabin, replied, "Thanks Burt. When you see Mr. Samuels, please tell him I'm aboard and will head to the Officer's Wardroom after I put my things away." Watson nodded and disappeared through the watertight door into the control room.

The quarters were smaller than Rico expected. It had a pair of beds plus two small closets, a sink, and a small desk with a chair. The upper bunk was not made up so it was clear that it would be Rico's while he was aboard the Cardinalfish.

Rico did not have to wait long to meet Samuels, as he soon knocked on the door and stepped into the cabin. "Hi. I'm Mike Samuels and welcome aboard." He held out his hand. "Where you from? Are you married? You have kids? When did you go to nuke school?"

Rico, while shaking hands, replied, "Wait a minute, will you? I can only answer one question at a time. I am originally from Florida. Yes, I'm married. We have two kids. I attended sub and nuclear school in 2010. The Seawolf class submarine was the model taught. I was on two other boats before this one, and I proudly wear gold dolphins on my chest. Did I answer all of them?"

Samuels laughed. "When you're done here, go through the after hatch and down one ladder. That is the Officer's Mess and Wardroom area. I will meet you there. Please bring your security folder, your service record, plus your orders assigning you to this boat."

Rico nodded and replied, "Will do. By the way, you have a lot of activity going on. What's up?"

Samuels looked at Rico and replied, "As soon as we verify your security clearance, I or the captain will brief you. I'll see you in a bit, down below in the wardroom."

Samuels left the cabin and disappeared down the ladder at the end of the passageway.

Rico changed into a set of khakis after putting everything away. He found an open area in the overhead above his bunk and taped a picture of his wife and two sons. Staring at it for a few moments, he released a deep sigh. Looking at the picture, he silently said, "Well, sweetheart, I'm aboard and I hope this tour will be a good one and the officers and crew are good as well."

Rico closed the cabin door and went through the after hatch and down one ladder. He found Mike Samuels sitting at the table with a cup of coffee.

Samuels looked up and asked, "How about a cup of coffee?"

Handing Samuels his service record, security folder, and his orders, Rico replied, "Sure, I need one."

Samuels became serious as he read through Rico's service record. When he was finished reading, he looked at Rico and said, "Wow, your record is impressive! I think you are a good fit as our navigator. Both the skipper and the XO are academy grads, but they are not your typical academy ring knockers. They are both well-liked and good guys. Everybody on board, whether academy, Officer Candidate School (OCS), or enlisted, gets a fair shake."

Rico replied, "I already know that. I did some checking before I left DC."

Samuels responded, "So, I guess, then, that you checked me out as well?"

Rico quickly answered, "You bet I did. I checked out the whole wardroom."

Both men stared at each other for a moment and then laughed.

Then Samuels was serious again. "Rico, you are replacing Al Cadenhead, who was a really good navigator. He was transferred to the Tarpon as the XO when he was selected for commander. That boat is homeported in San Diego."

Samuels continued, "Allow me to tell you about the navigation department personnel. The quartermaster gang leader is a senior chief. He knows his stuff, works hard, and is on the ball. There are four junior petty officers under him, and they are all well-trained. Only three of them are qualified in submarines and wear silver dolphins on this boat. The fourth is like you and must requalify on this boat and learn all her systems. You know the routine. Finally, if something is wrong or is unusual, they will not hesitate to notify you and back you to the hilt."

Rico, with a reflective look on his face, said, "Well, that's great. Only three of them are qualified on this boat. We will work on that. I was expecting and hoping for a good group of men. Do you have any idea when we drop the mooring lines and pull out of here?"

Samuels answered, "You and your gang will get the mission specifics after you get the briefing on what has caused us to move up our patrol schedule and change our geographic operations area. We were not supposed to get under way until next Saturday, which would have given you almost a week to get familiar with the boat. But now, we are getting under way as soon as we secure loading everything and take on a specialized crew member. We have a boat that has not been heard from in a while. I am sure the captain will brief you when he meets you. Oh, by the way, your gang is not only men. You have a woman quartermaster in your gang."

Rico smiled and answered, "That's cool."

Getting Acquainted

Rico returned to his cabin after Samuels was finished showing him around. He sat down at the desk and thought about what he had seen throughout the boat. She was big, beautiful, powerful, and awesome! It would take a considerable amount of time to learn and remember all the ship's systems that were new on this class of submarine. The extra compartment added on amidships was amazing! What kind of special missions would this big and bold beauty be carrying out?

He turned his focus to writing a letter to his family back home:

Dearest Sharon and boys,

Hi. Hope all is well with you at home. I miss you all already, and it's been only a couple of days. Thinking ahead a little bit, I hope the movers show up on time and the Housing Office here helps you get to our new quarters without any trouble or delay when school is out for the summer.

I am aboard the Cardinalfish, and she is beautiful! She is everything that I can imagine in a submarine. Today, I met some of the officers and crew walking through the boat. My first impression is that this crew is an exceptional one. The best of the best are here, and I am proud and glad to be a part of it. My navigation team are true professionals without issues. I am glad for that, if true.

Mike Samuels, the head of operations, told me that most families really like their quarters here. There are lots of things for the kids to do so they don't ever get bored. He also tells me that the Wives' Club is good and quite active helping and supporting all the families here.

Sally, Mike's wife, will help you and the boys get acclimated to being in Hawaii. She will show you around Pearl Harbor and all its facilities. Sam says you'll have no problems picking out your favorite restaurant here as there are many to choose from. I hear their cash registers ringing already!

I will try to write as often as I can. I have a lot to learn here. We are going out on patrol soon so you may not get a letter until we hit a liberty port if that is in our patrol plan.

I love you all. Boys, please give Mommy a big hug and kiss for me. Sharon, know that you are always in my mind and heart. I hope to see you soon (when we get back).

Fondest regards to your family and mine. God bless you all.

All my love always,

Rico

Rico kicked off his shoes, climbed up into his bunk, and looked at the picture of his wife and sons. Tired from the long trip, he fell asleep thinking of his family, and all the things that had to be done before the Cardinalfish got under way.

Suddenly, hearing running water, he jumped out of bed and looked around. Samuels was at the sink washing his face.

Looking in the mirror, he saw Rico leap out of his bed. He turned around facing him, "Good morning. You sleep, okay?"

Rico replied, "Yeah, I'm okay, but too many new noises."

Samuels laughed, "I know what you mean. It's the same for me when I go to a new boat. The noises are never the same. Hey, it's Sunday morning and we have time to go to church. Do you go to church? Would you care to go with me? What denomination are you?"

"Hey! There you go again, asking multiple questions before waiting for an answer."

Samuels looked down at the floor. "Yeah, I know. It's a bad habit I have. I need to work on it."

Rico looked at his watch and, seeing it was only 0630 (6.30 a.m.), asked, "Is the captain aboard yet?"

Samuels answered, "Yes. I told him you were asleep, and he told me not to awake you. We aren't shoving off yet as we are waiting for a special crew member to report aboard. He's coming in around mid-morning. The skipper may brief both of you at the same time, or he may not."

"Okay, that's fine. By the way, I'm Catholic," replied Rico.

"Great! I'm going to the eight o'clock Mass after a cup of coffee. Care to come along with me?"

Rico replied, "Sure, just give me thirty minutes and I'll meet you in the wardroom."

Rico appeared in the officer's mess twenty-eight minutes later where Samuels was eating an English muffin and having his coffee. He walked over to the coffee pot, poured a cup, and grabbed a cheese Danish.

He sat down across from Samuels and asked, "Are we walking to the church from here?"

Samuels responded, "Why don't we go in my car, so we don't get all sweated up?"

Rico nodded and smiled as he took a bite out of the Danish.

The interior of the church was beautiful with its stained-glass windows and marble floor. The interior was more Hawaiian than traditional. The two men sat five rows back from the altar. The priest, walking towards the altar, stopped when he saw Samuels and Rico.

He held out his hand to Rico and said, "I think Mike has brought us another practicing Catholic. I'm Father Miles Barrett. I'm the chaplain and priest here at Pearl Harbor. Welcome to our church."

Rico, shaking hands, replied, "Thank you, Father. I and my family are practicing Catholics. If you require a registration form, I'll fill it out after Mass. My two boys are experienced altar servers, and my wife regularly sings in the choir. Can you use them?"

Father Barrett responded, "My prayers are answered! I'm going to have experienced altar servers for a wonderful change. I'll look forward to meeting them and listening to your wife sing at Mass."

Rico asked, "Are you the same Father Barrett that was the chaplain for twenty-four years with the Marines?"

Father Barrett smiled, "I am the very same. Before you ask me, I signed a contract to be here for the very same reason I think you are here."

Rico, with an inquisitive look, asked, "Father, what do you mean by that?"

Father Barrett answered, "To be where I am needed and to be where life is not so boring."

Rico, now smiling, just nodded.

Father Barrett sat in the pew and faced the two men. "By the way, I hear the Cardinalfish is getting under way early. That's too bad for their families. May God go with you and the rest of your crew."

Surprised, Samuels asked, "How did you know that father? Do you also know where we are going?"

Father Barrett made the sign of the cross and answered, "There isn't too much that gets past me being a chaplain. No, I do not know your destination or mission. But it becomes obvious that you are leaving early when one sees all the trucks on the pier and food plus weapons being loaded on board."

Both men looked at each other and said nothing.

After Mass, the two men returned to the Cardinalfish and entered the control room. They found Watson going through the latest messages on the message board. He looked at Rico and Samuels and said, "The entire crew was recalled, and the CO and XO are now aboard as well."

Mike accepted the message board from Watson and read several of the messages. After reading them, he gave the message board to Rico to read.

After reading the messages, Rico turned towards Watson and asked, "Where is my team right now?"

Watson answered, "All of them are waiting for you in Navigation. The captain would like to see you first in his quarters before you go and meet them. I believe the XO will be there as well."

Rico nodded and climbed the ladder up to the next level and then aft into officer's country. He stopped in front of the captain's quarters and knocked on the door. He entered the cabin after hearing, "Come in."

Both the CO and the XO stood up. "I'm Captain Eric Williams and this is Commander Billy Doyle. Welcome aboard, Mr. Petrone."

Rico replied while shaking hands with both men, "Thank you, sirs. I am glad to be aboard."

All three men sat down, and the captain began speaking. "May I call you Rico?"

Rico smiled and replied, "Yes, sir, please do."

The expression on the captain's face changed from a smile to a more serious expression. He let out a sigh and said, "This is a hell of a way to get acquainted, but we received advanced orders ahead of our normal scheduled departure time. I assume you have read the message board. We have a boat overdue reporting in and COMSUBPAC has us going to find out what is going on with her. After reading your record, I know you have been on two other boats that were hunter killers. Have any of those patrols taken you to the China Sea?"

Rico responded, "Yes, sir. I had one patrol in that area."

"That's good, particularly good. I am meeting and talking to you ahead of our special passenger because you need to get us ready to depart as soon as he arrives. We're going into the Devil's backyard!"

The captain turned to the XO and asked, "Do you have anything you want to add, Billy?"

Doyle nodded and said, "Rico, we didn't plan this kind of reception for you. We expected to give you some time to become familiar with the navigation gang and the boat while heading to our patrol area at normal speed. But now you'll have to hit the deck with your running shoes on. If you need anything or have something that doesn't look or feel right, do not hesitate to call or come and see me. Of course, you'll have to requalify your gold dolphins here as she is totally new and unfamiliar to you. So, I expect that when you are not on duty, sleeping, or working with the NAV gang, you'll work on requalifying on this boat. It's critical for you to be fully knowledgeable on all systems on this boat." The XO handed Rico his requalification book for the systems on the Cardinalfish.

Rico, taking the book, replied, "Yes, sir. I am prepared to do whatever it takes to be qualified on this boat and to assume any additional duties that are needed or required."

Doyle smiled and said, "I know you will. Otherwise, you would not have been sent to us." He held out his hand and again shook hands with Rico. "Welcome aboard, mister. Now, get this boat ready for sea and her patrol."

After leaving the captain's cabin, Rico found Samuels in the control room. He asked, "Ops, is there anything else I need to know before I go to the NAV space?"

Samuels nodded and replied, "Yeah, we now know the name of the boat. It's the Tarpon. As I said earlier, our last navigator is on board her as the XO. Her patrol area is a hot spot in the China Sea. Now we get to go in and either get her out or find out if she has been crippled or destroyed. Let's hope that boat is okay, and the crew is still alive and well."

Rico asked, "What was her mission?"

Samuels answered, "Their mission was to get sonar signature recordings on that new Chinese nuclear aircraft carrier. The Japanese made a couple of passes over her and filmed her. Plus, we have satellite films of her as well. She is one big monster! She carries about one hundred twenty planes and helicopters. If accurate, that's thirty more than our biggest carrier. She has a bigger crew by two thousand. Try to imagine going up against that kind of fire power in an open armed confrontation."

Rico, smiling, said, "Her size just makes her a bigger target for the good guys regardless of the size and number of her destroyer and submarine screens. You know their technology is behind ours. So, any confrontation gives us a slight edge."

Samuels answered, "Let's hope we never have to find out."

The Navigation Team

Rico stepped through the forward control room hatch and into Navigation. A senior chief quartermaster and three men and a woman were waiting for him. They stood up when he entered.

Rico smiled and held out his hand. "Hi, I'm Mr. Petrone and I'm your new navigator."

The senior chief shook hands with Rico and replied, "I'm Michael O'Hara. This is Quartermaster First Class Robbie Reynolds, Second Class Quartermasters Tom Taylor and Gary Crown, and this is Third Class Quartermaster Barbara Mahoney."

Rico shook hands with all of them and said, "I'm glad to meet all of you. I have heard good things about you, and I am pleased to be working with all of you. Please take your seats."

Reynolds asked, "What's going on sir? Why were we all called back to the boat early?"

"Team, we are going out early because one of our boats failed to check in and we have been ordered to go and find out what's going on with her. Her designated patrol area was the China Sea."

Mahoney asked, "Which boat is it?

When Rico told them it was the Tarpon, all of them took a long look at each other but remained silent. Mahoney put her hand over her mouth as tears welled up in her eyes.

Rico paused a moment, and then began speaking. "We don't know Tarpon's status. I know your last navigator was transferred to that boat and became the XO. I also know that, while he was here, you were a close, tight-knit group. Let's all hope the boat is safe, and the crew is alive. Before we get started preparing for this patrol, I would like to know a little about each of you. Senior Chief, you're first."

"Senior Chief Mike O'Hara. Seventeen years in the Navy and most of it is sub time. I'm a plank owner here and was aboard this boat when it was commissioned. I'm married, and we have two daughters. Their names are Foamy and Neglect!"

Rico tried not to laugh but he couldn't hold it in. Once he was composed again, he replied, "Excuse me, Senior Chief, but I don't think that those names are actually the names of your daughters." He asked O'Hara again, "The names please, Senior Chief?"

O'Hara, cleared his throat and answered, "Our oldest daughter is named Maureen, after the actress, and the youngest is named Scarlet."

With a straight face, Rico replied, "That's genuinely nice, Senior Chief. Do you live at Tara Plantation or is your place "Gone with the Wind?"

Everyone laughed except for O'Hara. After a moment, he sheepishly smiled.

Rico turned his attention to Reynolds. "Okay, Reynolds, your turn."

Reynolds responded, "Sir, please call me Robbie. But the crew knows me as Robbie the Robot. As you can see, I am not a small man. I am six-feet-five inches tall and weigh in at two hundred fifty pounds.

You will notice that I am not overweight. Because of my size, I get most of the heavy-duty stuff aboard this boat. I have twelve years in the Navy and all of it, like Mike, has been mostly aboard subs. I made chief on the servicewide written exam and am waiting to put on my chief's hat in a couple of months."

"That's great, Robbie. I can't wait to help you wet down that chief's hat. Are you married?"

Reynolds answered, "Yes, sir, to the Navy."

Rico pointed to Taylor.

"Tom Taylor, from Dallas, Texas. I'm engaged to be married when this boat has some extended homeport time. I've been to all the navigational and electrical navigation support schools including A, C, and advanced schools. Been in the Navy nine years. Gary and I went through all of those schools together."

"That's great," said Rico, now pointing to Crown.

"Gary Crown, sir. You know my background thanks to Robbie the Robot. I'm from California and when I am not aboard the Cardinalfish, I'm at the beach doing my thing: surfing. I'm not married but I have a girlfriend who lives with me. She's a nurse at the base hospital."

Rico looked at Petty Officer Mahoney and said, "I apologize, Mahoney. It should have been ladies first."

Mahoney replied, "It's okay, sir. Around here, I'm just one of the guys."

Both Taylor and Crown laughed. Crown said, "Don't shoot pool with her. She'll clean your pockets!"

Rico laughed and responded, "That's okay, guys. You don't want to play Texas Hold'em with me. Your background, please, Mahoney?"

Mahoney's face was as red as her hair, which was cut in a page boy style haircut. "Sir, I've attended Quartermaster A and C schools. Been in the Navy four years of a six-year tour. I am considering reenlisting for six more. I chose submarines because I didn't like doing all of those push-ups the Marines have to do or run all day long like a wounded gazelle being chased by a lion. I am not married, and I like to ride dirt motorcycles in competition."

Rico, walking to the navigation table, said, "Well, you won't be riding bikes for a while, but I am glad to have all of you in this department. Okay, team, we must prepare for this trip. We'll need to lay out the dead reckoning tracks and go through all the Notice to Mariners to ensure our computer and paper charts are all up to date. We'll also need to go through the chart portfolio that has the bottom contour charts for the China Sea included in it and select and correct the appropriate charts."

O'Hara smirked and cleared his throat. "Sir, when we returned to the boat, you were attending Mass this morning. While you were gone, I laid out the dead reckoning tracks on the China Sea charts and went through the Notice to Mariners for them as well. We are good to go except we need to know if we are sailing the great circle northern or the southern route. Once we know that, we can bring out the correct bottom contour charts and make corrections. We'll update the tides and currents as we prepare to sail through each of the designated patrol areas."

Rico replied, "I'll read the operations orders and ask the captain or the XO which route to take. Additionally, I'd like you to check out all the electrical navigation equipment. I want to be sure we don't have any equipment issues. Check with the navigational electronics technicians and have them report the operating status. Make sure the non-operating equipment is tagged out and ask when it will return to full operational condition. Okay?"

O'Hara replied, "Aye, aye, sir. Is there anything else you need?"

Rico answered, "Yes, there is. How did you know we were going to the China Sea?"

O'Hara responded, "Sir, Mr. Watson mentioned China Sea when he called me back to the boat."

Rico replied, "Very well. Can one of you get me a copy of the Watch, Quarter, and Station Bill? I want to see what all of your assignments are for different evolutions and casualties."

O'Hara turned to Mahoney and ordered, "Get him a copy, Red."

Mahoney, going to the control room replied, "I am on it for every evolution you can think of."

O'Hara, not laughing, raised his voice a little, "Come on, Mahoney, go get it."

Rico held up his hand as if to say "enough." Speaking softly, he said, "Okay, here's how things are going to work around here. You all can rag on each other when I or anyone else wearing shoulder boards isn't in here. But when I or they are in here with you, I want complete attention on what we are working on with no fooling around. Your last navigator probably worked the same way as I do. Okay?"

The entire navigational team responded, "Yes, sir. Aye, aye, sir."

One Addition

Rico left Navigation and headed for the control room via his cabin. When he got to his cabin, he was surprised to see an Asian man speaking to Samuels.

He walked in and asked, "Is everything alright, Mike?"

Samuels, standing up, replied, "Come on in, Rico. There's someone I'd like you to meet."

The man stood up as Rico entered the cabin. The man was much taller than Rico expected. He was clean-shaven and had a flattop haircut. He looked quite young, but his temples were slightly gray.

Smiling, the man held out his hand and said, "Hi, I'm Lei Wang Joe Skiboski. It's a pleasure to meet you. We are going to be shipmates for this patrol."

With a puzzled look on his face, Rico looked at Samuels and, while shaking hands, said, "Lei Wang Joe who?"

Both Samuels and Skiboski broke out laughing. Samuels sat on his bunk and Lei Wang sat at the desk leaving no place for Rico to sit, so he remained standing.

Samuels started the conversation. "Rico, you can call him Lei Wang Joe, or just Lee. That's what we call him. He's from the Naval War College in Newport. You may have seen him there when you were giving your presentation on the use of petroleum products as offensive and defensive weapons. He teaches Chinese military organization there. He speaks fluent Chinese and is a terrorism specialist."

Lee, still smiling, responded, "Rico, I not only teach Chinese military organization, but I also teach Chinese military intelligence and counterintelligence. I am also a graduate of the Naval Academy in Annapolis. I entered the civil service arena after my obligation to the US Navy was over. I will be the Cardinalfish's evaluator, analyzer, and interpreter for this trip. To remove any questions, my Polish father met my mother in China when we were on friendlier terms with that country. The 'Lei Wang' is from my mother's side of the family and the 'Joe Skiboski' is my father's name. Does that clear things up for you, Rico?"

Rico was now laughing. "I'm not laughing at you, Lee. I'm laughing because I thought I had one heck of a handle, but you have me beat by a mile!"

Lee asked, "What is your full name, Rico?"

Closing the cabin door, Rico replied, "Do both of you promise to keep it quiet and not tell anyone else?"

Both men agreed, holding up three fingers and saying, "Scout's honor."

Rico sighed and in a low voice said, "My full name is Enrico Pasquale Giuseppe Petrone."

Both men started laughing. Rico laughed as well.

The door suddenly opened and the XO entered the room saying, "Enrico Pasquale Giuseppe who?"

Now, everybody was laughing. Samuels stood up and said, "We're breaking this up for another time and place. XO, the operations department is ready for sea."

Rico followed by saying, "Sir, the navigation department will be ready for sea as soon as we determine the sailing route and read the op orders. Which route do you want to travel, the northern or the southern route to our patrol area? Also, may I read the op orders?"

The XO passed the message folder he was holding to Rico and said, "I came in here to have you become familiar with our op orders. When you are finished reading it, please pass it to the other two gentlemen. The last reader will drop it off on the control room table after you all read and sign it."

All three men replied with, an "Aye, aye, sir."

The XO smiled and, as he was leaving the cabin, turned to the three and said, "My name is normal. Your names must have come after a lot of heavy drinking and carousing around!"

The laughing began again as the XO closed the door.

Before reading the operation orders, Lee said, "Rico, I sat in on one of your presentations at the War College. I thought it was somewhat of a fairytale until it was used against us during Desert Storm. Burning oil wells and creating large oil spills aren't exactly fun things to deal with while you are in a combat situation."

While reading the operations orders, Lee asked with a surprised look on his face, "Okay, you guys, why do we have to destroy the Tarpon if she is disabled? What if the crew is alive and we can't get them off? What do you know that I don't know?"

Samuels called the control room and requested that Lieutenant Watson come to the cabin if he wasn't busy. Moments later, Watson knocked on the door and entered the cabin.

Samuels faced Watson. "Burt, if you have read the op orders, can you answer some questions that Lee has?"

Watson replied, "That depends on the questions, and what his security clearance level is."

Samuels said, "He holds a top-secret clearance like the rest of us."

Lee asked the same questions to Watson.

Watson began, "What I'm telling you is classified and is never to be discussed. Seven months ago, the US Navy accepted a Northrop Grumman, a high-tech torpedo. This new torpedo is an interchangeable offensive to defensive weapon. The offensive posture is called the CRAW, which stands for compact rapid attack weapon. When changed to a defensive weapon, it's called the CAT, which stands for countermeasures anti-torpedo. When Tarpon deployed to the China Sea for those sonar tapes, she was carrying some of these new torpedoes.

"They are also carrying Harpoon and Tomahawk missiles, just like us. They cannot and must not fall into Chinese hands. If they get them, their technology moves forward a giant leap. As for the crew, I'm glad I don't have to make that decision. That decision rests solely on the shoulders of Captain Williams, our commanding officer. I'm willing to bet that he already has guidance and orders from COMSUBPAC on that issue. I also believe that the Tarpon crew knew the score concerning that issue before leaving San Diego to get the sonar tapes in the China Sea."

There was dead silence in the cabin. Both Rico and Lee were shocked at what they just heard. Samuels already knew that information as the operations officer.

Watson's final comment leaving the cabin was, "May God help them and us."

Meet, Greet, and Under Way

The below decks watch section leader picked up the control room hand microphone of the 1MC system and said, "Now hear this. Now hear this. Quarters for all hands will be out on the pier at 1300. I repeat, quarters for all hands will be out on the pier at 1300. Watch section two below decks watch will remain onboard and on watch. All officers will meet in the Officer's Wardroom with the captain in fifteen minutes. That is all."

Samuels looked at Rico and Lee and said, "Okay, guys, let's go hear what the skipper has to say."

The three men made their way to the officer's mess area and took a seat after grabbing a cup of coffee.

All the officers stood and came to attention when the captain entered the mess area.

"Seats, gentlemen. As you know by now, we're going out on a hunting trip. The Tarpon may be in trouble or worse. She hasn't re-ported in at her scheduled time. It's our job to find her and bring her and the crew back to Pearl, if possible. If she has been destroyed, well, that's a different story and we will address that issue when and if we find her."

He looked at Rico and Lee and said, "Mr. Petrone and Mr. Skiboski, will you please stand up?"

The two men, now standing, were introduced to the rest of the wardroom. Williams continued, "Mr. Petrone reported aboard yesterday and will assume the full duties as the ship's navigator. Mr. Skiboski is here for evaluation and intel purposes. He will also act as our onboard interpreter when we pick up Chinese communications. Lee, your berthing assignment is up forward in the chief's quarters. We call that area the 'goat locker.' You may hear both terms while aboard the Cardinalfish. It goes back to early times when the chiefs of the Navy were responsible for the food and stores aboard ship. Goats were part of the food supplies.

"Mr. Samuels, have the COB escort Mr. Skiboski to the goat locker and assign him a bunk. Also, make sure that he knows which ship's compartments are out of bounds."

Samuels acknowledged the order.

Captain Williams continued, "Our ship's complement for this patrol is fourteen officers, one civilian, and one hundred twenty-six enlisted men and women. As we head out from Pearl Harbor to our assigned mission area, you can expect multiple practice drills and evolutions. I want this crew and you razor sharp before we get to the China Sea. Mr. Petrone, we'll be taking the southern route to the China Sea. Once we pass the outer harbor marker and get to deep water, we'll dive the boat. Mr. Samuels, rig the ship for dive if you haven't done so already. If any of you haven't read and signed the op orders, please do so at this time. Are there any questions?"

There were none but there were plenty of worried and concerned looks. You could hear a pin drop as they all left the mess area for their own workspaces.

Senior Chief O'Hara looked at Rico as he entered Navigation and said, "The southern route chart is ready, sir."

Rico responded, "Senior Chief, I am worried about you. I'm here only two days and already you can read my mind. How did you find out before me?"

O'Hara answered, "Sir, Captain Williams is my double-deck Pinochle partner."

The navigation group all smiled as the senior chief picked up the chart showing the dead reckoning tracks to the China Sea.

Rico looked over the chart and said, "This looks fine. Are the bottom contour charts set up as well?"

Crown answered, "Sir, yes, sir. We're good to go all the way to and into the China Sea."

Rico nodded and said, "Now is the time to call home to your families before we muster on the pier at 1300. Be sure to tell them that we will be gone for a while, but don't tell them where we are going. It's standard routine to keep that to ourselves and it's better for them that they don't know."

The navigation team left for the designated cell phone area at the shore end of the pier. Crown stayed behind as he was the on-duty quartermaster. He looked at Rico and said, "Sir, I've already called home while you were with the captain. I didn't mention where we are going."

The 1MC came on again. "Now hear this. Now hear this. All-hands quarters on the pier in ten minutes. That's all-hands quarters on the pier in ten minutes. That is all."

Rico led his team into the control room and up the ladders to the topside main deck. They crossed the brow and took a position, at parade rest, next to the operations department.

The XO stood directly in front of all the ship's departments with his back to the ship's crew. He ordered the ship's crew to attention as the captain came out onto the main deck, saluted the topside watch and then the American flag, and crossed the brow to the pier.

He looked up and down the crew standing at attention. He then faced the XO and ordered, "Report."

The XO saluted the captain, did an about face, and shouted, "Report in by departments!"

Each department reported, "All present and accounted for."

Once the report was verbally given to the captain by the XO, he ordered, "At ease and gather around, shipmates."

The crew encircled the captain and waited for his comments.

Williams began, "Shipmates, we have been given a difficult mission. Our job is to go and find the Tarpon. As you know, she has not reported in and is now considered missing. I know I can count on all of you to professionally do your jobs to the best of your abilities. We don't know what to expect, but we will persevere. Why? Because we are the best of the best. We are the Cardinalfish, and we lead and set the example for the entire US Navy Submarine Force. Good luck to all of us. XO, set the maneuvering watch and prepare to get under way."

The XO came to attention and saluted the captain, saying, "Aye, aye, sir. All departments, you are relieved from quarters. Set the maneuvering watch and prepare to get under way."

The department heads returned the XO's salute. The crew began climbing down through the topside hatches and the various ladders to the boat's interior.

The two tugboats were already alongside the Cardinalfish with lines tied to her fore and aft. All the Cardinalfish's hatches were closed and secured as the boat was gently pulled away from the pier. The captain and two lookouts were stationed on top of the sail as the gigantic submarine started to move under her own power for the open waters of the Pacific with the two tugs assisting her.

The Maneuvering Watch

Rico walked into Navigation to check on the preparations as the boat moved away from the pier. Senior Chief O'Hara turned on the plotting table used to navigate and clear the harbor.

Rico asked, "Senior Chief, are we all set all the way out to the harbor entrance buoy?"

O'Hara answered, "Sir, yes, sir. Maneuvering tracks for us have been laid out and set into the computer. We're good to go." He continued, "Sir, for your information, Petty Officer Mahoney is on the bridge as the starboard lookout. Petty Officer Crown is on the helm in the control room, and Reynolds is off watch because his duty section is the first watch once we dive the boat."

Rico nodded and said, "Very well. I think I'll see if there's room up on the bridge. I would like to get familiar with how we leave and arrive here for when I have to do it as the officer of the deck."

The senior chief paused for a moment and replied, "Sir, I have got it here. If I need you, I'll give you a call. The bridge, as you know, is kind of small, but I think your idea about going up is a good one for when you take command of the boat."

Rico left Navigation and entered the control room. He climbed up the ladder between the bridge and the control room. Captain Williams was the officer of the deck and the conn and in command of maneuvering the boat.

Rico stood underneath the bridge hatch and raised his voice to be heard, "Sir, I request permission to come up."

Williams looked down through the trunk hatch and saw it was Rico and replied, "Permission granted, Mr. Petrone."

Rico climbed up into the bridge area of the Cardinalfish and stood next to Captain Williams. He slowly turned full circle taking in all the view. He was finally heading out to sea. A feeling of exuberance came over him as he inhaled the smell of the salty air and watched a school of dolphins keeping up with the boat's speed and maneuvers. He felt terrific!

Williams said, "It feels good heading back out to sea, doesn't it, Mr. Petrone?"

Rico replied, "Yes, sir. It took me two years to get back to submarines. This boat is phenomenal! She is everything a sailor could want or need. It feels good to be back at sea."

The captain laughed, "Once a sailor, always a sailor. Right, Rico?"

Rico responded, "Sir, yes, sir. There's nothing like it in the world."

Williams removed his binoculars and handed them to Rico, saying, "You have the deck, Mr. Petrone."

Rico was surprised to hear those words. With a grin from ear to ear, he called down to the control room, "Control, bridge, Mr. Petrone has the deck."

The control room responded, "Bridge, aye. Mr. Petrone has the deck."

A couple minutes later, O'Hara called to the bridge, "Bridge, this is Navigation. Three minutes to starboard turn."

Rico replied and repeated, "Bridge, aye. Three minutes to starboard turn."

The boat's radio operator on watch informed the two tugs, one on the port side, forward and carrying the harbor pilot, and one on the starboard side, aft and alongside the Cardinalfish, of the impending turn in three minutes. Both tugs gave their ship's horn one short blast to acknowledge the communication.

Three minutes later, O'Hara recommended commencing the starboard turn. All three vessels turned simultaneously and headed towards the open sea now directly in front of them.

Twenty minutes later, the harbor pilot walked to the starboard side of the forward tug's bridge and gave a casual salute to the men on the bridge, yelling, "Good luck, and good hunting. May you return safe and sound with all hands."

Both Williams and Rico saluted back and waved as the towing lines of the two tugs were dropped from the Cardinalfish.

Williams looked at Rico and ordered, "All ahead two-thirds. Make your course two hundred seventy degrees and secure the maneuvering watch. Duty section one has the first watch."

Rico repeated the orders Williams had just given to him to the control room. The orders were repeated back to the bridge by control.

Subsequently, a public announcement was made by the control room throughout the boat, "Now hear this, secure the maneuvering watch. Section one has the first watch. Set condition one."

Rico took one last deep breath of fresh air, handed the binoculars back to Williams with a smile on his face, and said, "Sir, thank you for allowing me to take her out of the harbor."

Williams smiled, and nodded, "Not bad for your first time leaving Pearl."

Rico responded, "Thank you, sir. I request permission to go below."

Williams answered, "Very well. Go below."

After Rico entered the control room from the bridge, Watson climbed up to the bridge and became the officer of the deck and the conn, relieving Captain Williams. Down below, Samuels entered the control room and assumed his duties as the operations officer.

Williams told Watson as he was leaving the bridge, "Burt, dive the boat after we cross into international waters at the usual water depth. Make your depth is six hundred feet and increase your speed to twenty-five knots. If Tarpon is down and the crew is still alive, we need to get there as soon as possible."

Watson repeated the captain's orders and said, "Aye, aye, sir."

10

Silent Running and Routine

Lieutenant Watson phoned the captain as the boat passed a half mile beyond the harbor entrance.

Captain Williams picked up the phone after two rings. "This is the captain."

Watson responded, "Sir, we have plenty of water depth beneath us. I request permission to dive the boat."

The captain replied, "Very well, mister. Once we are at depth, pass the word for all officers not on watch to meet me in the wardroom. You have the deck and the conn. I've written sailing instructions in the operations logbook in the control room. If there is a need for any changes or recommendations, please notify me, as I will be here in my cabin after I meet with the officers."

Watson responded, "Aye, aye, sir."

Watson turned to the port and starboard lookouts and told them to make a complete three-hundred-sixty-degree visual search for any vessels in the area. He then called the radar and sonar watch standers to conduct a scan to search and identify any contacts (ships) in the area. There were none. After getting that information, he called the chief of the watch in the control room and verified the water depth.

A couple minutes later, the chief of the watch notified Watson that the water depth was one thousand feet and dropping off.

When the lookouts reported no contacts, Watson turned to both men on the bridge ordering, "Lookouts below." The diving Claxton sounded twice, "Oooga, Oooga." Watson, gave the order over the 1MC, "Dive, dive."

The air and water vapor spouted into the air as the vents on all the ballast tanks opened along the top of the boat. The flood ports of these tanks, being open, allowed sea water to rush in and fill the ballast tanks, replacing the ambient air. The big boat nosed in a downward direction as Watson scrambled down the two ladders and into the control room. The quartermaster of the watch secured both watertight hatches to the bridge once Watson and the lookouts were inside the boat.

Watson removed his binoculars and looked at the diving indicator board. The ballast tanks, the negative and safety tanks, and the trim tanks all showed green. Everything was normal and in order for the dive.

After relieving Samuels of the deck and the conn, he ordered the men on the diving planes, "Ten degrees down bubble and make your depth six hundred feet."

They both responded, "Ten degrees down bubble to six hundred feet. Aye, aye, sir."

Watson answered them, "Very well." He then ordered the helmsman, "Increase your speed to twenty-five knots, course two-seven-zero degrees."

The helmsman responded, "Increase to twenty-five knots, course due west. Aye, aye, sir."

The helmsman then reported, "Speed is twenty-five knots, and steady on course two-seven-zero degrees, sir."

Still staring at the depth gauge, Watson replied, "Very well."

He walked forward and stuck his head into Navigation. He verified the course with the quartermaster of the watch. Once satisfied, he telephoned the captain and informed him that the boat was on course, depth, and speed.

Williams replied, "Very well, Mr. Watson. Carry on and maintain silent routine."

Watson answered, "Aye, aye, sir. Maintain silent routine."

The control room phone talker notified all compartments to set silent routine. The chief of the watch reported that all compartments had set condition to silent routine.

Watson relaxed a little bit as conditions with the dive were in order. He responded, "Very well," and asked for a cup of black coffee.

All the officers not on watch stood up as Captain Williams entered the wardroom.

He smiled and said, "Seats."

He was holding a large manila envelope that had a large red stamp that read, *TOP SECRET. Cardinalfish Mission Orders. Open after clearing Pearl Harbor.* He sat down and signed the custody sheet for the envelope and its contents and handed the custody sheet back to the classified materials control officer. He tore open the envelope and began to silently read the enclosed paperwork.

After he was finished reading the orders, he said, "Gentlemen, I'll begin with a little bit of background and historical information. Over the last few years, you all know that the Chinese government has been quite successful in hacking into our classified military, Navy, and weapons files and taking information relative to our advanced military offensive and defensive capabilities. Their newest carrier is a good example of that. However, their technology is far behind our own.

"The Tarpon's mission was to enter the South China Sea, retain a stealth posture, and obtain sonar signature tapes for identification purposes on this new carrier and, once back home, have it disseminated to our aircraft and helicopter groups, and our surface and submarine fleets. The last message from the Tarpon to COMSUBPAC stated that they were successful in obtaining the sonar tapes. They also said that they were being followed by a group of Chinese warships. Their sonar heard something that they could not identify. They thought it might be a weapon of some sort.

"COMSUBPAC gave them permission to investigate and, if possible, obtain information and details. The Tarpon never acknowledged that message and was not heard from again. When she failed to report in on time, we changed a satellite orbit and had it pass over the South China Sea. The infrared pictures show an image of her water submerged wake nearby a small Chinese battle group. The next satellite pass over the area showed nothing. She was gone but the Chinese ships remained in the area.

"Our mission is to find her, rescue the crew if alive, and obtain whatever data the Tarpon found that might be critical to the defense of the United States. From this point on, and until we reach the South China Sea, we will conduct various drills and exercises to ensure we are battle-ready to handle all scenarios and situations.

"Weapons, I want your times for loading fish in the tubes reduced to a faster time. Operations, I want your radar and sonar watches and equipment checked out at regular intervals to ensure satisfactory operations. Engineering, I want your team to be able to give full and emergency reactor power when I need it or call for it. Computer techs, I want all your computers up and operational. Navigation, I want your team to be ready to make recommendations for course and depth changes. We will be running at deeper depths to ensure we aren't detected by ships, subs, or planes, and finally, we will be maintaining silent running and routine all the way to our designated operations area. That is all, gentlemen."

The XO stood up and replied, "Hell, that's enough, sir!"

Counseling
and Kudos

The entire crew became more confident and comfortable with each passing drill. The fire drill and the flooding drill took on a special meaning as they realized that this trip wasn't the usual surveillance trip. Add to that the possibility of one hundred forty Tarpon shipmates sitting at the bottom of the ocean with no way out. The possibility of them being dead added to the tension felt throughout the boat. The Cardinalfish crew was determined to rescue them or take their revenge on the perpetrators.

Captain Williams approved various contests and competitions, easing some of the tension and pressure. There was a beard growing contest going on and most of the crew were more than eager to participate. Even Lei Wang Joe Skiboski took a shot but for only for the first five days. His beard looked like a short-haired French poodle whose snout had mange! The crew really appreciated Lee participating and working alongside them and he quickly became part of the crew.

The COB won the singles Cribbage contest and Lieutenant Watson was the chess tournament winner. The Pinochle competition ended in a draw with partners in the wardroom tying a pair of reactor sailors from the aft end of the boat.

Three-and-a-half days after leaving Pearl Harbor, the Cardinalfish sailed past Guam at a depth of six hundred feet and still on a westerly course and at the same speed. All at once, sonar identified and reported a Russian trawler starting engines and turning on a parallel course. Her distance was less than two thousand yards.

Williams was notified, came into the control room, and immediately ordered, "Make your course zero-zero-zero degrees (due north), decrease your speed to fifteen knots. Planes, give me a twenty-degree up angle and smartly come up to three hundred fifty feet. Sonar, identify all thermoclines (warm water on top of cold water that can block out sonar) and their depths and tell me if, and when, that Russian matches our course and speed. We don't want to give him any additional information on US submarine technology. They always show up at the most inopportune moment."

Sonar reported several thermoclines with one at approximately at four hundred feet and another slightly above six hundred feet.

When the boat settled on course north with a depth of slightly below four hundred feet and a speed of fifteen knots, Watson reported the same to Williams. Sonar reported the trawler matching the boat's course and speed.

Williams replied, "Very well. Helm, all stop. Planes, give me a zero bubble and hold us at this depth. Mr. Watson, quietly fill the auxiliary tanks from sea, watch the depth gauge, and tell me when we drop to below four hundred fifty feet."

Watson repeated the order and answered, "Aye, aye, sir."

Lee came into the control room and asked, "What's going on?"

Watson replied, "We're a mouse playing with a Russian cat. We're about to drop off his sonar and go below a four-hundred-foot thermocline. We'll be long gone before he figures it out."

Lee looked at Captain Williams and said, "Oh, is that all?"

When the boat completely dropped below the thermocline, it maneuvered into the Russian's baffles (sonar dead zone). The Russian, losing the sonar signal, sailed on various courses for twenty minutes or so and then turned back towards Guam.

Williams asked Rico for a course recommendation to get back on track for the due west course. Once the boat turned back on her base course of due west, she dropped back down to six hundred feet and increased speed to twenty-five knots.

Rico was incredibly pleased at the superior performance of his navigational team tracking and plotting the whole incident. All the bottom contour navigational fixes were right on the money. The boat's set and drift were computer-adjusted as necessary. After they were all seated in Navigation, he said, "Team, I am very pleased with your performance of duty so far. Your professionalism and working knowledge are outstanding. It is really a pleasure for me to be part of this team. You and I both know that we must expect the worst once we get to the South China Sea. So, if there are any questions or problems, I'd like to get them out of the way now before we get to our patrol area."

The team was silent for a moment and then Petty Officer Mahoney spoke up. "Sir, may I speak with you in private after this meeting? I have a request I would like you to consider."

Rico was surprised and asked, "Can it wait until after the patrol or does it have to be addressed now?"

Mahoney replied, "This request has been on my mind since we left Pearl. I think it needs to be addressed, now, before we get to our patrol area so that my mind is free and clear."

Rico replied, "Well, okay then. If there aren't any other questions or problems to be addressed, you are all dismissed."

Mahoney sat across from Rico in Navigation. He left the door open.

"Okay, Miss Mahoney, what can I do for you?"

Mahoney was a little nervous, so she let out a sigh and began, "Sir, I'm sorry, but I really need to ask you a personal question. I have been seeing a great guy for a while now and before we left Pearl, he asked me to marry him, and I could not give him an answer because of my duties and responsibilities here. I know we'll be facing situations like this all the time because that's our job and the nature of the beast. I love my job and I cannot imagine doing anything else except being a quartermaster aboard a submarine."

Rico asked, "Can you please tell me a little bit about your boyfriend?"

Mahoney smiled and responded, "Sir, his name is Martin, and he is a career active-duty Marine. He's a sergeant major and assigned to a combat unit. We are like two ships passing in the night. He's really a great guy and has a good sense of humor."

Rico smiled and responded, "So then, what's the problem? Look, if you both care for each other and you both like your jobs, you can find a way to work things out."

Mahoney had tears in her eyes as she spoke again. "Sir, I'm afraid that I might not make it back to him if I continue being a quartermaster in subs. So I am thinking about not reenlisting and leaving the service."

Rico thought for a moment and replied, "I'm married with two sons. My wife stays home and takes care of things on her own. When I return from one of these trips, I give her a break and take on the home duties and responsibilities. She gets a break from everyday life. You and your beau will have to work that out between you to find a mutually agreed upon solution. When you are both called away from home, well, that's when family and close friends help you."

Mahoney nodded her head and responded, "I understand, sir, but I'm still afraid of losing him, or him losing me. I don't want him to become a single parent because of my job. I don't want to be one if I lose him as well. I'm afraid."

Rico said, "Mahoney, I want to ask you a question. How many of your shipmates are married or how many of them have boyfriends or girlfriends?"

Mahoney responded, "Quite a few, sir."

Rico continued, "So there you are. You are not alone. You are sitting in the same boat as the rest of us on board this sub. We have learned to deal with the situation, and you must learn to do the same. There are no easy streets when you are a member of the military or, for that matter, in any precarious job. I understand why you are afraid. Every one of us on board this boat has fears. So, how do we all deal with it? I'll give you the thoughts of a friend of mine who is much more philosophical about it than I am. I think it will help you."

Rico sighed and went on, "Everybody, in a time in their life, experiences fear. For those facing combat, fear takes on a much different perspective. Fear is a part of your total faith that never works out. It can't be ignored. You must face it head on and put it behind you. Where fear is, happiness and satisfaction are nonexistent. Fear is never a reason for quitting. It's only a flimsy excuse for walking away.

"You need to understand that, or you will never realize your dreams while solely living with just your fears. You can't allow your fears to be bigger than your entire faith. Fear is a mind killer. It will leave you trapped, helpless, and powerless. If you allow it to go unchecked, it could and would affect your job, your personal welfare, this crew, and the safety of this boat. You need to know and remember that your fear lets you know what you are doing and what you aspire to do is worth it. You will gain strength, courage, and confidence with every experience you have when you look fear square in the face and spit in its eye. And by the way, there is no such thing as a fearless warrior."

Rico stopped for a moment and asked Mahoney if she would like some water. She answered, "No thank you, sir."

Rico took a drink of water and continued, "You need to have the courage to pursue the life you have always dreamed of and were meant to have, despite the fear you are experiencing. By doing so, you will unleash the best and most powerful version of you that has ever existed or will exist. If you don't face it, the regrets you will have to live with throughout the rest of your life may just destroy you."

Mahoney, faintly smiling, answered, "Thank you, sir, for talking to me about this. You have given me a lot to think about and address. I really appreciate it, sir."

Rico smiled and said, "You're welcome. I know you will continue to do your job to the best of your ability. You are a credit to the navigation team, and I am glad to have you here as part of it. By the way, have you spoken to anyone else in our group about your marriage proposal?"

Mahoney responded, "No, sir. I have kept this quiet, and I would like it to remain so."

Rico replied, "It's our secret. Please feel free to come and talk to me at any time but please remember that I am not a marriage counselor. Maybe when we get back to Pearl, you both will consider seeing a counselor and then tie the knot."

Mahoney replied, "Yes, sir, and thank you, sir."

After Mahoney left, Rico went to his cabin. He closed the door, sat down at the desk, and pulled out paper and pen to write a quick note to his wife. "Honey, today I think I found my second calling. I'm either going to be a marriage counselor or a religious minister in my next job. If you were here and we were face to face, I'd expect you to laugh and answer, 'That will be the day!'"

12

The Warrants

Admiral Blejong walked into his lush, manicured botanical garden. He marveled at its beauty and thought back to a time when he was a fifteen-year-old cadet in the Chinese Navy living here with his parents. Now sixty-five, he still remembers how the garden looked like a weed patch after the Vietnam War was over in 1975. He was pleased that the garden still flourished even after all this time. But he couldn't understand why the free world didn't embrace its meaning. Its major aesthetic design is a simple, minimalistic natural setting created to inspire quiet reflection and meditation.

He knew he always needed and used the garden to help him before making strategic and difficult decisions. Maybe the garden was the main reason that he was still the head of all Chinese Naval forces. That, and the fact that he was extremely good at his job in a flourishing modern Chinese Navy. He relished wearing an admiral's uniform. He wondered what he would do if he lost it all. He knew that his position was part of the reason he was still alive and in power.

He had summoned Captain Wu over an hour ago. Where was he and what was he doing that made him so late in coming? How dare he keep the top admiral of the Chinese Communist Navy waiting!

At that very moment, his servant entered the garden and walking behind him was Captain Wu. He saluted, bowed, and politely apologized for being late.

Blejong returned the salute and asked, "Why are you so late? I called for you over an hour ago. You know I do not like to be kept waiting."

Wu, bowing again, apologized once more. He remained bent over and replied, "Admiral, I was in the midst of making arrangements for a deep submersible vehicle to dive down to that American submarine we destroyed. She is down at about seven hundred fifty feet."

Blejong paused for a moment and responded, "Very well, my friend. I forgive you but don't let it happen again."

Captain Wu rose and said, "Thank you, Admiral. What was it you wanted to see me about?"

Blejong motioned Wu to follow him into his office. Once both men were seated, he asked Wu, "Did we have any damage to our ships or the ji guang weapon?"

Wu answered, "No, sir. Everything worked well and there were no issues of any kind. Not only is it my duty to destroy her for trespassing, but I took great pleasure in doing it. They must know that we will protect our waters and our country's sovereignty. Those warrants you gave me are quite explicit and allow me and my ships to deal out Chinese justice."

Blejong responded, "You and I both know that there will be serious repercussions if we do not completely destroy that submarine. You are to obtain her technology and anything else you deem important to our cause and our country as soon as possible and then destroy her. Moreover, President Lin has no knowledge of what we are doing. He must never know. You know what that would mean for both of us if he ever found out."

Wu answered, "I understand, sir. But weren't those warrants originally issued by Lin to our Coast Guard for foreign flag fishing vessels trespassing into our waters and not for adversarial warships?"

Blejong, now irritated, replied, "Yes, they were. I, without Lin's approval or consent, amended those warrants to include all foreign flag vessels, fishing vessels or otherwise. Our government wants Taiwan back as part of our country as soon as possible. Lin wants to annex all the countries and territories adjacent to the China Sea because they either abut or are inside our latest water boundaries. Some of those are allies with the Americans. The Americans are our main concern. We claim China Sea sovereignty boundaries beyond the China Sea and along the western shorelines of Malaysia and the Philippines. Those countries, plus Vietnam, Japan, Indonesia, and the territories of Taiwan and Hong Kong, all want and claim ownership and wish to remain independent.

"Annexation is a chess game. We must make subtle moves and hide our main intention until it is time to make them all Chinese territories. We have started the game. We made artificial islands and are also using existing islands for new military bases. We created military bases on Fiery Island, Subi Reef, and Mischief Reef in the Spratly Islands. Those islands have been claimed by Malaysia, Taiwan, Vietnam, and the Philippines. Our main problem is and will always be the Americans. They will try to block us at every move."

Blejong continued, "They have in place and are creating new bases in the Philippines at Manila, Fort Magsaysay, Ebuen Air Force Base, Lumbia Air Force Base, and Antonio Bautista Air Base to counter our three in the Spratly Islands. They are prepared and determined to keep the Philippines as an ally. Their best counter move would be to make them an American state. That becomes an unattainable and immovable obstacle for us. Those bases are within four hours of our homeland by air and well within striking distance of our capital. They are using submarines, aircraft, and satellites to monitor our every move."

Blejong sighed and said, "Lin wants to try to do it peacefully. You and I both know that it cannot and will not be done in that manner. We must use extreme force so that all our forces will be feared by all countries. Once that is demonstrated, then we will more than likely have a free hand to take our countries and territories back where they belong, under our Chinese rule."

Wu responded, "I understand, sir. I agree with you but have nothing to say on the matter, except that I will follow your orders. Is there anything else you want to tell me?"

Blejong answered, "Yes, there is. I gave you five copies of the warrant. There's one for you and the other four go to the commanding officers of your included four ships. These warrants are to ensure you know what my expectations are in carrying out your mission. Additionally, our surveillance satellites are looking for another American submarine that will more than likely come our way. You are to prepare to engage her and destroy her like we did the first one. Our new mystery weapon cannot be traced so the Americans will never know what happened to both. I will radio you, using secure communications, of when and where you can find her. Remember, no loose ends!"

Wu replied, "Yes, sir. I understand and will obey your orders."

Blejong, now standing, said, "You are dismissed, Captain. Good fortune to you and to our country."

Wu stood up, bowed, and saluted Blejong with the admiral returning the salute. Wu left the quarters knowing that he was free to do whatever he wanted to, for any foreign flag vessel trespassing in the China Sea. He relished and anticipated taking on the American Navy.

13

The Cable Layer

The Hong Kong Consulate General's Office notified their diplomat in Washington, DC, that their cable layer, the Liberator, was missing in the China Sea. Their diplomat asked to meet with a representative from the US State Department. The subject was an urgent one. US Diplomat David Ridings met Liang Jiayi behind closed doors. A translator, accomplished in both languages, was summoned to Ridings' office.

After exchanging greetings, Jiayi said, "Mr. Ridings, I am here to discuss with you a serious and urgent request from my government. I know you can help us as you are attempting to maintain peace with the Chinese. They are trying to annex all countries and territories adjacent to the China Sea.

"To begin, Hong Kong made an agreement and signed a contract with the government of Vietnam. That agreement called for a suboceanic fiber optic cable connecting our two countries for exchanges of communications, negotiations, and agreed upon sales of imports and exports, including crude oil, natural gases, and chemicals. The cable is also a backup to our orbiting satellites. Our vessel, the Liberator, has not been heard from in two weeks and has disappeared while in the process of laying the cable from Hong Kong to Vietnam. Your navy in Japan monitors vessel traffic in and out of the China Sea. May we prevail upon you and your government to assist us by searching for our cable-laying vessel and her crew?"

Ridings rose from behind his desk and sat in the chair next to Jiayi. "Sir, we are more than willing to help you find your vessel. But it may not be in the immediate timeframe. I say that because I do not know the status of our military and commercial vessels transiting that area. Please allow me to inquire of our secretary of state, Mrs. Susan Nardi, and I will get back to you at your embassy here in DC. I would also recommend that you speak to the secretary of the United Nations as he may be able to help you as well if we cannot assist you in a timely manner."

Jiayi nodded and thanked Ridings for his help and assistance.

The two men stood up and shook hands. After the Hong Kong diplomat was gone, Ridings made two phone calls, one to Nardi, and one to the US Navy Department.

Several days later, Ridings got an answer. He called Jiayi and told him that a review of film from past satellite orbits showed the Liberator transiting the China Sea and laying cable. She was intercepted and boarded by the Chinese Coast Guard. An hour and forty minutes later, there was no evidence of the vessel or her crew on the subsequent satellite orbit over that area. He informed Jiayi that the US would continue searching for the vessel and her crew.

14

The Diversion

Rico was suddenly awakened by someone calling his name. He turned on his small overhead lamp and focused his eyes on the XO standing next to him.

He looked at him and asked, "What time is it?"

The XO replied, "It's 0320. Throw some clothes on and meet me in the wardroom as soon as possible."

Rico was surprised. "What's up, sir?"

The XO replied, "We'll tell you when you get there." The XO left and closed the cabin door behind him.

Rico rolled out of the bunk and threw some cool water on his face. It felt good. He stared into his bloodshot eyes in the mirror as he quickly combed his hair and put on a wrinkled uniform. Five minutes later he sat down in the wardroom. He was surprised to see Captain Williams, Lieutenant Watson, Samuels, Lee, and the XO seated at the table.

The captain, faintly smiling, said, "Grab yourself a cup of coffee, Rico. It will help to wake you up. I see you are not a happy morning person."

Rico said nothing, made a smiley face expression, poured a cup of coffee, and sat down at the table.

Williams passed the message board he was holding around the table for all to read. He spoke after everyone read the messages on the board. "Gentlemen, COMSUBPAC has amended our sailing orders. Rico, set a course for a place called North Reef. It's an island but named North Reef. It is part of the Paracel Islands. I believe it is about halfway between where we are now and Sanya, China. A satellite passed over that geographical area and picked up unusual images on the beach of that island. COMSUBPAC thinks it's debris, possibly from Tarpon. We are ordered to divert to there and investigate. Rico, we need to know the depth of the water around that island and its reef and if there is a deep access for us or a team to get close to the beach."

Watson asked, "Captain, did COMSUBPAC identify what the images are and if that island is inhabited?"

Williams answered Watson, "Negative on both counts. That's why we have been ordered to check it out. However, the images on the beach may be parts of a shipwreck. They weren't there when the satellite made its next to last pass over those islands about an hour and forty minutes ago. The changing tide may have put them there."

Samuels asked with a pensive look on his face, "Do they really think they may be pieces from the Tarpon?"

Captain Williams released a deep sigh and said, "God, I hope not. We've been ordered to check it out and so we will. Rico, give me an update for arrival time and water depth once you have everything set up and include the course change. Burt, I want all weapons loaded and ready, if need be. Mike, we'll use our passive sonar as we get close to the beach and the radar if we are alone in that area. Make no mistake, gentlemen, we will arrive on scene armed and battle-ready."

Rico headed for Navigation after leaving the wardroom. Reynolds was the quartermaster of the watch. He was a little surprised to see Rico. He said, "Good morning, sir. Are you okay?"

Rico nodded and said, "Reynolds, I need the bottom contour charts and the regular charts for a place called the Paracel Islands. We'll need to set up the tracks to get there."

Reynolds, responded, "Aye, aye, sir. Do you want me to wake up Senior Chief O'Hara?"

Rico answered, "Yes, please do. I want to put more than two heads together for this one."

O'Hara appeared in less than ten minutes and asked, "What's up, Mr. Petrone?"

Rico began, "O'Hara, we are being diverted to the Paracel Islands to a place called North Reef. We'll need to approach that island submerged to prevent detection and try to get in as close as possible to the beach. A satellite made a pass over that reef and picked up images on the beach that we need to investigate. Once we have the tracks set up and have all the pertinent info, we'll brief the captain, the XO, and anyone else who has the need to know."

Reynolds reappeared carrying several charts, the islands' archaeological information, and the latest navigational position fix for the Cardinalfish. The fix was less than an hour old. Rico examined that last fix along the track line on the navigational chart that was in use for this part of the voyage.

Reynolds handed Rico a book that had a description of the Paracel Islands. Rico found the description and read:

" North Reef is situated approximately 56 km north from the Crescent Island group and about 70 km west-northwest from the Amphitrite Islands. The North Reef is the most northwesterly feature of the Paracel

Islands. Most parts of that island are submerged and mostly reef. There are rugged rocks all around the outer perimeter that are barely above water. There is a passage into the lagoon on the southwestern side of the island. The average tidal water depth into the lagoon is 20 meters. The reef extends a half mile to the south and southwest."

It was after 0430 (4:30 a.m.) when Rico and the senior chief finished laying out the track and gathering the pertinent information for North Reef.

Rico called the XO and asked for a meeting in the wardroom in ten minutes. The XO passed the word to Captain Williams, Lieutenant Watson, Lieutenant Commander Samuels, and Lee for the meeting.

Once they all arrived and were seated, he laid the charts on the table and began, "Gentlemen, I'll start from our current location. We are currently located one thousand one hundred five miles from North Reef, in the Paracel Islands. At our current depth and speed, we will arrive southwest of the Reef in thirty-seven hours. The access point requires that we sail west and then south a bit more to avoid the reef marine growth and its outer cropping. The water depth into the lagoon from its entrance is only sixty-six feet. The entrance is approximately four-tenths of a mile long.

"We cannot get any closer than three-quarters of a mile due to the extensive reef growth and lack of maneuverable water depth. Captain, with your permission, sir, I would like to recommend sending in one of our two-man miniature subs to investigate the satellite findings. It will have no problem getting to the beach. Additionally, North Reef is uninhabited. The only occupants are birds and aquatic animals of a medium to large variety (seals)."

The captain reviewed all of the information and replied, "Make it so, XO. Nice job, Rico, and NAV team. Well done!"

It was the XO's turn to speak: "Captain, I think for this mission we should ask for volunteers. Quartermaster Second Class Taylor is our best enlisted diver and Lieutenant Watson is our best qualified officer. It's Watson because he is the weapons department head and has spent a lot of time retrieving our exercise torpedoes when we practice firing them. He'll know if any of that debris is weapons-related."

The captain looked at Rico and asked, "Rico, do you have a problem sending Taylor if he volunteers?"

Rico replied, "Personally, no, sir. But I think you should give whoever goes an idea of what to expect on that reef as well as the trip in and out. After all, our info is from books and hasn't been updated in quite a while. Add to that our satellite's next pass is after we arrive there."

The captain smiled and asked Watson, "Do I see a volunteer sitting in front of me?"

Watson smiled and replied, "Be glad to sir, since I love being in the water and you know how much I like to see new places."

Rico answered the captain, "Sir, I'll ask Taylor when he comes on watch at 0745 this morning."

The captain responded, "Very well. Now let's all get some sleep as it's been a busy night shift. Tomorrow, more than likely, will be as well."

Rico asked Taylor right before he took the navigation watch at 0745 (7:45 a.m.) about volunteering.

Taylor replied, "Of course, sir. I'll be glad to take a ride in the mini sub with Burt . . . I mean Mr. Watson!"

Rico had him report his decision to Samuels and Watson. The agreement to go by both men was passed along to the captain.

15

Entering the
China Sea

Rico entered Navigation after being called by the quartermaster of the watch. "What's up?"

"Sir, we will enter Chinese waters in forty to forty-five minutes," Taylor answered. "The captain asked to be notified before we cross the water boundary."

After looking at the latest navigational fix on the chart, Rico answered, "Thanks, Taylor. I'll notify the captain."

Samuels ran into Rico in the passageway as he was knocking on the captain's door. "He's in the control room."

Rico replied, "Thanks. By the way, we hit Chinese territorial waters in about forty minutes or so."

Samuels stopped and stared at Rico for a moment and said, "Well, I guess now the real fun begins. We need to get to North Reef undetected and at the same time remain covert all the time we are here while looking for the Tarpon. That'll be fun. Not!"

Rico said, "Mike, I've been thinking about this whole situation. Quite honestly, I don't like it. If the Chinese destroyed or crippled the Tarpon, they know the US will send a boat searching for her. We're the searchers. In addition, COMSUBPAC has us going to North Reef to check debris on the beach. That reef is square in the middle of the China Sea. I think the Chinese are using the Tarpon, no matter what condition she is in, as bait to bag themselves another boat. It's like their using a double-edged sword! This whole area is going to be crawling with Chinese ships, boats, and planes."

Samuels responded, "I agree with you. Let's go talk to the skipper and the XO."

Both men entered the control room where the captain was talking to the COB. Samuels, standing close to Williams, asked, "Sir, may Rico and I have a word with you and the XO in private? It's important.".

Captain Williams stood up and replied, "Let's go to my cabin. We'll grab the XO as we pass his cabin."

Williams closed the cabin door when all four men were seated inside. He asked, "Okay, gentlemen, what's on your mind?"

Rico cleared his voice and began to speak. "Captain, North Reef is at the north end of the Paracel Islands. The Chinese will be waiting for us north of those islands with bated breath if they have become aggressive and attacked the Tarpon. May I suggest slowing down, going deeper, find ourselves a thermocline, hide under it, and ride it from the south up to North Reef instead of coming in from the north?

"Additionally, the latest weather report indicates that there is a large low-pressure area moving off the Chinese coast towards Japan. It will strengthen in size and power as it travels over the water. They will have a hard time trying to find us in those heightened seas. If we come in from the south, we can use our passive sonar to search for the

Tarpon enroute to North Reef. But coming in from that direction and finding nothing, we only have the northern part to search."

The captain looked at Samuels and asked, "Do you agree with Rico?"

Samuels responded, "Sir, yes, sir. I think he has a good idea as to how to proceed."

The XO quickly jumped in and said, "Rico has made some good points. I agree with them, Captain,"

The captain stood up and replied, "Let's all go to Navigation. I want to look at the area and bottom contour charts. Mike, ask Sonar to check for deeper thermoclines in the area. Then, for the moment, slow us down and take us deeper, under the thermocline, if there's deep water beneath us. You all know that as we get closer to North Reef, there'll be shallow water. So, I'll make the decision how to proceed after I see the charts, check the weather, and think about what all of you just said."

The four officers entered Navigation and surprised Petty Officer Taylor, who was still on watch. Clearing his throat, he jumped up and said, "Oh, hello, sirs. May I help you?"

Rico, smiling a little, asked to see the Cardinalfish's current position on the track line on both sets of charts for the China Sea. He also asked Taylor for the latest weather forecast.

Captain Williams checked it all over and asked Doyle for his thoughts.

Doyle responded, "Sir, it's risky business either way. But there is one thing we haven't considered or discussed yet. That is the Tarpon's mission and patrol area. Her mission was to get sonar recordings on the new Chinese nuclear aircraft carrier. To get them, they had to be far to the west and close to the coast where that carrier would likely be conducting sea trials, operating, or anchored. If the debris on North Reef is part of the Tarpon, she was trying to get the hell out of there and they either crippled or destroyed her. The water depth around the Paracel Islands has an average depth of approximately four thousand feet and the deepest depth in that area is eighteen thousand two hundred feet. Both of those depths are below our crush depth. So there's plenty of deep water to hide in but the reefs and shallow water will give our position away. Also, they probably have listening devices set up on the sea floor just like we do. I'm thinking they will find us anyway on whatever course of action we take."

Rico added to the XO's comments by saying, "That's true, XO. But there is something else we should consider. Captain, may I recommend we set up a decoy by coming up to a depth that will give away an infrared wake while still on this northern course? But only for a few minutes. Their satellite or one of their search aircraft will pick it up and notify their fleet that's probably already able to move north or south. Once the wake is reported, those ships will stay north of North Reef while we go south. Doing so just means they won't find us. Additionally, we have a lot of water maneuverability and multiple thermoclines to ride and hide in and under until we get close. This boat is better constructed than any of our previous submarines. She's quieter, faster, and can go deeper. Don't forget her weapons array and countermeasures abilities."

The captain, holding up his hand, replied, "Okay, guys, I've heard enough and I have made my decision. We'll create a wake and keep their fleet on the north side of the island. We'll come in from the south. We'll use the passive sonar to search for the Tarpon as well as search for other contacts in that area as we move through it. But North Reef comes first. I've a hunch that what we find there might give us some insight and help. Mr. Petrone, amend your course tracks for the southern approach to North Reef and let me know twenty minutes before we hit the China Sea border. Who has the deck and the conn right now?"

The XO answered, "It's Mr. Watson. He just came on watch."

Samuels caused all of them to laugh by responding, "Damn, that guy sure does get around, doesn't he?"

Rico responded to Captain Williams's orders by saying, "Aye, aye, sir. I'll set them up per your orders and instructions and get back to you twenty minutes before we enter Chinese territorial waters."

Samuels left and entered the control room to have Watson come up to one hundred feet for five minutes and then return to the previous depth, per Captain Williams's orders.

Carte Blanche

Admiral Blejong contacted Captain Wu on his ship, the Chang Ling. He had an important message to pass along. He was not only worried, but he was also mad. The Americans were entering the China Sea with a second submarine just as he predicted, but sooner than expected. He knew they would be searching for the Tarpon that Captain Wu's fleet recently sank. The Chinese Navy was still preparing to steal her advanced weaponry and technology. Blejong took a moment to decide what he wanted to say and how to say it.

The conversation began across the secure telephones, "Captain Wu, this is Admiral Blejong. We have another intruder entering our territorial sea. One of our surveillance aircraft, using infrared scanning, picked up its wake. They are taking a northern route. You are to follow your orders and the warrants I sent you. I trust your judgement in handling this important matter. They are not to find the Tarpon. You are to destroy this second boat. First, make sure you follow our specific protocol. Ensure there are no American survivors from either submarine."

Wu answered, "Admiral, I understand. When will the salvage group dive on the Tarpon?"

Admiral Blejong replied, "It is supposed to happen in three to six days. This bad weather is holding us up. We are waiting for the shipment of specialized equipment needed to get down to that depth. All of the Tarpon crew should be dead by that time."

Captain Wu responded, "Sir, I will do my best, and use everything within my weapons arsenal to keep them away from the Tarpon. Are you sure they are coming from the north?"

Admiral Blejong said, "I just told you they are taking the northern route. You will need to get them to follow you or maneuver them into our specialized weapons area. That way you can destroy both American submarines at the same time. But take their weapons and technology first. When the American president starts asking questions, we will create a fake sonar tape and tell them they collided with each other and were destroyed. You will need to attack and use the ji guang weapon on the forward portion of this second submarine."

Wu answered, "Aye, aye, sir. Admiral, I will review the warrants again. I will notify you when we are finished with these cowboys. Goodbye, sir."

Blejong hung up his secure phone and stared out the window. The gardens were beautiful this time of year. He thought to himself, "These Americans are not cowboys but devils. We do not have the element of surprise this time. They will be coming with blood in their eyes and hate in their hearts and minds.

Hide and Go Seek

Rico called the captain's cabin after hearing from Senior Chief O'Hara. "Captain, we will be in Chinese waters in twenty minutes."

Williams responded, "Meet me in the control room right away and make sure Mr. Samuels is there as well."

Rico responded, "Aye, aye, sir."

Captain Williams knocked on the XO's cabin door, stuck his head in, and said, "Billy, it's time. Come with me."

The XO followed the captain to the control room.

The captain looked at Samuels and asked, "Who's our best sonar operator?"

Without hesitating Samuels replied, "It's Petty Officer Harry Ross and he's on the sonar gear right now."

Ross had been with Samuels ever since Samuels was first assigned to submarines. They were close friends in addition to working together for years. The only difference was that Ross was staring the thirty-year mandatory retirement in the face. This patrol would be his last. He regretted leaving the Navy, but his wife, Joann, had plenty of honey-dos around their new home in San Diego to keep him busy for a while.

The captain called Sonar and said, "Sonar, this is the captain. Report all contacts."

Ross quickly answered. "Captain, I hold no surface contacts. But I hold a submerged contact at eight thousand yards, and she is just sitting still and listening. She's a submarine and not ours. The electrical hum indicates she is Chinese. They don't know we're here as their sonar is not operating."

Samuels whispered, "It's a lookout for just in case."

The captain responded, "Very well. Ross, do we have a thermocline below us and, if so, at what depth?"

Ross answered, "Yes sir, we do. It's at seven hundred feet."

The captain turned to Watson and said, "Mr. Watson, I have the deck and the conn. Quietly pass the word to all hands to rig for silent running and battle stations with no audio alarms please. All ahead, one-third. Five degrees down bubble and make your depth seven hundred fifty feet."

The bow and stern planes operators responded, "Aye, sir. Five degrees down bubble to seven hundred fifty feet." A couple minutes later, the boat was at the ordered depth.

At the same time, Williams asked Rico for a course recommendation. Rico reviewed their position on the bottom contour chart and gave him the recommended course.

The captain ordered, "Helm, left ten degrees rudder and make your course two-five-five degrees. Sonar and diving planes, keep us under this thermocline."

The Chinese sub never knew the Cardinalfish was there. She maintained her course and speed until she was well out of the area. Thirty minutes later, Ross reported to the control room that the sonar was all clear with no surface or submerged contacts in the area.

After ensuring that the sea around them was clear, the Cardinal-fish came up to two hundred feet and remained stationary. She was exactly three-quarters of a mile from North Reef.

The captain turned to Samuels and said, "Mister, you have the deck and the conn. Keep us in this position. Please call Mr. Watson and Petty Officer Taylor to the control room."

Samuels answered, "Aye, aye, sir," and called Watson and Taylor to come to the control room.

When both men arrived, the captain began to speak. "Men, we are now at the drop point for you two and your trip to the beach. We are three-quarters of a mile off the North Reef and about a quarter of a mile away from the lagoon entrance. Remember that the two-man sub can only do four knots. The water depth, as you already know, is sixty-six feet. You can be seen and detected from the air. The sun will be starting to set so it will be sunset nautical twilight when you get to the beach. Hang close to the west side of the lagoon entryway until you get to the beach. Your mini sub has a glass bubble so you can gauge your close-ness to the reef edge and hide in its shadow by eyesight. Do not brush against the reef. Do not take any of the debris that you find. I repeat, do not take any of the debris that you find. The Chinese may have already been here and seen what's here. If you were to take anything, they would know that we were here, and we don't want that to happen. Take pictures to document what you see and find. Any questions?"

Watson smiled and said, "Sir, would you mind holding a couple of pieces of that strawberry shortcake the cooks made for tonight's dessert?"

Williams, not smiling said, "I suppose you want me to hold some of the vanilla ice cream for you as well."

Watson laughed and replied, "Well, sir, Taylor and I are partial to chocolate but if you have nothing else, I guess vanilla will have to do."

The XO was laughing as Williams responded, "Get the hell out of here and go take your pictures."

Both men entered the mini sub and completed their prelaunch checklist. All was in order and satisfactory. The mini sub holding tank was sealed, pressurized, and filled with sea water as the two men gave a thumbs-up. The small craft slowly dropped out of its cradle and through the opened lower access hatches of the Cardinalfish's auxiliary compartment. She maneuvered up to one hundred feet. Watson checked his small chart for the proper course to the lagoon entrance. Once the entrance was found, they stayed close to the west wall and headed for the beach. Water clarity was good due to the slight current and it being only sixty-six feet deep.

The depth read twenty feet when she was laid to rest on the bottom. The wave action from the latest storm moved the mini sub around. Watson tried to keep the sub in position. Taylor opened the glass bubble and swung out of the sub. Hanging onto the starboard handle, he put on his swim fins and checked his waterproof camera, his depth gauge, and his oxygen gauge. Taylor took a few moments to look around for any large marine life that might be swimming around or laying on the bottom. He saw only small reef fish and an octopus trying to hide in a small pothole in the channel's sandy bottom. Satisfied that all was okay, he began swimming for the beach.

Taylor removed his mask as he lay in the rough shallow water on the beach. After looking around and seeing no one, he removed his fins, and ran for some underbrush. Just to play safe, he maintained a stooped over position as he walked in the bushes along the beach. He spotted something lying in the high tide water mark on the beach just ahead of him. It was close to dark but still light enough for pictures without the flash. The object was part of a small wood cabinet with a corkboard piece still attached to the partial door. The corkboard had a picture on it with some writing. He looked at the picture and read the writing after wiping away the sand. He centered the corkboard and took the picture. There was some paper flipping back and forth in the breeze near a single sneaker farther down the beach. He quietly moved to it. He picked up the paper, read it, took a snapshot of it, and put it back down.

Suddenly, the sound of a diesel engine pierced the air. A Chinese fishing boat was headed for the beach. He guessed it was coming for either fresh water or just some playtime. Now in a stooped-over position and still inside the shoreline bushes, Taylor worked his way back to the point where he came ashore. Using his knife, he made a small partial cut on a palm branch and then tore it from its tree. Making sure he could not be seen by the now beached fishing boat, he backed up towards the water as the palm branch took away his footprints from the sandy beach. Once in the water, he put on his fins and swam back to the mini sub.

Watson turned the sub around as Taylor, now inside and buckled up, closed and locked the bubble. As they approached the Cardinalfish, they found the lower hatches opened and the interior lights became a homing beacon for the mini sub. Once inside, the sub was anchored and locked into place on its cradle and the seawater drained out of the compartment. Watson and Taylor took off their diving gear, put on their clothes, and headed for the control room.

The captain, waiting in the control room, asked the two men, "How was the trip? Did you take the pictures? Do you have anything else to report?"

Both men responded, "It was uneventful with no problems."

Taylor replied, "Sir, per your orders, I got a couple of pictures and left everything on the beach as it was.

Looking at the digital pictures, Williams said, "Oh, my God," as he read the top paper. The words "Watch Procedures and Protocol for Maneuvering" were at the very top of the first page. The document was in English.

The captain passed the pictures to the XO. Attached to the corkboard in one of the photos was a partial picture of a young woman clad in a skimpy, two-piece yellow polka dot bikini. The writing in the lower right corner read, "To the crew of the USS Tarpon, good luck, and smooth sailing. With Love, Desiree Chamberlain."

The captain asked the XO, Samuels, Rico, Watson, and the Cardinalfish security officer to go to the wardroom after reviewing the pictures and wait for him.

Once they were all seated, Williams asked, "Your thoughts, gentlemen?"

The XO replied, "Well, there is no doubt. They took out the Tarpon. As far as I'm concerned, we are now at war with the Chinese."

Samuels responded, "We can't be sure it was the Chinese at this point in time nor can we ascertain she was attacked. We must have definite proof, but it does appear to be the Chinese since we are in Chinese waters. It might be that some sort of material casualty happened to the Tarpon. We need to find her."

Rico answered, "Gentlemen, from my perspective, we have to remain stealth and continue our search, and find the Tarpon. After finding her and seeing her, we might be able to determine the cause or causes. We can't jump to conclusions here. There's a lot more at stake now. I'm not talking about just a confrontation with the Chinese; I'm talking about the global aftermath of any such offensive actions."

They all waited for the captain's remarks. He sat in silence for a few moments, looking down at the tabletop and playing with a folded paper napkin. He began, "I agree with Mr. Petrone here. We must play hide-and-go-seek with the Chinese, or whoever it is, until we find the Tarpon. Then, and only then, will I make a recommendation to COM-SUBPAC and Commander in Charge, Pacific Fleet (CINCPACFLEET). They'll let the Navy and the president decide what actions to take unless whomever it is attacks us. It's not our call. In any case, once we know the truth with documentation, we'll go back to international waters and send a report of what we found.

"Our mission is to find the Tarpon, rescue the crew, if alive, and then destroy her to prevent access to her weapons and technology. If she was taken out by the Chinese, then woe be to them as they will have to deal with good old Uncle Sam and his ire." Williams continued, "You are all dismissed except the XO and Mr. Petrone. I wish to have a few words with you."

The captain began, "Rico, I want you to set up a search grid that allows us to sweep to the west, southwest, and then to the north to see if we can find any indication or evidence of the Tarpon since we found none coming in from the south. Set up the navigational tracks and come back to me with them and your recommendations. I would also like to say to you, in front of the XO, that I think your performance, recommendations, and cool headedness are clear indications that you should have command of your own boat and the sooner the better. Thank you, Rico."

Rico left the wardroom with a big smile on his face and headed for Navigation.

18

Leaving, Finding, and Hiding

Walking into Navigation, Rico found Reynolds leaning over the chart table plotting and marking a navigational fix on the boat's intended track.

He turned, saw Rico, and asked, "You okay, sir? You look like you just ate a Cheshire cat!"

Rico, smiling, replied, "Nope. It was just a tin of sardines in mustard sauce."

Reynolds stared for a moment, and said, "I'd rather eat anchovies in olive oil, sir!"

They both chuckled and Reynolds asked, "What can I do for you, sir?"

Rico replied, "We need to get out of here via a north, northeastern route. Let's look at the bottom contour charts for going west a bit and then northwest, but not too close to the Chinese coast."

Rico and Reynolds worked together to lay out the tracks and put the planned route together. When it was completed, Rico phoned the captain and asked to meet him in the control room. The XO and Samuels were with Rico when the captain entered the control room.

Williams asked, "Okay, Mr. Petrone, what do you have for me?"

Rico laid out the charts and verbally went over the tracks, the water depths, and the estimated times of arrival (ETAs) to each course change.

The captain nodded while asking, "Are there any potential navigational hazards along our intended track?"

Rico pointed to a graphic on the chart and responded, "There's a sea mount right here about four miles due west of North Reef."

Williams acknowledged Rico's data and said, "Very well. From here, we'll move away from North Reef due west and put some deep water under us."

The captain turned towards Samuels and asked, "Who has the watch in Sonar right now?"

Samuels answered, "Section two has the current watch, so it will be Petty Officer Rocky Ramirez. He's as good as Ross, sir."

Williams responded, "Very well. I want passive sonar working as we move. I don't want any surprises and run into a Chinese sub or a bunch of surface craft. Continue with silent routine and battle stations and get us moving out of here and into deeper water. Do it quietly with no cavitation please."

Samuels responded, "Aye, aye, sir. All ahead one-third, left ten degrees rudder, come to two-seven-zero degrees, continue silent running and battle stations." The helmsman and the two men on the planes repeated Samuels's orders as the ship slowly moved ahead while changing direction.

The fathometer read a depth of two thousand feet ten minutes after changing course to due west. Samuels ordered the boat to go deeper to six hundred feet

Twelve minutes later, Petty Officer Ramirez called the control room. "Sir, I have picked up an anomaly at seven hundred fifty feet. It's on the side of the sea mount, slightly to our port side and near dead ahead of us. Our range to the mount is four thousand yards. I hold no other contacts at this time, sir."

Samuels responded, "Very well, Ramirez." He turned to the helmsman and ordered, "Planes men maintain your depth at six hundred feet." He then picked up the phone and notified the captain and the XO of the sonar report. Both men came to the control room.

The XO called into Sonar and asked, "Ramirez, what information do you have on the anomaly?"

Ramirez answered, "Control, it is metallic in nature, and it is quite large. It appears to be resting on some sort of a shelf on the side of the sea mount. Well, sir, it might be the wreck of a submarine."

After hearing the report, the captain asked Samuels, "How long can you hold us at this depth?"

Samuels replied, "As long as you want, Captain. We're pretty much sitting on top of a thermocline."

Williams gave the next order. "Mike, close the yardage to the mount to one thousand yards and maintain that distance and hold at our depth and then have Watson come to the control room, please."

Samuels responded, "Aye, sir. Can and will do."

The captain spoke to Watson as he entered the control room.

"Mister, in our auxiliary space, we are carrying drones and a small DSRV (deep submersible rescue vessel). Send out a drone and take a look at what's on the side of that mount. It might be the Tarpon, or what's left of her. If it is her, we'll send over the DSRV and hope there are survivors. She can carry twenty-four people, including the two operators. The water depth here is way too deep for the two-man sub.

If there are survivors, would you be willing to take the DSRV out and attempt a rescue?"

Watson, without hesitation, replied, "Yes, sir. I'd be glad to, sir. Who's my second operator?"

"I am," said Taylor, as he was passing through the control room. Rico, now standing in the control room, was surprised to hear and see Taylor, who added, "That is, with Mr. Petrone's permission."

Rico smiled and said, "Looks like you two boys are going out together again."

Williams agreed and ordered a drone to be deployed to the sea mount.

The drone turned on her underwater lighting as it slowly approached the anomaly. A silhouette of a submarine appeared out of the darkness. The stern of the boat aft of the reactor spaces was missing. When the drone moved closer to the opened hull, a male body appeared tangled in the wreckage. The dolphins on his shirt identified him as an American. Now there was no doubt that this was the missing Tarpon.

The drone was recalled and Captain Williams, now considerably upset, spoke to Samuels and Rico. "Well, we now know what happened to her. We need to determine if there are any survivors inside the remnant pressure hull. Deploy the DSRV. We'll use Morse code instead of the UQC, as it is less likely to be detected."

Watson and Taylor headed to the auxiliary space. It took them twenty minutes to check out all the DSRV systems. The two men climbed aboard her and finished the prelaunch checks. They secured the hatch as it was moved to the seawater holding tank for pressurization, flooding, and release.

Watson answered the voice in the headphones he was wearing, "Roger, we are ready to go. But don't forget there is six hundred feet of water pressure outside, so flood the holding tank slowly, if you please, before you let us out. We have sensitive ears." Both Watson and Taylor laughed at the operator's response from inside the auxiliary space as the tank slowly filled with seawater.

The DSRV dropped out of the Cardinalfish and stopped at seven hundred feet for a pressure check and any water leaks. Everything was shipshape. They slowly continued down to seven hundred fifty feet and moved ahead. The sea mount became visible on the video screen. The passive sonar on the DSRV was working and giving distance and depth readings to Watson and Taylor.

Ramirez, using Morse code, spoke to Watson, "Wreck approximately at your depth. Steer three-zero-one degrees."

Although the water temperature at this depth was extremely cold, both men displayed sweat on their faces. They both knew they were facing instant death if any kind of a mistake was made.

Ten minutes later, Watson reported that he had visual contact. Out of the darkness, they recognized the dim view of the dead sub sitting on a shelf with an approximately fifteen-degree list to the starboard side. The stern of the sub was dug well into the sea mount shelf. The DSRV moved forward along the side of the boat, at main deck level, to a point just forward of the sail. The "number buttons," welded onto the steel hull for identification purposes, identified the boat as the Tarpon.

While sitting there, the two men looked at each other as their sonar suddenly picked up tapping emanating from inside the hull. The DSRV maneuvered closer and hovered over the high-pressure escape trunk access hatch to the interior of the boat. Watson, doing this on his own, was playing a hunch. Taylor tapped out SOS. The Tarpon responded with their own SOS from inside the hull. It brought smiles to both Watson and Taylor. Suddenly, they heard a rumbling sound that increased in volume. Rocks and sand from above rolled down upon the Tarpon. The starboard list increased a little bit more.

Watson looked at Taylor. "We've got to get them out now. If the list gets any bigger, we'll never get them out."

Taylor answered, "Sir, let's go. I'll tell the Tarpon to be patient and that we need to clear away some debris so we can attach and seal against the hull. Cardinalfish will also hear it. Let's hope they don't tell us to abort."

Watson responded, "If they tell us to abort, we never heard that message. It was garbled. Got it?"

"Yes, sir. I got it and I agree. Wait a minute, there's another message from Tarpon. They've got twenty-six alive and some are injured. Lucky for us this DSRV can carry twenty-four people. Counting the two of us, we only have to make two trips."

The DSRV's hydraulic arm began clearing away the rocks that prevented them from attaching to the escape trunk. Now on top of the hatch, the DSRV sealed itself to the hull. The seawater between the DSRV and the Tarpon escape trunk hatch was pumped out to allow the transfer of survivors. The access tunnel was pressurized at same time to equalize the outside water pressure with the inside pressure of both the DSRV and the Tarpon to prevent an implosion.

Once the access tunnel was water-free and pressurized, Taylor dropped down inside the trunk and tapped three times on the hatch. At first, there wasn't a response. He tapped three times again and heard a response from those still alive and trapped inside the dead sub. Once all the hatches were opened, Taylor shined a light into the sub. He saw a Master Chief Petty Officer, presumably the COB, with a big smile on his face and tears running down his cheeks. Taylor asked, "Master Chief, how many?"

He responded, "Just like we sent you. There's twenty-six. We lost one hundred fourteen men and women to Chinese treachery."

Taylor informed the chief that it would take two trips and that it was best to transfer the worst cases first. Watson and Taylor successfully took the first twenty-two men and women from Tarpon to the Cardinalfish. Captain Duggan, the Tarpon skipper, and the COB plus two others, were the last to leave the dead sub.

Watson deliberately maneuvered the DSRV parallel to the hull so Captain Duggan could see what was left of his sub. At first sight, he was totally surprised and in shock at what he saw. He cursed the Chinese. Then, he became uncontrollably angry. He openly wept when he saw his XO's body tangled in the wiring and cables hanging outside of the hull with his arms and legs moving with the current. Taylor and the chief had to hold him until he calmed down. He realized and thought that he was responsible for the deaths of one hundred fourteen crew members. Turning off his thoughts and emotions, he retreated to a dark place inside his mind and shut down the outside world.

As the DSRV maneuvered away from Tarpon to return to the Cardinalfish, Watson and Taylor made a video of the stern of the Tarpon. The propeller shaft room, just aft of the reactor spaces, to the outside stern of the boat was completely missing. It looked like it had been sliced off by a carving knife. There weren't any jagged edges on the port side. But the starboard side showed a tearing aspect as the remnant portion of that compartment could not hold the weight of the rest of the sub's stern.

Once all the survivors were aboard the Cardinalfish and the DSRV was hauled in and secured in the auxiliary space, both Watson and Taylor relaxed. There was no way they were going to talk about what they saw. The video they took would do all the talking that was needed.

They made their way back up to the control room to cheers and pats on the back. Captain Williams congratulated both men and told them, "Well done."

Then, facing the Tarpon captain, he held out his hand, saying, "Welcome aboard, Captain Duggan. It's a pleasure to see you again."

Duggan, now aware of his surroundings, pushed Williams's hand away and gave him a hug. With tears flowing down his cheeks he replied, "Thank you. You're an angel sent by God. Thank you, thank you."

Williams didn't know what to say. He turned to his own XO and said, "Billy, have medical check out all these men and women to make sure they are all okay. Give them anything they want and show them where the vacant bunks are so they can get some sleep. Oh, and have the cooks make a hot meal for them."

The XO answered, "Yes, sir. It will be a privilege, sir."

Captain Williams invited Captain Duggan to his cabin after he had showered and had clean clothing and a hot meal. Duggan answered, "Captain, I would like to put my thoughts together and rest a bit. Then I'll brief you on what we did and how I think we were crippled."

Williams nodded in agreement and said, "Okay, but if you were attacked, I think we should talk right away and relay the information to COMSUBPAC and CINCPACFLEET."

Duggan reluctantly nodded in agreement while replying, "I concur, sir. I probably won't be sleeping for a while anyway. Maybe it's the right time to put things on the table, so to speak."

19

A Tale of Woe

The Cardinalfish corpsman knocked on the wardroom door. "Permission to enter, sir."

Captain Williams responded, "Come on in, Doc, and have a seat. Captain Duggan and I were about to talk. If your other duties are taken care of, I'd like you to stay if you don't mind."

Corpsman Ernie Robins took a seat directly across from Williams and Duggan. Robins had been in the Navy for almost four years. He was born and raised in Memphis, Tennessee. When his four years were up, he intended to go to college and then medical school. Most of the crew called him "Doc," but the crew with southern roots called him "Doc Cash." The moniker came from the late country western singer Johnny Cash. Robins had the same deep voice and twang in his voice, but he could not carry a tune.

Williams said to Duggan, "Captain, this is our onboard corpsman, Doc Robins. He and I came aboard together and became shipmates when this boat was commissioned. He's quite a knowledgeable character. He decided to be a corpsman after his mother died of cancer. She is the reason he became a corpsman and is the best there is. I'm glad to have him as part of this crew."

Robins smiled and replied, "Thank you, Captain, for those kind words. I came to inform you that all the Tarpon crew that we rescued have been checked out. I gave all of them a mild sedative to relax them. Some are still in shock, but I think they will come around. They are all thankful to be alive. They are angry and want retribution on the Chinese fleet that sunk their boat. I'm also here to give Captain Duggan a shot as well."

Captain Duggan responded, "Doc, everything will be crystal clear as I talk to your captain about our mission and the sequence of events that led to my losing the Tarpon. Please hold that shot until I ask for it or you see a need to give it to me. But I'm okay and right for the time being."

Williams smiled and asked, "Are you ready to talk about it?"

Duggan replied, "I guess now is as good a time as any. Time to get it over with. Please get your yeoman and a recorder and we'll start. Oh, and if I may, I'd like to ask for a good stiff drink from your medical locker, Doc, if you please."

After hearing that comment, Robins reached into his medical bag and gave Duggan a small bottle of brandy. He accepted it and just stared at it in his hand.

Robins smiled and said, "Captain Duggan, I gave that to you to drink. You have had a rough time and you need it. If one is not enough, I have more in my medical bag and in the medical cabinet."

Duggan opened the bottle and downed all the brandy. He said, "You are right, Doc, I needed that. But I'm okay for now and I don't want another one. It will put me to sleep, and I need to be alert to talk to Captain Williams about our mission."

Williams picked up the phone and rang for the yeoman. He asked him to come to the wardroom and bring a recorder. Williams, Duggan, and Robins all went to the wardroom where they were met by the yeoman.

Captain Williams looked at Duggan and asked, "May I call you Peter, or do you prefer being called Captain?"

Duggan took a deep breath and said, "Pete or Peter is best since I don't have a boat anymore. You ask the questions and I'll try to answer all of them."

Williams grabbed a cup of coffee and sat back down. "Okay, Pete, let's start. What was your mission and please tell it in your own words?"

Duggan stared at the table. His eyes filled with tears as he sighed. "As you know, the Chinese now have a new aircraft carrier. She is bigger and faster than anything we have. She can carry more planes and equipment than we have, and she has a larger ship's crew. Our mission was to get as close as we could to her homeport anchorage and get sonar tapes on her as she got under way and remained under way at various speeds. We have those tapes."

Duggan reached into his pocket and pulled out a thumb drive. He handed it to Captain Williams. "There they are. We got them at an extremely high cost: one hundred fourteen of my crew."

At this point, Duggan began to openly sob and cried, "Why? Why am I alive and most of my crew is dead? Why? Those tapes weren't worth the cost. What a burden for the rest of my life."

Robins opened his bag and pulled out another small bottle of brandy and handed it to Duggan. Duggan opened it and drank it all. He used his handkerchief to wipe the tears from his face. After gathering his composure, Duggan turned to Williams and said, "Captain Williams, I hope this never happens to you."

Williams asked, "Do you want to wait a minute or two before you continue?"

Duggan answered, "No, let's keep going. Maybe it will do me good to get everything out in the open."

He continued, "They detected us on the way out to deep water. They came after us with a couple of subs and at least three destroyers. We played hide-and-seek while we tried to get away. They were the cat, and we were the mouse for three-and-a-half days. Every day and night it was touch and go. Every day I thought, "Do I defend myself or do I just try to get away? Do I go offensive or remain in a stealth posture? We both know that any kind of weapon used by me could start a global war. I had no authority to do so and no way to communicate to Pearl. Then it happened."

Williams, surprised by Duggan's last sentence, asked, "What do you mean?"

Duggan was wringing his hands as he answered Williams's question. "As you already know, the US uses an electrical system based on one hundred ten volts and sixty cycles. The Chinese use two hundred twenty volts and fifty cycles. We can detect the sixty cycles or fifty cycles or whatever cycle each foreign country uses. When that electrical hum emanates through the water, it's picked up by our sonar, so we know the country of origin. The first hum we picked up was Chinese. Based on sonar, we also knew there were three destroyers. Then we identified two submarines and an AUV (automated underwater vehicle).

"As we tried to get away, there was a new hum in the water. Sonar could not identify what it was or who the originator was. This new hum had a lower tone than our sixty cycles and the Chinese fifty-cycle electrical system. The sonar computers initially identified it as an anomaly. It was intermittent as we changed maneuvers, depth, and speed. The hum was sometimes mobile and sometimes stationary. It was confusing."

Duggan stood up and started pacing back and forth in front of the wardroom table. He stopped and looked at Williams and said, "After trying to escape them for three-and-a-half days, suddenly that low electrical hum was close aboard. Then suddenly we heard a 'pop' that sounded like a balloon when it bursts. At the same time, I was notified in the control room that we had uncontrollable flooding aft of the reactor spaces. Our executive officer volunteered to go back and assess the damage and help with damage control and assist the reactor teams as necessary. You, of course, knew him as he was your navigator before he came to us and became the XO."

Williams held up his hand and stopped Duggan from continuing. He asked, "You are telling me that Commander Cadenhead is dead?"

Captain Duggan, still crying, said, "We had to try and save the boat, so he went back there and sealed the watertight door while staying in the flooding spaces. Our COB and our on-watch duty reactor officer saw the smile on his face and a thumbs-up as the water went up over his head and then he disappeared. You rescued twenty-six of us today because of him. The whole crew could have been lost. By the way, I think there might be some of my crew still alive in the spaces we could not enter. My God, what makes a man do such acts of heroism, knowing that he is going to die?"

Duggan became visibly shaken again as he continued describing the sequence of unimaginable events. He continued, "The flooding happened so quickly that we couldn't control it. The boat started going down by the stern. We blew all our tanks, the ballast, the negative, safety, trim tanks, and auxiliaries. We put high air pressure into the boat, and we just kept going down with a seventy-degree down angle by the stern. The water depth was below our crush depth. Hell, the whole crew and I all knew that implosion would be our eventual end."

Duggan stopped talking. Robins handed him a towel to wipe the sweat from his face. Williams got up and passed him a hot cup of coffee. He drank some of it and said, "Let's keep going."

Duggan continued, "With that kind of down angle, you had to hold on to anything you could find to keep from falling towards the stern. Then we got lucky. We hit the side of the sea mount and started sliding instead of just dropping into the depths. The slide slowed us down quite a bit and then we came to a sudden stop with a slight starboard list. I have no idea what stopped us. Sonar was still working, and I asked for a reading. The operator told me we were lying on a shelf on the side of the mount at seven hundred fifty feet. The emergency air was still operating but I don't know how or why. At least we could breathe. The only food we had was in the officer's wardroom and our drinking water had to be rationed. We were too deep to be able to send out an emergency message or a distress signal or even release the emergency communications buoy. We knew that another one of our boats would come looking for us when we failed to regularly report. It took a while for you to find us but thank God you did."

Williams was shocked. He couldn't believe what he just heard. He looked at Robins and asked for a brandy. All three of them drank the brandy as Duggan continued.

"I can tell you, without any hesitation, we don't know what it was. We never saw what it was, but we did hear it and it sounded like bees buzzing. That weapon, whatever it was, is brand new and we don't have one. The flooding, obviously, could not be stopped. The shaft revolutions per minute went up through the roof. I have no idea who scrammed the reactor because we had no communications with the spaces being flooded. But I'm pretty sure it was Cadenhead."

Williams asked Duggan if he wanted to stop. Duggan replied, "No, let's keep going. I feel better getting it off my chest. The brandy makes me talkative!"

Duggan looked at Robins sitting with his head down and shaking it. He asked him, "Are you okay?"

Robins answered Captain Duggan while looking at Captain Williams, "Sirs, with your permission, I would like to pass the word of Commander Cadenhead's death to the rest of the crew."

Williams answered, "No, son. I'll do it after we are through here. It's my job and not yours."

Williams picked up the phone and asked that Commander Doyle come to the wardroom. Billy Doyle came in and took a seat next to Robins.

Captain Williams spoke to Doyle with a somber voice, "Billy, Al Cadenhead is dead."

Doyle was now the one with a shocked look on his face. He stared at both captains in disbelief.

Williams said, "Billy, the Chinese have got to be using the Tarpon as bait. I want this boat to remain at battle stations and ready for anything right now. Do it by voice if you must but no loud announcements or audible alarms. Check with the sonar watch and have him remain in passive sonar and identify all contacts. Then have him find a thermocline for us to hide in or under. Oh, have Watson and Taylor man the DSRV to destroy the Tarpon. Do it pronto and then we're getting the hell out of here and back to international waters!"

Doyle responded, "Aye, aye, sir," and left the wardroom for Sonar, but not before Williams gave him a request.

Williams said, "Have Mr. Petrone report to me. I want to talk to him right away."

Rico showed up and took a seat. Captain Williams explained what Duggan had told him about the strange new weapon that they heard on the Tarpon.

Rico commented, "So, this is a new and unknown weapon, sir?"

Duggan replied, "Yes, I'm positive it is."

Rico replied, "You know one of my quartermasters was on the DSRV as an operator. He and Lieutenant Watson pulled all of you off the Tarpon. He said that when he was leaving with the last group, they passed over the Tarpon's stern and they were surprised and confused at what they saw. The port side of the pressure hull, aft of the reactor spaces, looked like it had been cut, like a knife through butter. The starboard side had a partial clean cut, and then it either broke off or was torn off. The reactor room was totally open to sea. They said Captain Duggan saw it as well."

Williams asked, "Do you have any ideas about what it was that caused such damage?"

Rico replied, "Sir, the Tarpon's lead sonar tech and one of the reactor officers are two of the survivors. Maybe their tech and Ross, working together, can duplicate the sound or sounds they heard and then try to identify it."

Williams said with a slight smile, "Get them on it and make it fast!"

Rico replied, "Yes, sir."

As Rico left for Sonar, Williams called to him, "Mister, give Samuels a course to get us out of here as quickly as you can and do it quietly. Before we leave, the DSRV has a mission to complete on the Tarpon. We're not leaving anything valuable or useful for the Chinese to pick up."

Rico responded, "Yes, sir. I'll get with Samuels and give him the course as soon as I work it out."

Captain Williams asked, "Captain Duggan, is there anything else you want to add or say about what happened to you?"

Duggan looked at Williams, stood up, and said, "I think the Chinese more than likely hacked into our experimental military technology database. They've been trying to do that for a while as we all know. They had to use a remote drone to find us and then attack us with whatever that thing was. They are using drones, or something similar, that may be automated. They had to get it from our database. But there is one more thing. When they attacked and destroyed my boat, they knew another boat would come searching. Somewhere out there, they are waiting for you. You are now their main and next target!"

Aloha Tarpon

After meeting with his remnant crew members for a prayer meeting for the dead, Captain Duggan returned to the wardroom for dinner.

While they were eating, Williams looked at Duggan and said, "Captain, I'm sure you know that before we leave this area, we must destroy the Tarpon."

Duggan dropped his fork onto his plate and replied, "Sir, there may be some of my crew alive in some other compartment of the boat. You can't destroy her until we are sure that no one is alive."

"Captain Duggan, I more than well understand your feelings and your concerns. Our DSRV, on its last trip when they retrieved you, told us that there was no way anyone else could or would survive. You were lucky to be on the upper deck in the control room. If you were at battle stations, as I'm sure you were, most of your crew would have been on watch on the lower decks or back aft. You should realize that only twenty-six of you survived and you are the lucky ones."

Duggan spoke in a louder voice, "Captain Williams, I disagree and protest your decision. Some of my crew still must be alive and I will not allow you to destroy my boat. If you destroy her, I'll recommend a general court martial when, and if, we get back to Pearl."

Williams, showing annoyance, replied, "Captain, you do what you have to do and so will I. If Tarpon is not destroyed, the Chinese will get their hands on all our updated technology and weapons, and that includes our newest torpedo. We cannot allow that to happen. When you left Pearl you had orders, you followed them, and you completed your mission, and I intend to follow mine to the letter. There are no exceptions."

Captain Duggan stood up and shouted, "Sir, whether it be one life or one hundred fourteen lives, I cannot allow you to destroy Tarpon until we know for sure. I will do anything and everything I can to prevent you from doing so."

Williams, displaying his anger, yelled, "Duggan, sit down and be quiet. You so much as think about damaging my boat, I will restrict you to your quarters, and put you under arrest. You will not interfere with the duties and responsibilities given me by COMSUBPAC."

Duggan sat down and, staring at his plate, replied, "Sir, I still have a responsibility to my boat and my crew. Why can't you understand that?"

"Captain, the rest of your crew is dead and so is your boat. The DSRV, as we speak, is laying timed demolition charges in the open aft section of your boat, in her sail, and in the escape trunk. Remember, the Chinese that destroyed the Tarpon will be coming for us as well. We must be well out of the area before those charges go off. No more discussion on this matter is required or necessary."

Williams faced Rico. "Rico, did you give our recommended course to the officer on watch in the control room?"

"Yes, sir. We are good to go whenever the DSRV is back aboard and you are ready."

Williams picked up the phone and dialed the control room. "Mr. Watson, when the DSRV is back aboard and secured in her cradle, we will leave on Mr. Petrone's recommended course at two-thirds speed and at our current depth."

"Sir, yes, sir. We just finished securing the DSRV inside our auxiliary space. Request permission to proceed per your orders."

Williams looked directly at Duggan. "I am as sorry as you are about this, Captain Duggan. Very well, Mr. Watson, execute."

Duggan cupped his hands over his face, outwardly crying, "No! No! For heaven's sake, no!"

Thirty minutes later, Sonar reported hearing an explosion far off in the distance. The Tarpon was no more.

Being Cheated

The Chang Ling set sail for Tarpon's location with their DSRV aboard. Standing on her bridge, Captain Wu was smiling and thinking about the possibilities of a promotion to admiral, commanding an aircraft carrier, or even a large battle group. The promotion depended upon his success in obtaining the Tarpon's technology and weapons systems. There was a rumor among the upper Chinese Naval echelon that the US Navy recently created a new torpedo that far exceeded anything that the Chinese had in their arsenal. Wu, driven by ambition, realized that he needed to get the technology and weapons from Tarpon. He was ruthless and set out to accomplish his mission, no matter the cost.

The seas picked up a bit as a rain squall penetrated the area. At a speed of ten knots and encountering three- to five-foot seas, the task force would reach Tarpon's location in thirty minutes. Sonar called the bridge and reported a contact at seven hundred fifty feet and stationary. The distance to the contact was three thousand yards. Wu acknowledged the report and ordered the DSRV to prepare for diving. Immediately after giving his order and directly in front of the group of ships a deep explosion occurred, sending a huge column of water into the air. Wu ordered all stop and instructed Sonar to conduct an active sonar search of the immediate area. Sonar reported back that there were no contacts detected in the area and that the original contact at seven hundred fifty feet no longer existed and its parts were probably resting on the sea bottom.

Wu immediately broke out into a tirade. He was beside himself. All his aspirations disappeared with the explosion. What could he do now? How could he explain his failure to Admiral Blejong? After all, the DSRV being delayed caused this catastrophe. He had to come up with an idea or a plan that would appease Blejong, but also eliminate his embarrassing failure. Reporting to Blejong came first. He was cheated by the Americans and their navy. "They will pay for taking away my destiny and putting me in this precarious position," Wu thought.

He entered his cabin and called Admiral Blejong on the secure telephone. He tried to remain calm when the admiral answered his call.

"Good day, this is Admiral Blejong."

"Admiral, this is Captain Wu. I am calling to give you some unfortunate news. We are unable to dive on the American submarine. She has either been destroyed by survivors in the submarine or by another submarine. Considering the amount of damage we inflicted on it, I believe that there are no survivors. I think there is another American submarine in the area. Our only possibility of now obtaining American weapons and technology is to find her and destroy her in the manner of how we destroyed the first submarine."

Blejong was extremely irritated. "You think? You think? Explain to me why you didn't get there first. Explain to me why you weren't using your passive sonar to detect this latest submarine in our waters. Explain to me why I shouldn't take your head!"

"Admiral, I am just as upset as you are. After all, we are talking about my life. I, again, submit to you the factors leading up to this unfortunate event which was not caused by me. The DSRV was late in arriving and being transferred to my ship. Secondly, the submarine could have been destroyed by its own crew. Thirdly, my fleet has not received any information or notification from our communications group that any of our satellites detected the second submarine entering our waters. I know the only way I can remain alive is to get that second submarine. I will give you my life if I am not successful."

There was dead silence on the other end of the phone. The response was cold and candid. "Captain Wu, I am holding you solely responsible for this failure. I am now in the same position as you but with our president and the upper echelon. The only way you and I will remain alive is for you to complete your mission. There are no more excuses, factors, or other possibilities. The fate and future of China and her ability to annex other countries and territories solely rests in your hands. The Americans will do everything they can, short of an all-out armed confrontation, to prevent that from happening. Our destiny is to be the world's leading country and to dictate and rule over all others, including the United States. If you fail, I fail. If I fail, China fails. And if you do fail, don't come back alive."

The Reactor Officer

Lieutenant Commander Ziegler entered the wardroom looking for Captain Williams.

"Sir, may I have a few words with you? My name is Ziegler. I was the lead reactor officer on Tarpon."

Williams replied, "Have a seat. You're known as Ziggy, aren't you?"

Ziegler answered, "Why, yes, sir. How did you know?"

"You were a 'swab' at the Naval Academy when I was a differential mathematics instructor. Correct me if I am wrong, but you were not only a science whiz, but you also competed in track and field, didn't you?"

Ziegler smiled, "Why, yes, sir. Thank you for remembering that."

"What did you want to see me about?" asked Williams.

While wringing his hands Ziegler said, "I would like to give you some information that I think is important."

Williams asked, "Would you like something to drink?"

"No thank you, sir."

Ziegler appeared distressed. "Sir, I was in the wardroom with other officers having dinner when the alarm went off and the flooding began. I hurried aft to the reactor space, but the XO beat me there. He had dogged the watertight door and jammed it to prevent any of us from entering. Once there, I motioned him to pick up the phone. Once he had the phone, he told me he wasn't letting me in and asked me to tell him what to do. The background noise was getting louder, and it was hard to hear him. He could hear me, but I could not understand him because of the noise from the incoming seawater and that very loud hum. Alarms were going off throughout the boat.

"Cadenhead was in front of the reactor control panel, Ziegler continued. "I asked him to tell me if there were any indicators showing red. He nodded yes. I asked him if the reactor in the red. Again, he nodded yes. I told him to scram the reactor by hitting the big white button that was on the extreme right of the panel and waist high. He did what I told him to do. At that point in time, the water went up over the sight glass in the door and he smiled at me and gave me a thumbs-up. Then, he was gone."

Williams, leaning on the table with his head down, asked, "Mr. Ziegler, can you tell me what the conditions of the boat were while she was taking on the water?"

Ziegler stared into space for a moment and was visibly shaking. Taking a deep breath, he continued, "We were in the wardroom having dinner when suddenly we heard this really loud, low-pitched hum penetrating the hull. It sounded like an animal snarling and growling and getting ready to pounce. That was followed by a loud 'pop' like a balloon bursting. The boat's flooding alarm sounded. We heard the diving officer give the order to blow all tanks. He ordered all ahead emergency and full rise on both sets of planes. The boat just hung there and then she started to descend by the stern towards the bottom. We were at four hundred fifty feet at the time. We could feel the stern taking a downward angle. At that point, I began running to try and get to the reactor room. The final down angle had to be sixty to seventy degrees.

"You would not believe the kinds of objects and items that were flying by me towards the stern. When she hit bottom, she rolled a bit rather than remaining level. That's when I got to the reactor room and saw the XO inside. We hit the bottom hard. I was unable to determine our speed as we hit due to my location. But I can tell you there were a lot of injuries. You probably know because you saw what we looked like when we came aboard the Cardinalfish from the DSRV. As the senior officer present apart from Captain Duggan, I took a muster in the control room. Our corpsman tended to the injured. I looked at the depth gauge and it showed seven hundred fifty feet. I was shocked because the depth in the area was twelve hundred to four thousand feet.

"We took an inventory of food and water and confirmed the oxygen system was still running, but I didn't know for how long. Food and water were the limiting factors. The water temperature at that depth is what was bad. It was very cold. We had no additional clothing or way to heat the compartment. We couldn't release the rescue communications buoy as it was fouled in some way because of the impact with the bottom. If we released it, or if we used the underwater telephone, which wasn't working, they would know we were still alive and come back to finish us off. We knew that COMSUBPAC would send another boat to look for us when we didn't send in a situation report.

"After things settled down, some of the others were worried about the reactor and the possibility of exposure to radiation. I told them what Commander Cadenhead had done and we were safe for the moment and not in any danger from the reactor. After a while, we gave up tracking time. The hours turned into days. It was too depressing and the fear and tension of not being rescued increased. I don't know how long we were down there, but I can tell you, it was a long time. Most of us forgot time. The crew started showing signs of stress. Some crouched and stayed in a corner. Grown men and women openly cried and screamed. Some prayed and some cursed. The compartment turned into hell!

"Finally, sonar, still intermittently working, picked you up and identified you as an American boat. We remained quiet and waited for you to use the DSRV, if you were carrying one. When we heard her close aboard, we started tapping SOS on the hull. Then she locked onto the escape trunk. The cheering was deafening. Guys hugged each other and some of the crew cried, while others said a prayer of thanksgiving."

Williams, now shaking his head in disbelief, asked, "While you all were waiting to be rescued, how was Captain Duggan?"

Ziegler, with sweat covering his face, answered, "He was in and out of reality. When he was bad, we humored him by pretending to follow his orders. He kept calling for Cadenhead. I don't think he knows why he is alive today. The XO saved our butts. We twenty-six owe him our lives."

Ziegler, now weeping, said, "I am telling you this because Al knew that if there were any survivors, they wouldn't have a chance if exposed to the continual radiation coming from the running reactor and the loss of some of its shielding. Radiation poisoning is a hell of a way to die! It's the worst! We twenty-six are alive because of what Commander

Cadenhead did. He gave up his own life to save others. I think he is a genuine hero."

Williams, now pensive, sighed and replied, "Once we get back to Pearl, and we will get back to Pearl, I suggest you go see the squadron commander and tell him what you just told me. I'll follow up and have Captain Duggan make the trip with you. That way, you can be sure Commander Cadenhead gets the recognition he deserves. He'll be honored and remembered for a long time."

Williams patted Ziegler on the back and said, "I know this conversation was extremely difficult for you. Thank you so very much for coming to me and being able to talk to me about it."

Ziegler nodded, stood up, put his hands flat on the table with his head down, and replied, "It should have been me in the reactor room. I just didn't get there fast enough. May God, Al Cadenhead, and his family forgive me. I can't forgive myself."

23

Fatal Interdiction

Two Japanese boats, bottom fishing, were picked up on the radar screen of both the Chinese Coast Guard patrol boats two miles inside the northern boundary of the China Sea. The patrol boats changed their course and headed straight for the fishermen at top speed. When they were in range, a shot was fired across the bow of the lead Japanese vessel. The boats, still in Chinese territorial waters, came to all stop and waited to be boarded and inspected. They were boarded in the past and after it was determined that they were just fishermen, were escorted and led out of the area. Today was different. The Coast Guard sailors, heavily armed, boarded both of their boats.

The captain of the Amibune Maru, questioning their authority, was immediately shot and thrown over the side. The three remaining crew members of that boat and the four Sakura Maru crew now knelt on the stern of the lead Chinese patrol boat. Staring at each other, they could not believe what just happened and now feared for their own lives.

Lieutenant Aiguo Bohai laughed. "Any of you speak again, you will be joining your captain. You are trespassers in Chinese territorial waters. We have warned you before. Maybe this time, you will remember to never fish in these waters again."

The crews of both patrol boats, except for the men manning machine guns and the machinery spaces, boarded, and ransacked both fishing boats. Two dories, the inflatable life rafts, and personnel life jackets were machine gunned. Anything of value was destroyed or taken by the Coast Guard.

The seven men, still kneeling, watched as both fishing vessels were scuttled.

Bohai, now standing over them and smiling, ordered his men to throw these men over the side. He climbed back aboard his patrol boat saying, "It's time to leave."

The dead fishing captain's brother tried pleading with Bohai.

Bohai replied by throwing them into the water. Now in the water, the seven men watched the patrol boats sail away. They searched for anything that would keep them afloat. The thought of the circling sharks possibly attacking them filled their minds. Their anxiety ran high.

Just as they could no longer see the patrol boats, a yellow and white canister popped up to the surface. It was the inflatable life raft that was covered by the onboard, unused fishing nets. The men swam to the raft, inflated it, and climbed aboard, knowing it would be a long time before anyone found them. They hoped and prayed mother sea would provide them with fish and maybe some fresh water.

24

Foul Play

The Cardinalfish came up to periscope depth after sonar confirmed no contacts submerged or on the surface. Lieutenant Commander Bill Fenton had the deck and the conn and ordered the radio floating wire antenna be deployed to the surface. Fenton was a Navy reservist who had been recalled to active duty specifically for the Cardinalfish. His specialties were computer engineering, design, and language. He, like Rico, was adept at his specialties.

The on-duty radioman came into the control room and handed Fenton a received, decoded message. The message read: "Satellite orbit over the China Sea has identified seven people in a life raft. If possible, investigate, identify, and rescue survivors." The location latitude and longitude were included in the message.

Fenton asked the radioman, "Have you sent and received all messages and has the captain seen this message?"

The radioman replied, "Yes, sir, to both of your questions, including the situation report on the successful rescue."

Fenton immediately ordered the floating wire antenna recalled and ordered, "Make your depth five hundred feet."

After reading the message, Williams telephoned Rico and asked him to see him in Navigation. Both men looked at the China Sea chart displayed in the navigation table. Williams asked, "Rico, how soon can we get there?"

Rico incorporated the radio message latitude and longitude into the computer. Facing Williams, he replied, "Four hours at this speed, with nothing in our way or us being detected, sir."

Williams answered, "Make it so, Rico." He left Navigation and went to the control room. "Bill, we're going to that life raft location. Make sure the boat is at normal battle stations instead of relaxed and ready for anything just in case it's a trap. Rico will give you the course change. I want three volunteers for a diving mission. One of them must be Lee Skiboski. I believe he is a qualified diver. These people may be from the Tarpon, or they may be from China or some other country. Lee's going along to remove any language barrier."

Fenton replied, "Aye, aye, sir."

It was a dark moonless night when the Cardinalfish was within one thousand yards of the raft. Fenton ordered Ramirez to make a sonar sweep and report all contacts. There were none. At sixty-five feet, Fenton raised the periscope and immediately made a three-hundred-sixty-degree visual sweep of the horizon. No contacts were sighted.

The Cardinalfish closed the distance to the life raft. Fenton notified the captain and was instructed to call the three divers to the control room.

Williams, now in the control room, looked through the periscope and noted the seven men. He had Lee look. Lee turned to Williams and Fenton and said, "The name on the raft is Sakura Maru. They more than likely are from Japan."

Williams asked Lee, "I know you speak Japanese and are you willing to talk to the survivors?"

Lee replied, "Yes, sir."

Williams responded, "Okay, we'll send out three divers through the escape trunk and have them approach the raft. We don't need a Chinese satellite taking our picture. Lee question them, and if you believe their story, we'll surface and expeditiously take them aboard. I don't want to be detected, even if the Chinese are expecting us."

The seven men were surprised when the three divers surfaced beside their raft. Lee removed his mask and mouthpiece and spoke to them. He turned and faced the head of the periscope and gave the okay sign. The Cardinalfish moved close to the raft, surfaced, and took aboard all seven men plus the three divers. Once in the control room, the rescued men were openly weeping and bowing and thanking Buddha and Williams for being saved. The Cardinalfish then dove to five hundred feet and proceeded on her intended mission.

Lee remained with the men and interrogated them once they were fed, clothed, and medically checked. They returned to the control room with Williams waiting for them. The remaining fishing boat captain spoke first. "We were inside the boundary of the China Sea and fishing from two boats. My twin brother was the captain of the Amibune Maru. We fish for our families and sell nothing unless we have something large and desired by others. The Chinese Coast Guard approached and boarded us. They were heavily armed. We are fishermen and nothing else. We were told we were trespassing in the China Sea. My brother questioned their authority. He was immediately shot and thrown to the sharks.

"They beat us up, ransacked both boats, and took whatever they wanted. They opened the scuttles to both boats, destroyed all our life-saving gear, or so they thought, and left us to die or fend for ourselves. One life raft surfaced in its container. It was under the fishing nets and was not found by those Chinese devils. We treaded water until their Coast Guard was out of sight. Then we inflated the life raft. It had no oars or sails, but we had some food and a fishing line. We have been floating around in the raft for nine days. We want to go home."

Lee relayed all that was said to Captain Williams.

Williams replied, "Nope, we can't do that just yet. We have more people to be concerned about and you know who I'm talking about. Please explain to them that we will have them home after we complete our mission. Also tell them that while they are aboard this boat, they will remain completely quiet, make no noise, not touch any of the equipment, and immediately follow all our instructions. Mention that the Chinese are, more than likely, looking for us as well."

Lee nodded and relayed what Williams just said to the seven men. He turned and replied, "Captain, they understand and will follow all of your orders. They want to report the incident to their home government. They are extremely angry. This captain wants revenge on them for killing his brother. You, of course, know what that means."

Williams nodded and answered, "Yes, Lee, I do. Another international incident between those two countries. We already have a vigorous boiling pot between them. Bill, call a security team to the control room and have these men put in quarters that are out of the way as much as possible where they can be watched twenty-four-seven."

Fenton responded, "Aye, aye, sir. Chief of the watch, make it so."

Chief Gibson called for the security team and the men were led away to their quarters.

25

Sonar Contact

Rico phoned Captain Williams and gave him a quick brief about routes to return to international waters once the mission was complete. "Captain, this is Rico. We have two choices for getting out of these waters. I think and believe our best bet is to go south again, and then east. It's the quickest way out. The southern route has plenty of deep water. It will be difficult for them to find us unless they are a sub sitting on or under a thermocline, or a destroyer hiding behind one of the islands.

"Going north, in my opinion, is inviting trouble," he continued. "Travel time is longer, and the waters are slightly shallower. Add to that their northern naval bases are closer to any interception course they would use to cut us off from getting home."

Captain Williams responded, "Very well, make it so and notify Mike Samuels in the control room of the courses we'll need to get out of here."

Rico replied, "Aye, aye, sir. Southern route it is."

He went to the control room and gave Samuels all the data necessary for getting back to international waters.

Samuels, in turn, spoke to the operations duty section to bring them up to speed on what was expected of them. The crew remained at battle stations. Samuels asked Ross and Ramirez in Sonar to report to the control room, as they weren't in the duty section currently on watch. Once both men showed up, Samuels talked about what he wanted and expected from the sonar gang. "You men have done a great job so far by being on the ball and keeping us out of trouble. You'll need to keep that up for at least another sixteen hours or until we get to international waters. Captain Duggan made it noticeably clear that the Chinese have a weapon that we don't know anything about, and it is not in our onboard database. So, anything that you detect out of the ordinary, I want to know about it right away! Is that clear?"

Both men responded, "Yes, sir, very clear."

Samuels continued, "This duty section is due to be relieved by section three in fifteen minutes. Ramirez, you are a member of that duty section. I suggest you start relieving the current watch turnover right now, so you have a good complete picture of what's out there."

Ramirez replied, "Yes, sir. I intended to do that right after you were finished talking to us."

Samuels smiled and said, "Well, if you're ready to relieve, get going."

Ramirez left for Sonar.

Ross turned to Samuels and said, "I'll be in Sonar continuing to work with the Tarpon sonar tech to try and identify that unknown sound. When Ramirez needs an extra set of ears, I'll be right next to him, sir."

Samuels smiled again and said, "And what big ears you have, Grampa!"

Ross laughed and replied as he left for Sonar, "The better to keep us from sinking, sonny boy! Ah, sir."

The first few hours were quiet. Then, as the Cardinalfish made its turn to the east, a blip showed up on the sonar screen. Ramirez analyzed the vessel's propeller cavitation emanating from the surface craft. It was a Chinese Type 055 destroyer. The database identified the destroyer as the Chang Ling. He tapped Ross as he called the control room and asked for Samuels.

"Control, this is Ramirez in Sonar. I hold a contact bearing two-seven-zero degrees. Its range is ten thousand yards dead astern of us. It's a Chinese Type 055 destroyer called the Chang Ling. I know she has picked us up as her sonar is actively pinging. She is not advancing on our position but has matched our speed. She is just hanging back there as if to be waiting for others to show up, or there may be some sort of ambush ahead of us."

Samuels responded, "Very well. Let me know immediately if there is any change in her speed or position or if any other ships or contacts show up. Be aware that they could be waiting for their submarines to catch up with us, or they could be ahead of us. So, stay sharp!"

Ramirez responded, "Aye, aye, sir. I understand and will do."

After he was finished getting the information from Ramirez, Samuels called Captain Williams in his cabin and reported the sonar information.

When the captain entered the control room, Samuels went to the International Book of Ships in the ship's computer and called up the Chang Ling. She was one of the newer destroyer classes of ships the Chinese were building. She had a length of five hundred fifty feet and her maximum speed was identified as thirty-two-plus knots. She carried a crew of three hundred ten and had a sailing range of seven to eight thousand nautical miles. All her guns and torpedoes were remote-controlled plus she could carry two helicopters for antisubmarine warfare.

Samuels read the file on the destroyer to Captain Williams.

Williams looked at Samuels and said, "She has a lot of firepower and can raise hell with us for a long time. See that all watch sections get extra food and drink as it could be a long time before the next meal while being thrown around by that ship."

Samuels responded to Williams, "Captain, she is obviously matching our course and speed as if she is waiting for others to catch up to us, or ahead of us. Those others could be more destroyers, or even a submarine or two."

The captain, thinking for a moment replied, "Mike, work with Rico and start changing a course to port or starboard every thirty minutes. Don't make the course changes sinusoidal. Also change our depth by one hundred to one hundred fifty feet when you zig zag but don't go any shallower than three hundred fifty feet. Change our speed as well but don't show them the thoroughbred they are following. We're still in Chinese waters and they don't have any idea of who we are or how much fire power we have."

Samuels looked at the captain and replied, "Aye, aye, sir. According to our navigational plot, we will cross into international waters in about two hours. I'll also talk to Sonar and have them keep looking for thermoclines to hide in and under, in both shallow and deep depths."

Williams smiled and said, "Very well, Mike. Have fun doing your thing! Oh, one other item. Have Lee drop into Sonar and let him listen to their conversations. Maybe we can get insight into what their intentions are."

Samuels answered while smiling, "Sir, yes, sir. I think Lee will enjoy that!"

26

The Wolves' Blockade

Rico entered the control room and scanned the instrumentation. Samuels was leaning on the dead reckoning tracer (DRT) table and studying the past movements of the Cardinalfish and trying to decide which way to go next.

Rico asked him, "How's it going? Have there been any changes? Who's relieving you for the next watch as the deck and conn officer?"

Samuels smiled at Rico. "Whoa! Now who's asking multiple questions without waiting for an answer?"

Rico just stared at him, shook his head, and said, "Holy cow, it's contagious!"

Samuels, laughing, said, "No changes yet. If you were qualified in this boat, it'd be you. But I think it will be the XO as the rest of the boat is remaining at battle stations."

It was Rico's turn to pass a ridiculous remark. "Well, I could relieve the watch anyway, but only if you wanted me to take her down to the bottom."

Samuels looked at Rico and said, "Don't even kid about that. Do you know how deep crush depth is for this boat? It's so deep, the Devil himself would ask to come aboard!"

Rico laughed and said, "Oh, my goodness! We can't allow that to happen as he doesn't have a security clearance or wear a dolphins insignia!"

Both men were laughing when the phone rang.

Samuels picked it up and answered, "Control. Samuels."

It was Ross. "Mr. Samuels, we have picked up multiple contacts. Two of them are two additional destroyers. The other two are submarines. The subs are doing a poor job of trying to hide in a thermocline at five hundred feet. They are all Chinese and now there are a total of five combatants."

Samuels replied, "Roger that. Have they picked us up yet?"

Ross answered, "The Chang Ling lost us in that last zig and depth change. She doesn't know where we are yet, but she is working on it. The other four don't have us either, but we are closing the range to them. They are all ahead of us."

Samuels replied, "Very well. Roger that and have you figured out Duggan's mystery weapon yet?"

Ross answered, "No, not yet, but we think we are close."

Samuels answered, "Roger that. Hurry up, will you?"

Rico worked on a course and depth change for the Cardinalfish on the DRT table as Samuels finished talking to Ross.

Samuels acknowledged Rico's course and depth changes. He turned to the helmsman and the planes men and ordered, "Right twenty degrees rudder. Make your depth six hundred feet and remain at all ahead two-thirds."

Rico looked at Samuels and asked. "Why are we going deeper?"

Samuels answered, as he was ringing up the captain, "Thermocline and because when they finally pick us up, we have better depth and speed options below that thermocline. They may get confused and think of us as one of their submarines being mixed in with them."

Williams picked up the phone said, "Yes, Mike. What is it?"

Samuels reported the changes made in course and speed. He also notified the captain of the four additional ships that sonar picked up.

After the report, the captain replied, "Very well. Continue evasive actions. Get with Mr. Petrone and have him work out courses and depths for an alternate entry into international waters. I'll be there in a couple of minutes to take command of the boat. Also, ask Rico how far to the entry point."

Rico answered the last question with, "It's twenty-five thousand yards."

Rico returned to Navigation to work on alternate courses and depths after receiving the orders from the captain via Samuels.

When Captain Williams arrived in the control room, he took the deck and the conn from Samuels. At the same time, Ross picked up the Chinese talking on the UQC. As Lee was writing down their conversation, Ross reported the talking to the captain. Ross was continuing to monitor all the ships while Ramirez was recording the Chinese talk emanating through the water. Suddenly, the conversation between Chinese ships ceased. Lee took his notes to the control room.

Captain Williams asked Lee, "Were you able to understand what was coming across the UQC, and if so, what are their intentions?"

Lee replied, "Captain, I translated all of it. I don't think you will like what they were talking about. The three destroyers will be tracking us from the surface while the two Chinese submarines work at trying to prevent us from entering international waters. That prevention includes ramming us, if necessary. They also mentioned another vessel called the Quanling that is enroute to this location. She is one hundred fifty feet long and about fifteen feet across. This is slightly smaller than any conventional sub and although she is quite compact for a submersible, she is still too large to be described as a mini submarine. She was launched last year by the Chinese. She is the world's largest AUV."

Rico returned to the control room as the conversation between Lee and Captain Williams was taking place. After hearing what Lee had to say, the color drained from Williams's face.

Rico looked at all four officers and said, "Captain, I'm willing to bet that this AUV is carrying the secret weapon, which can possibly be controlled by any ship, plane, or submarine. They don't intend to blockade us. Their intention is to destroy us inside Chinese waters. If so, and if I am right, we are in for a rough time and big trouble. We'll need to send all this information to CINCPACFLEET and COMSUB-PAC as soon as possible. We cannot do it from six hundred feet. In any case, we would be in violation of treaty requirements for being inside Chinese territorial waters without permission. We now must figure out how to evade this pack of wolves and get past them and get to international waters. They have no authority in that location."

Captain Williams responded, "I hear you and agree with you, Mr. Petrone. I'd like you to stay here with the XO and Samuels and put together a battle plan that will allow us to get to international waters."

All three officers replied, "Yes, sir, and will do, sir."

Lee inquired, "Captain, you sound worried. Are you?"

Williams answered, "I'm not worried about a blockade. What I'm worried about is destruction of this boat and the lives of the crew. They destroyed Tarpon. Their intention is to take us out as well."

27

Failure to Report

The Chang Ling and the two other destroyers made life miserable for the Cardinalfish. The numerous depth charge patterns prevented her from getting close to the surface to make the required scheduled situation report ("sitrep") to COMSUBPAC.

The 0800 (8 a.m.) morning sitrep sat in the radio room waiting to be sent. Lieutenant John McCoy, the communications officer, requested to speak to the XO.

McCoy, a former enlisted radioman, obtained his officer's commission by going through OCS. After OCS and four years ashore, the Cardinalfish was his first submarine. At times, he found that being the comms officer and having to learn all the systems on the boat was not an easy job. Creating and handling the unclassified messages weren't a problem, but the classified and encrypted messages made him uncomfortable. Additionally, the depth charging was new to him. He was having difficulty adjusting to it and trying not to show his fear. Knowing he was not alone in being scared, he wondered if they were going to make it to international waters and a safe area.

Doyle stuck his head inside the radio shack and asked, "What's up, Lieutenant?"

McCoy stood up and replied, "XO, we didn't send out the morning sitrep because of the Chinese. Do you have any idea when we will get close to the surface so I can send it?"

"It could be quite a while. Keep a copy of it and each subsequent sitrep ready to go in your computer and you can send them when I give you the word. Okay?"

McCoy, outwardly trembling, answered, "Sir, yes, sir. Any idea when that will be?"

"Well, I can see you are a little shaken. I'm scared as well. Hell, we're all scared and that includes the captain. That's part of our job. You knew that when you accepted your orders and came here, didn't you?"

While wiping the sweat from his face, McCoy responded, "Yes, sir, I do understand. But I never thought it would be this bad. The explosions from those ashcans (depth charges) are so loud that they rattle your teeth and your bones!"

Doyle nodded in agreement and stated, "Yes, they do. They remind me of some of those heavy metal band concerts I used to attend."

Smiling, McCoy responded, "Sir, I'm a little too young to remember those groups."

"Well, maybe after all of this, I'll let you listen to some of that music. But for now, I know you'll do your job to the best of your ability. Once we ditch these guys, I'll get you the word to send. Will that be alright?"

McCoy, answered, "Sir, yes, sir. Maybe you'd like to listen to some of my country western music?"

"Thank you, for offering, I'd like that but hold it for later."

In the meantime, back at Pearl, COMSUBPAC's chief of staff was notified that the morning sitrep from the Cardinalfish hadn't come in and was overdue. The boat was immediately listed as potentially missing. A request was made to review the film from the latest satellite orbiting the China Sea. It showed three ships, presumed as Chinese, laying down depth charge patterns in the South China Sea. The chief of staff notified COMSUBPAC of the situation.

COMSUBPAC replied, "Well, at least we know she's still alive and kicking. Send a message to the carrier battle group anchored outside of Tokyo Bay. Tell them to get under way and head for the South China Sea. Also, please get in touch with our secretaries of the Navy and Defense. One of them will need to talk the secretary of state and have her contact the Chinese diplomat in Washington, DC. I think it would be advantageous to ask the Japanese fleet to join our carrier battle group for a "military exercise" in that area. Maybe the Cardinalfish can break away from those destroyers and whatever else the Chinese might throw at them. In the meantime, we'll sit and wait to receive her messages when she is able to transmit them. Please, keep me posted."

COMSUBPAC's chief of staff answered, "Aye, aye, sir. Will do."

28

Run and Hide

Doyle, Rico, and Samuels continued putting together what they thought would be a way to escape into international waters. Every time the Cardinalfish made course and depth changes, she was blocked by a Chinese sub or by a destroyer. The Cardinalfish was able to remain in a stealth condition by using countermeasures, speed, and course changes as well as changes in depth. All the tricks in the book were used to get around the Chinese. A destroyer or a sub always found her and got in her way. At times, escape seemed impossible.

Then, the Chinese changed the rules of the game. The destroyers waited for their submarines to find the Cardinalfish by using their active sonar. They reported the current location of the boat topside to the destroyers. Then the destroyers moved in for the kill.

For the next six hours, all three destroyers took turns running in close to the possible location of the Cardinalfish and laying down a pattern of depth charges. The explosions rocked the boat causing minor damage to the Cardinalfish. Damage control teams worked around the clock to stop any leakage that occurred during the depth charging. Captain Williams wondered how long the crew could take this kind of punishment before someone cracked up.

Robins tended to crew members who were injured during the Chinese attacks. So far, the injuries were bandages and pills with no broken bones.

Now, all five Chinese vessels were simultaneously using their sonar to try and pinpoint the Cardinalfish to find her and send her to the bottom. Sweat and fear appeared on everyone's faces. No one was exempt. Nevertheless, Williams was proud of his crew.

Rico looked at Samuels and said, "You know, something's fishy around here."

Doyle heard Rico's comment. "What are you talking about?"

Rico replied, "We all know they have ASROC (antisubmarine rocket) capabilities, but they aren't using them. Also, those subs aren't using their torpedoes and that AUV is standing off somewhere and just sitting there. It's like they want to get us to a designated area. I think they want to do to us what they did to Tarpon. I think, because we are the latest and newest boat, they want to steal what's on board and put it to use on their vessels. They'll cripple our boat like they did the Tarpon and then take what they want. Then they'll destroy what's left. CINCPACFLEET and COMSUBPAV will never know why or how."

Doyle nodded in agreement.

Williams had enough of being blocked and tossed around by the depth charges. He wrapped his arms around the attack periscope when the next surface attack began. He looked at Rico and asked, "How deep is the water around us?"

Rico answered, "It's well below our crush depth."

Captain Williams, smiling, ordered, "Planesmen take us down to crush depth and once we get there, helmsman reverse our course and ring up all ahead flank. I want to head towards the Paracel Islands. I also want dead silence throughout the boat. I don't want to use the word 'dead'! I'll call it extreme silence or playing possum. Sonar, are there any thermoclines between our current depth and our crush depth?"

Ramirez responded, "Captain, there are two. You'll pass through both on the way down. You'll see them on your control room screen as we go through them."

Captain Duggan came into the control room as the big boat nosed downward to deeper water.

He stood beside Williams and asked, "What the hell are you doing?"

Williams answered, "We're going to crush depth."

Duggan continued, "I see you are going through the same steps I took to try and get out of these waters. I hope you are more successful than I was."

Williams smiled and said, "We will be. We have a higher level of technology on this boat than you had on the Tarpon. We're bigger, faster, and can go deeper than the Tarpon. The only concern I have is that unknown weapon that took off your stern."

Minutes later, the planesmen reported that the boat had reached her crush depth.

At the same time, the helmsman responded, "All ahead flank and reversing course, Captain."

Williams replied, "Very well. Maintain course and speed when we steady up on the new course. We'll keep going that way for a little while and see what happens."

Rico stood beside Williams and said, "Captain, all of these vessels came at us from the west. We are now going west. We still have plenty of room to maneuver and change our course to the northeast, away from the AUV, as she came in from the northwest. There is deep water on a northeasterly course."

Captain Williams thought about it for a moment and then respond-ed, "Very well. Helmsman, change course to zero-zero-zero degrees."

The helmsman repeated the captain's order, swung the boat to the right, and steadied up on course due north.

After an hour or so, sonar reported that the destroyers had split up and were searching in three different locations all in the west and south. The Chinese submarines were searching north. Captain Wil-liams thought about making a run towards the east and international waters. Ross, picking up Chinese chatter again in Sonar, removed that idea from Williams's mind.

Lee reported to Williams, "Captain, the two Chinese subs have picked up our trail. They reported to the lead destroyer that they dis-covered high propeller turns and a low-level cavitation that identified the contact as the Cardinalfish at a very deep depth. They also said that they cannot pursue at that depth because their crush depth limit is well above ours."

Williams called Captain Duggan and Rico over to the chart table and asked, "Pete, what do you think about sitting on the bottom?"

Rico answered before Duggan had a chance to answer, "Captain, it's way too risky at this depth to try and sit on the bottom here as it is outside of our depth limit. Allow me a moment or two to look at the bottom contour chart."

The bottom chart was called up on the table's screen. It showed a plateau or mesa two hundred feet above their current depth. Williams saw Rico point to the higher bottom and nodded.

The good part was that it was located to the east. The bad part was the chart had no description or indication of what the bottom consis-tency was on the mesa. It could be old hardened jagged lava, coral, or just rocks and sand.

Williams ordered the planesmen to come up two hundred fifty feet. They responded to the order and raised the diving planes upward to create a five-degree up angle. At the same time, the helmsman was ordered to come right another fifteen degrees and steady up on a course of zero-one-five.

Captain Williams ordered an "all-stop" to allow the Cardinalfish to slow down and coast over the top of the mesa. When she was located dead center over the mesa he ordered, "Samuels, let her settle down on top of the mesa."

Samuels responded, "Aye, aye, sir. Put her on solid ground, I hope."

The Cardinalfish dropped softly onto the mesa top. The bottom was composed of mostly small rocks and sand. When settled, she had a slight list of eight degrees to port as she quietly lay on the mesa.

Duggan smiled at Williams and said, "Way to go, Eric. You did it."

Williams responded, "Piece of cake for this boat. She's the best in the fleet! We'll sit here a while and just listen to what they have to say."

Lee walked up to Captain Williams and said, "If you need or want me, sir, I'll be in Sonar listening to their lingo."

Williams smiled and said, "Very well, mister. Report anything that you deem important for us to remain covert and alive."

29

Deja Vu All Over Again

Lee listened through the extra pair of sonar headphones while the Cardinalfish continued sitting on the mesa. The Chinese destroyers were now using their active sonar and maneuvering back and forth on the surface, trying to find the Cardinalfish with no luck. The sound of their propellers faded after three hours of active sonar pinging. Lee thought he heard something, so he had Ross turn up the volume. What they both heard was another Chinese conversation.

Lee jotted down the conversation and left Sonar and walked into the control room.

Captain Williams, setting his coffee cup on a paper napkin on the table, asked, "Okay, Lee, what have you got? And I hope it will give us some idea as to how to get us the hell out of here very quickly and quietly."

Lee replied, "Captain, I've got good news and bad news. Which do you want first?"

Williams, now frowning, answered, "You might as well give me the good news first. Then the bad news shouldn't be so hard to swallow."

Lee, raising his eyebrows and making a face, answered, "Yes, sir, here's the good news. They don't know where we are, and they are arguing as to how to find us. Now for the bad news. They sent one of the three destroyers to lead their AUV to our last position. Her estimated time of arrival is in about two hours. Ross and I think it's the Chang Ling now leading it back here and will be the ship autonomously controlling it. Oh, and captain, she is carrying an offensive weapon or weapons."

Before Lee had a chance to finish, Captain Duggan, sitting next to Williams, began to shake uncontrollably. He grabbed Williams by the arms and said, "Eric, we have got to get out of here now. My crew and I can't go through another sinking. Let's get the hell out of here before it's too late."

Williams removed Duggan's hands from his forearms and replied, "Pete, it will be okay. We have some time to decide what to do and how to evade the rest of these Chinese ships. You have got to keep it together or I'll have to remove you from the control room and restrict you to your quarters under guard. Remember you have to remain quiet, so they don't pick us up on sonar."

The XO looked at the ship's corpsman standing next to Rico across from both Captain Williams and Duggan. He raised his hand and motioned Robins to come and talk to him.

Robins walked over and asked, "Yes, sir, do you need something?"

Doyle replied, "Yes, sure do. I want you to give Duggan a shot or something that will let him sleep for the next eight hours. We can't afford to have him fall apart at the seams if we must fight. Can you accomplish that?"

Robins answered, "Yes, sir. I can use a syringe and he won't even feel it."

Doyle said, "Okay, Doc, you're the man! Do it."

Robins left the control room to get the sedative.

Lee continued his briefing of the Chinese conversation at the same time the XO was talking to the ship's corpsman. "The Chinese think they can trick us into thinking they are gone but they are sitting close by. One of their submarines is sitting and hiding in the thermocline well above us. Because of the warm water on top of the cold water, they haven't detected us just yet. Our sonar is blocked out by the very same thermocline. Ross and Ramirez are passively searching for that sub as we speak."

Williams acknowledged Lee's report and asked, "Does sonar know the location of the other two destroyers and the second sub?"

Lee responded, "Sir, we have the two destroyers located but we don't have the second submarine."

Williams walked over to the phone and called sonar.

Ross answered the phone, "Sonar, Ross here."

Williams spoke in a low voice. "Ross, what's your best guess for the second Chinese sub that's hiding out there?"

Ross responded, "Captain, the two destroyers and one sub are off the port quarter. Ramirez and I think the second is located within one thousand yards of our position. My best guess is that they know there's a plateau here."

Captain Williams, nodded to himself. "Ross, based on your sonar pattern, where's the best open area we can use to get the heck out of here?"

Ross replied, "Captain, before I can answer that may I ask you to please confirm the ship's heading?"

Rico walked over to the helm and read the compass repeater, "Captain, our last course, before sitting down, was zero-one-five degrees."

Williams, nodding again, repeated the course heading to Ross.

Ross acknowledged Williams and repeated the ship's heading to Ramirez. There was a brief discussion between Ramirez and Ross and then they finally agreed.

Ross replied to Captain Williams, "Captain, we are fairly sure that the second Chinese sub is off our starboard bow. The best open area is a course of zero-four-five degrees. You may want to have Mr. Petrone check his bottom contour charts for his opinion, sir."

Rico heard that conversation between Williams and Ross and replied, "I'm on it, Captain." He called up the bottom contour chart that included the mesa and the surrounding area. After reviewing all the information at hand, Rico answered Captain Williams, "Sir, that looks like the best heading to evade these destroyers and subs. I know I don't have to say it, but I will. Sir, we'll need to get and stay below a deep thermocline that's well below where that second sub is sitting to prevent detection."

Williams acknowledged Rico, and again, contacted Ross in Sonar. "Harry, have you got a thermocline that we can hide in to get out of here?"

Ross replied, "Sir, you have one in a narrow band about two hundred feet above us and it looks like it goes forever on the heading you intend to take."

Williams responded, "Well done, Sonar!"

Ross replied, "Sonar, aye. Thank you, sir."

Williams turned to Rico as well, saying, "Well done, Rico."

Rico responded, "Thank you, sir."

Williams turned to Samuels and ordered, "Mr. Samuels, bring us up fifty feet ever so quietly and all ahead dead slow once we are up above the mesa. Helmsman, right ten degrees rudder and bring us to the right to course zero-four-five degrees once we are up fifty feet."

The helmsman replied, "Left ten degrees rudder, all ahead dead slow. Once we are fifty feet above the mesa plateau, come left to course zero-four-five. Aye, aye, sir."

Rico stayed at the navigation table and watched the cursor move in an arc towards the right.

The Cardinalfish slowly and quietly moved up off the mesa and to her ordered depth and hugged the thermocline that was located above them. When on the ordered course, the helmsman informed Mr. Samuels and Captain Williams.

Williams waited for thirty minutes and then ordered all ahead one-third and maintain battle stations and silent routine.

Once at that speed and depth, Ross reported a sonar contact coming out of the Cardinalfish's baffles. After notifying the control room of the sonar contact, the contact began using their active sonar. It was the Chinese submarine running at full speed to cut in front of the Cardinalfish and prevent her from moving closer to international waters.

It was cat and mouse time again as the two Chinese subs and two destroyers maneuvered to prevent the Cardinalfish from leaving Chinese territorial waters.

30

How Deep Can
We Go?

Captain Williams tried every trick in the book to get away from the two Chinese destroyers and two subs chasing them for two-and-a-half hours. He changed depths. He put the Cardinalfish under a thermocline to prevent detection, but the Chinese subs dove below it as well and found the Cardinalfish. When the destroyers came in for a depth charge run, he altered his course and speed to avoid the exploding charges.

There were times in those two-and-a-half hours that he wished he were in an old diesel boat so he could release some of his diesel fuel oil and block the incessant sonar pings and escape into international waters. He also released sound producing countermeasures to divert both the Chinese destroyers and subs, but they always seemed to stay on the boat's stern and then move forward and attack the Cardinalfish. The last trick he tried was to release some bedding, old uniforms, and crew personal effects and belongings through the torpedo tubes and allow them to float to the surface. When seen by the Chinese, they would think the Cardinalfish was hit and sunk. It was an old trick, and it also didn't work.

The two destroyers maneuvered to set up another depth charge attack on the Cardinalfish. This time they came in tandem. The first destroyer laid down her charges close to the boat. When they exploded, the Cardinalfish slightly heaved upward and rolled to starboard. At the same time, the sail planes operator reported loss of power and immediately announced the failure and shifted to emergency power. Several of the Tarpon survivors were sitting in the crew's mess area and having coffee. They broke out into sweat and tears as the depth charge run caused the boat to heel over, bringing back the horror of being sunk by the Chinese. Several of the Cardinalfish crew tended to them and attempted to keep them quiet.

Using the sound powered phones, the damage control party leader reported the damage as irreparable. The sail planes had to remain in emergency power. Ross, also reporting in, informed the control room that they had to shift to emergency power as well.

When Ross's report came in, Captain Williams told Samuels to take over as he headed to talk to Ross. "Ross, how bad is it?"

Ross replied, "That last pattern was close off our forward starboard side and bow. It damaged our sonar gear. I think it's minimal as we still have sonar but only in the emergency power mode. If we take another beating like that last one, I can't guarantee you'll have sonar capabilities."

Williams released a deep breath saying, "Okay, Harry. I'll try to find a way to get us out of this mess and keep your sonar online."

Williams returned to the control room and reassumed command of the boat.

Williams, facing Doyle, asked, "XO, do you have any ideas that we haven't tried to keep these Chinese bandits off of our butts and get us to open waters?"

Doyle wiped the sweat from his brow and replied, "Captain, only one other thing comes to mind that we haven't tried. That's to put her on the bottom."

Williams asked Samuels to check with sonar for the water depth. Sonar reported the bottom at thirteen hundred feet.

Samuels looked at Rico and asked, "Rico, can we put her on the bottom?"

Rico, reviewing the bottom contour chart, frowned, and replied to all three men, "The bottom is possible. Even if we were to go to the bottom, we must be aware of the extreme pressure on our outer hull. Also, if the bottom terrain is jagged and rough, we could put a hole in the hull and that would be the end of us. I cannot tell you what the bottom is like here. There's no information on that. But I don't think the Chinese subs can go that deep. Their construction and engineering techniques are not as good as ours."

Captain Williams walked over to the chart table and looked at the bottom contour chart. Rico pointed to the current position of the Cardinalfish on the chart and then pointed to the documented water depth. He stared into Rico's eyes and then Doyle's and Samuels's.

He took a few moments and asked Rico, "Is there a better place close by where we can put her on the bottom?"

Rico replied, "Yes, sir. We'll need to alter course to the right to zero-six-three degrees. There is a rise of the bottom there that keeps us well above our crush depth. It's five hundred yards away from our current position. But again, you know we can't stay down there indefinitely."

Without hesitating, Captain Williams turned to the helmsman and ordered, "Right ten degrees rudder and make your course zero-six-three degrees."

The helmsman replied, "Aye, aye, sir. Right ten degrees rudder and steady up on zero-six-three degrees." When the course showed the boat on a course of zero-six-three degrees, the helmsman reported the same to Captain Williams.

Williams replied, "Helm, very well." Then he contacted Sonar, "Sonar, report all contacts and give me bearings and distances if you can."

Ramirez responded to Williams's order verbatim. Two minutes later, Ramirez reported the courses and distances of the two Chinese destroyers and submarines.

Rico informed Williams when the boat was over the plateau, which was verified by sonar as well.

Williams responded with "Very well," and immediately turned to Samuels, smiled, and said, "Okay, Mike, put her down on top of the plateau."

Doyle walked over to Captain Williams and whispered, "I changed my mind. I don't think it's a good idea. Don't do it, Captain."

Williams stared at the Doyle and said, "Billy, we are going down to sit on the plateau."

He turned to Samuels again and ordered, "Mike, I said bring her down."

Samuels looked at Rico who shrugged his shoulders and smiled. Samuels wasn't smiling and, while looking at Doyle, replied, "The Captain ordered it and so we are going. Planesmen down five degrees bubble and take us down to twelve hundred seventy-five feet and level off. Then we'll put her down nice and easy."

Captain Duggan's cabin was within hearing distance of the orders through the control room's watertight door, and when he heard "put her on the bottom," he jumped out of his bunk and ran into the control room.

He grabbed Captain Williams by the throat and screamed, "You are going to kill us all. You cannot do this. My crew and I have been through all of this, and you know what happened to us. Now is the time to surrender, to give up and keep us alive."

Rico, Samuels, and Doyle, all jumped on Duggan and pulled him off Williams. Rico turned to the COB and ordered, "COB, get Doc Robins to sedate him. Have a security team put him in his quarters, under arrest, and lock the door. Is that clear?"

The COB responded, "Aye, aye, sir. I read you loud and clear."

Two of the crew, acting as a security team, took Duggan, now in handcuffs, to his cabin. Robins sedated him. The security team removed the handcuffs after Duggan stopped struggling and calmed down. He laid down on his bunk and was strapped in with the door being locked behind him.

When the Cardinalfish was sitting on the plateau, Captain Williams turned to the XO and all the crew standing watch in the control room and said, "They build them really good, don't they Billy? All of you should be proud you're assigned to the Cardinalfish. She's the best there is. We'll remain here for a while and maintain silence throughout the boat. Pass the word to shut down all unnecessary equipment until we have to move again."

Rico thought to himself, "I'm going to treat all of the construction personnel of this boat to a free lunch when and if we get out of this. Thank God it's American-made!"

31

Listening In

Captain Williams checked the clock hanging on the officer's wardroom bulkhead as he grabbed another cup of coffee. It read 0505 (5:05 a.m.). The Cardinalfish had been on the bottom for almost two hours. He walked into the control room and told Rico, who was still at the chart table studying the bottom contour charts, to pass the word for all hands not on watch to check for leaks or water in all the boat's compartments. Rico complied with the captain's order. Rico reported to Samuels, in the control room, that all compartments had reported in and there wasn't any evidence of leaks or water throughout the boat. Samuels replied, "Very well," and passed that information to Williams.

The XO was also in the control room and, when hearing the report of no leaks or water, said to himself, "Yes Captain, we'll have to send a special letter to Mare Island Shipyard for doing such a great job in the construction of this magnificent boat."

Williams said to Samuels, "Very well. That's great. We'll sit here a while longer and maybe get a better idea of what the Chinese intentions are concerning us."

Most of the watch in the control room was at relaxed battle stations. Some were reading books or technical manuals while others sat with their arms folded and their eyes on the ship's indicators, gauges, and panels. Down in Sonar, Ross, Ramirez, and Lee were wearing their headphones, listening for any sound of the Chinese battlegroup while having their eyes focused on the multiple sonar screens.

The silence was broken when Ross stuck his head into the control room and told Samuels that conversation was taking place between some of the Chinese ships on the underwater telephone.

Lee, sitting in the chair next to Ross asked, "Are you recording this conversation?"

Ross replied, "Yes, sir, right from the beginning." Ross had a strange look on his face as Lee was still wearing his pajama bottoms. The bottoms were pale blue with miniature images of Big Bird all over them.

Lee laughed at Ross's expression and replied, "They were a present from my children for my birthday last month. I can tell you where they got them if you want a pair."

Ramirez, quietly laughing behind the two men, responded, "All we need now is the Cookie Monster to show up and we'll all be set!"

Samuels, hearing the conversation in Sonar, stuck his head in the compartment and said, "Keep it down in here. We don't need the Chinese to know where we are and that we like chocolate chip cookies."

At the same time, Samuels noticed Lee's pajama bottoms and responded, "Oh, my God. Rico, come see this. Sonar has been turned into Sesame Street!"

Rico smiled and added his two cents in a low gruff voice, "Cookies, cookies, cookies. Cookie Monster love cookies! Where are the cookies?"

The XO walked into the control room and, hearing the conversation in sonar, replied, "Knock it off and get back to business. There will be no more play acting out kiddie characters! You all got that?"

The three men responded, "Aye, aye, sir." Samuels and Rico said nothing and went back to work.

Lee turned to Ross and asked, "Can you play the beginning of the conversation for me so I can catch up?" Ross did as Lee asked.

Lee grabbed a pen and paper and began writing his notes. It didn't take long for Lee to catch up on the Chinese conversation. When he finished translating the conversation, he went to the control room and asked Williams and the XO to meet him in the wardroom. The three men sat at the table but only after Lee grabbed a cup of coffee and a Danish.

The XO asked Lee, "Well, what did you find out?"

Lee began, "Well, to begin with, they are all cussing up a storm. That's because they know we are still here somewhere, and they can't find us. The destroyers want to try and flush us out by using depth charges, but they don't have many left due to most of them being used earlier in trying to destroy us. The two subs are maneuvering up and down and using their sonar to try and find us. Both subs cannot go as deep as we are as they are older boats, and a deeper depth exceeds their crush depth. So, we are safe for the moment."

Williams interrupted Lee and asked, "Do you have any information on the Chang Ling and the AUV?"

Lee responded, "Yes, sir, I do. Both the Chang Ling and the AUV are thirty minutes away and both are shut down. The AUV is on the surface. There are electrical, sonar, and weapons engineers on the AUV. They are conducting final preparations and adjustments before they activate it against us."

"Captain Duggan was right," he continued. "The AUV is carrying the mystery weapon. She also has the usual torpedoes and counter-measures on board. The Chinese are bragging that they are the only ones who have perfected it and increased its range for complete target destruction. They did not identify the type of weapon. But the Tarpon sonar tech and our sonar gang are working on that low-pitch sound that was heard before the Tarpon was destroyed. Ross tells me that they are really close to determining what it is. We better find out soon because they are not far away, and we may not have any kind of a defense against that mystery weapon."

Williams and Doyle looked at each other and simultaneously asked, "Well, what do you think?"

The captain answered first, "What do I think? I think I need to light a fire under the sonar gang and get a confirmed answer. I think we need to add an electrical technician to that team as an extra sharp mind, ears, and eyes. Our time is running out and we need to know how to defend ourselves."

Doyle agreed with Williams and left for the control room.

Williams turned to Lee and said, "Lee, I have to ask you to remain awake and in Sonar to be there for any more conversations, but also to support their activities finding out what that weapon is. Oh, by the way, put on a pair of pants if you please."

Lee replied, "Captain, I am more than willing to do that." Lee left for Sonar after changing out of his pajamas as Captain Williams began writing the current details and events in the ship's log, the official record of the Cardinalfish.

32

Surrender: No Way

Lee and Ramirez suddenly heard a conversation they could not believe. Ramirez phoned the control room and asked to speak to the captain.

Williams answered, "This is the captain."

Ramirez said, "Captain, we have a UQC underwater conversation going on with the Captain of the Chang Ling. He wishes to speak to our commanding officer."

Williams replied, "Very well. I want to have Mr. Skiboski come to the control room."

Ramirez responded, "Aye, aye, sir. But it may be a trap. They could use your voice sound waves to locate us and take us out. It may be a genuine request, but I just want to remind you that they have been trying to destroy us for a while."

The captain replied, "Thanks, Ramirez. Let's just wait a little while and see what they do. We'll let him think we aren't in the vicinity. Then I'll make a decision."

Ramirez replied, "Sonar, aye."

Lee entered the control room and held his hand up as if to say, "Don't speak just yet."

Williams acknowledged Lee's gesture and asked him to stand next to him.

Lee replied, "Captain, before you respond to anything, allow me to give you my impression of what I think his intentions are when and if you decide to talk to him."

Captain Williams acknowledged Lee, and after hearing what Lee had to say, waited five minutes, and picked up the UQC microphone. "This is the captain of the American submarine. Whom am I speaking with?"

The Chinese voice responded, "I am the captain of the Chinese destroyer Chang Ling. I represent President Li Qiang Lin. My name is Captain Aiguo Huang Wu. May I have your name, please?"

Before Williams replied, Lee suggested that he give a fake name.

Williams nodded and replied, "My name is Captain Leroy Garrett, and your English is very good. Where did you learn to speak our language?"

Captain Wu replied, "I was a military attaché at the Chinese embassy in Washington, DC, for four years before returning to China. It was there I learned to speak your language, eat pizza and hot dogs, drink ice cold beer, and play poker."

Before Williams answered Wu, Lee replied, "Captain, I think he is arrogant and overconfident. He may be using this conversation to get a bearing on us, just like Ramirez insinuated."

Williams acknowledged Lee and replied, "I have already thought of that. We'll keep this short and sweet. Ramirez, can you diffuse my transmissions?"

Ramirez answered, "Yes, sir. I can make them sound distorted as if we are sending from a long distance."

Williams responded, "Do it."

Williams answered Wu, "What do you want, Captain?"

Wu replied, "Because I enjoyed being in your country, I wish to offer you the opportunity to surface your boat and surrender. Otherwise, we will destroy you, your crew, and your sub."

Williams responded with a smile on his face, "Captain Wu, did you offer the same to the first US submarine you destroyed?"

Wu, now laughing, replied, "Of course not, Captain Garrett. He was stealing sensitive Chinese information and trespassing. I had no choice but to destroy his submarine. You, on the other hand, were sent to find the first submarine and merely entered Chinese waters without permission. You are just a trespasser. That is why I am offering you a chance to remain alive."

Williams replied, "Well, first, Captain Wu, if you are so magnanimous, why the hell did you try to sink us in the first place? You are playing games with me. So, I am making the same offer to you. Surrender all of your ships to us before we destroy all of them."

Wu laughed out loud and replied, "Captain Garrett, you are not a very good poker player. I know, without a doubt, that you are bluffing. You do not have the high hand, so to speak. Five ships to one have you overmatched, outnumbered, and you have no chance of winning, or survival for that matter. You know you can't win."

Before Williams had a chance to respond, Lee spoke to Williams, "Captain, he intends to destroy us no matter what. He destroyed one boat so what does it matter if it's two boats? He knows if he is successful, he'll be promoted, and more than that, our government won't risk a nuclear confrontation. Coincidentally, he could take all our weapons and technology, which is why I think the Tarpon was destroyed."

Williams, nodding, answered Wu. "This is your last chance and warning, Wu. If you don't surrender to us and the United States, I will blow you out of the water without blinking an eye and with a clear conscience. Damn you and your government for taking American lives. The Chang Ling will be the first of your ships to go to the bottom. Why am I threatening you? Because you never gave our first sub a chance to leave your China Sea. That alone gives me provocation to send you to hell."

It was now clear that Wu was aggravated and extremely upset. He began yelling in Chinese and Lee interpreted his remarks for Captain Williams.

Lee started to translate, "Captain Williams, he is talking to a couple of technicians. One is a sonar tech, and the other is an electronics tech. They are activating the AUV. It sounds to me she is controlled by some other means instead of just the Chang Ling. Because he asked the sonar tech if they were close enough to the activate the tower. I don't know what that means. I don't know if he means the AUV or some other device."

Williams replied to Captain Wu, "Okay, Wu, get ready for the deep six."

Wu asked, "What do you mean deep six?"

Williams responded, "The deep six is six fathoms or thirty-six feet. It means you're going to be destroyed by me and your final resting place will be on the bottom. Captain Garrett signing off."

Williams, while keeping the UQC phone line open and transmitting, turned to the XO and ordered, "Battle stations, this is no drill. Rig the boat for extreme silent running."

Doyle replied, "Aye, aye, sir."

Doyle and Williams exchanged smiles as the battle stations were heightened and reset.

33

The Secret Weapon

Captain Williams contacted sonar and ordered Ramirez to make a complete passive sonar sweep around the Cardinalfish.

Ramirez responded after completing the circular sweep. "Control, this is Sonar. I have identified six of eight contacts. The six are the Chinese ships and the AUV. I cannot identify the two other contacts. They are sitting on the bottom. The three destroyers and the AUV are at four thousand yards and located on our port side. The two submarines are at two thousand five hundred yards and located on our starboard side and in front of us. I am working on identifying the two sitting on the bottom, but my best guess is that they may be stationary and are definitely Chinese in nature."

Williams, with a puzzled look on his face, asked, "Sonar, how did you come to that conclusion?"

Ramirez answered, "Captain, the sonar computer found and identified them by their fifty-cycle electrical hum emanating through the water. They weren't there in the previous sonar scan, but they are there now. It's as if someone turned on a switch and activated them."

Lee and Ross entered the control room upon hearing Ramirez make his report.

Captain Williams said, "Hang on a minute, while we start the cat and mouse game with these Chinese." The Cardinalfish, now off of the bottom, was creating a zig zag course through the water and making changes in depth and speed, while at the same time, trying to remain covert as the Chinese continued their search.

Lee couldn't wait any longer and interrupted the captain. "Sir, you need to stay away from those two unidentified objects. The captain of the Chang Ling ordered the towers to be turned on. Ross and I now believe they are underwater military emplacements holding some sort of weapon. We also think that they may be controlled by either the Chang Ling or the AUV or both."

Captain Williams acknowledged Lee's comments and ordered Watson, the weapons officer, to the control room.

Watson, upon entering the control room asked, "Did you want to talk to me, captain?"

Williams relayed Lee's comments about the towers and asked, "Burt, do you have any ideas about their configuration or operation?"

Watson thought for a moment and replied, "Yes, sir, I do. I am sure that they can be controlled by the destroyer or by the AUV. To have that ability, there must be a coupling device or controller of some sort. Both will be connected to a fiber optic cable lying on the ocean floor. If that's true, then both the ship and the AUV can send and receive signals from those towers. I believe the best way to take the towers out of commission is to find the coupler/controller device and neutralize it or destroy the towers. Then we only have to deal with the five Chinese vessels and the AUV."

Williams tried to suppress his smile saying, "Only just six vessels you say? Hell, that sure gives us a definite advantage doesn't it, Burt?"

Watson's face turned beet red and he replied, "Captain, we're here because we can, and because we can, we will!"

All the crew members in the control room responded in a low voice with "AAARG!"

Captain Williams answered Watson, "You are dismissed, mister. Return to your duty station."

Watson replied, "Aye, aye, sir."

Captain Williams turned to Samuels and said, "Mike, release a drone and locate that coupler/controller device and the towers. Doyle, you're the backup to me while Mike is gone. Work with Mr. Petrone for our best maneuvering solutions."

Both Samuels and the XO replied, "Aye, aye, sir."

The captain turned to Lee and asked, "Do you, Ross, and the Tarpon tech have any idea on the signal range for these towers?"

Ross replied, "Captain, I was reading Scientific America magazine while we were loading stores and getting ready to get under way for the China Sea. I read an article about a laser cannon being researched by the US Navy, but the range was only about five hundred yards and tested on only surface craft."

Lee interrupted Ross by saying, "No, no, you're wrong, Harry. We heard at the Naval War College that the distance could be hypothetically improved to a range of two thousand yards, but I don't know how. I'm not a scientist. Our navy is currently experimenting with that kind of weapon right now, but only on surface vessels, and I don't know about its range. Also, I do remember that Mainland China put down a fiber optic cable from the Port of Shenzhen, China, to Da Nang, Vietnam, less than six months ago. The device must be attached to that cable. Wait a minute. Didn't Hong Kong recently complain to the US about losing a cable layer about six to eight months ago? The towers must be why they stole the cable if they stole the cable."

Williams got a hold of Samuels and ordered, "Mike, look for the coupler device attached to a fiber optic cable from those towers out to two thousand yards. Start at two thousand and work towards them. Keep the drone close to the bottom. Ramirez will give you the bearings and range to them."

Samuels acknowledged Williams's instructions. The Cardinalfish dropped down to twelve feet above the bottom to open the doors to the auxiliary compartment. He placed the drone in the deployment chamber and pressurized the compartment. Once the depth pressure was equal inside and outside the boat, he automatically opened the hatch and lowered the drone into the water. When the drone was clear, the chamber doors were closed, and the sub rested again on the bottom.

At the same time, Rico verified the water depth, contacted Sonar, and asked Ramirez to search for a thermocline. Ramirez responded that he had identified one at nine hundred twenty feet. Rico passed along that information to Williams, who ordered the boat to just below that depth. The three destroyers, detecting the Cardinalfish again, began their depth charge runs on her.

34

Seek and Destroy

Samuels turned on the drone search light and camera after the drone was about two thousand yards in front of the towers. He contacted Ramirez after checking all the drone's systems and finding them satisfactory and fully operational.

"Sonar, can you give me the bearing and range to the closest tower?"

Ramirez replied, "Aye, aye, sir. May I ask why?"

Samuels answered, "That's so I can track the cable from the tower to the coupler device."

"The tower is at two thousand five yards on a bearing of one-one-six, sir," Ramirez replied, "We are dodging depth charges and those two Chinese subs are just sitting out there. It could be a little hard working that drone as we move around and change depths and speed."

Samuels replied, "No kidding! Thanks for reminding me. I'll run a dead reckoning trace from here and let you know when I find the coupler for location purposes."

The Cardinalfish was playing hide-and-seek with the Chinese. She continually changed course, speed, and depth and, for the moment, was successful in avoiding any close contact with the destroyers and the two subs. She also remained out of the range of the twin towers. The AUV appeared to be immobile for the time being. Captain Williams was taking a large chance in remaining outside the speculative range of one of the two towers, while staying within the controlling range of the drone. Samuels was working the drone on the ocean bottom and moving towards the tower location.

After six minutes, Samuels reported to Ross and Ramirez in Sonar that he found the tower. He moved the drone up and down and around the tower to have a good picture in his mind to report what he saw. He called the control room and asked for a messenger. Petty Officer Mahoney reported to the auxiliary compartment and Samuels.

Mahoney quietly closed the auxiliary space door where Samuels was operating the drone. He saw her and asked, "Petty Officer Mahoney, are you my messenger?"

Mahoney replied, "Yes, sir, I am."

Samuels asked, "Okay, that's great. Have you got a pen and paper with you?"

Mahoney replied, "Yes, sir, I am ready to copy."

Samuels began, "The tower isn't very tall. I'd say it's about fifteen to twenty feet high. It is about fifteen feet in diameter. It is more like a silo than a tower. There is a sliding access door about four feet down from the top and it is about six feet long and three feet wide. I think the top opens and the laser rises out of its housing and has a three-hundred-sixty-degree rotational ability. I suspect the power and the amplifying unit or units are below the laser. I'll call it a cannon because it's a weapon. The fiber optic power cable is easy to spot. These fools used a black cable with a bright red stripe running lengthwise along the cable. I'm now going to move along the cable and find the coupling device. You can run that description back up to the captain in the control room."

Mahoney answered, "Aye, aye, sir. But I would like to show you my drawing of it to see if it matches what you are seeing."

Samuels looked at the drawing and replied, "That's perfect. That's exactly what it looks like." He began moving along the cable as Mahoney left the auxiliary space for the control room. Thirty minutes later, a large rectangular box appeared on the ocean floor. Mike turned on the camera to a wide-angle picture as he got close to it and made a video of it. The Chinese writing on it became very evident as the drone hovered over the top of the device.

He phoned the control room and Commander Doyle answered, "XO, here."

Samuels responded, "XO, the cable is quite large, and this drone is not equipped with a burning torch, so I'm going to try and cut through it with the mechanical hand. There are two cable runs on the device and each one goes to a tower. It sends and receives signals to and from both towers. I intend to cut the cable twice isolating the controller. That way the signal goes nowhere. I'll let you know how it goes, sir."

Doyle responded, "Very well and good luck with that."

While Samuels was talking to the XO, the Cardinalfish was rocked and shaking from the last pattern of depth charges dropped by the Chinese destroyers. An audible alarm went off and the public address system announced, "Flooding in the auxiliary pump room. Damage control teams respond." Two bolts were missing from a valve housing in the pump discharge line. The pump was secured, and the damage control team sealed the valve with new bolts.

At the same time, Williams and the COB scrambled to shut down the alarm as its sound penetrated out into the water.

Samuels was laughing after hearing the announcement.

Doyle, now with Samuels in the auxiliary space, asked, "Mike, what's funny about flooding?"

Samuels answered, "Well, Commander, I'm thinking about that woman's voice the Navy uses to make automated announcements on subs. When I was a boot ensign, I was in love with it when I heard that sultry, sexy voice for the very first time. I know they use it because it gets your attention. I was determined to find out her name and where she lived after completing my first patrol. She lived in Portland, Oregon. I wrote her and asked her for a picture. She sent one with a cute note. I was surprised at what she looked like. I laughed like hell when I saw her in the picture."

The XO asked, "And?"

Samuels replied, "She thanked me for my sexy letter and was pleased and amused to receive it. She turned out to be seventy-four years old with four kids, six grandkids."

Doyle, now laughing, said, "I wonder how the Navy found her and why they decided to use her voice?"

Samuels responded, "Because confined men think about women, sex, and home every few seconds and so do the women crew members about men."

Samuels continued working to finish the two cuts on the cable. He opened and closed the mechanical hands numerous times while simultaneously twisting and turning the hand. Finally, Samuels saw the cable separate from the controller on the left side. Eventually he finished cutting the cable away from the controller's right side. With both towers now disabled, he turned the drone power off. It descended and sat on the bottom.

Samuels, wiping the sweat from his face with a towel, called the control room. "Control room, this is Samuels. The towers are deactivated, and I heard the damage control team has secured the flooding in the auxiliary pump room."

The XO replied, "That's a good job, Mike, and good news on the flooding. Now, get back up here. We need you up here in the control room."

When Samuels returned to the control room, Lee was interpreting what Captain Wu was yelling about through his UQC to his submarines. Samuels listened intently to what Lee was describing.

Lee said, "Captain Wu is screaming and yelling at his techs. They haven't figured out just yet how we were able to disable the controller for their twin towers. He is backing away from us and ordered the two subs to attack us when and if they find us. He knows by now that we have deactivated his two towers."

Williams contacted Ramirez in Sonar. "Ramirez, do those two subs have us in their sights?"

Ramirez responded, "No, sir. That's because we are deeper than they can go, and we are under a really nice thermocline right now."

At the same time, the two Chinese subs began using their active sonar and were constantly pinging looking for the Cardinalfish.

Ramirez reported that one of the subs located the Cardinalfish and was attempting to give chase as she went deeper.

Lee reported to Williams that Wu ordered the sub to follow us no matter how deep we go.

Williams asked Lee, "He ordered that boat to exceed their crush depth? What a fool!"

Lee replied, "Yes, sir, he is. He is determined and obsessed to take us out!"

As Lee was talking, a large explosion occurred. The XO had all compartments report in. None of them reported any additional damage.

Ramirez reported, "Sir, that explosion was that Chinese sub imploding. I hear her coming apart. I hear bulkheads collapsing. I can hear screaming and yelling in the compartments on that boat that are still intact, but not for long. She's going to the bottom in pieces."

After hearing Ramirez's report, Lee responded, "Captain Wu has ordered the two destroyers and the remaining sub away from us and intends to pursue us with the AUV. He'll try to repair or replace these twin towers and use them later."

Williams responded, "Very well. Let's really make him mad and drive him up through the roof. Mr. Watson load tubes one and two, flood them down, and very quietly open their outer doors."

Watson replied, "Aye, aye, sir."

A few minutes later, Watson answered, "Tubes one and two loaded and flooded down with their doors open, sir."

Williams answered, "Very well. Sonar, pass the bearing and range of those two towers to Mr. Watson for insertion into our weapons computer."

Watson contacted Williams and replied, "Target bearings and range are loaded, sir."

Williams answered, "Fire one, wait five seconds and fire two."

Watson complied with Williams's orders. Two explosions occurred five seconds apart. The twin towers no longer existed.

Williams smiled and said, "It will take some time for them to be reconstructed and operational. They can chew on that for a while. Mr. Samuels, change course to the east and all ahead full. We are running for international waters."

Samuels replied, "Aye, aye, sir. Helm, make your course zero-nine-zero and all ahead full. Keep her at this depth."

The helmsman repeated Samuels's order and began the turn to due east and the boat's speed was increased to all ahead full.

Rico scanned the bottom contour charts and responded, "We've got clear and deep water all the way to international waters."

35

Condition Red

As the Cardinalfish turned east at full speed, Williams spoke to the on-watch duty section, "Quartermaster of the watch, for the logbook, I have the deck and the conn. Mr. Samuels has the dive."

Petty Officer Crown, acknowledging the captain, made the entry in the boat's logbook at 0005 (12:05 a.m.).

Williams then contacted Sonar and said, "Ramirez, give me a status report on our Chinese friends."

"This is Ross, Captain. I have the sonar watch again. Ramirez is backing me up and working the recorder to make sure we have an accurate account of our submerged actions. There is a sub ahead of us and is waiting for us as we close the range. She'll be in torpedo range when we are two thousand yards closer. The destroyers and the AUV are falling behind because they can't keep up with us. They are at seven thousand yards and opening, sir."

Williams replied, "Very well." He then turned to Rico and asked, "Mr. Petrone, do we have deep water to either the north or south of us?"

Rico, after surveying the bottom contour chart, responded, "We have better water depth to the south of us, sir."

Williams again replied, "Very well. Helm, right ten degrees rudder. Make your course two- seven-zero degrees."

The helmsman acknowledged the order.

Williams replied, "Very well. Hold the turn until we steady up on that course."

Samuels and Rico looked at each other with a surprised look on their faces.

Rico asked, "Pardon me, Captain, why are we heading back into the Chinese hornet's nest?"

Williams smiled at Rico and replied, "Watch and learn, mister. These guys killed one hundred fourteen Americans and destroyed a multibillion-dollar US submarine. They have a penalty to pay and I'm collecting it. That's why. I am prepared to answer for my actions to COMSUBPAC, CINCPACFLEET, and the Secretary of the Navy, if necessary."

Captain Williams spoke to the dive officer, "Mr. Samuels, when we settle up on two-seven- zero degrees, kindly reduce our speed to all ahead two-thirds, if you please."

Samuels stared at Williams for a moment and responded, "Aye, aye, sir. Reduce our speed to two-thirds when heading due west."

As the Cardinalfish made her big sweeping turn, the Chinese submarine began closing the distance.

"Sonar, this is the captain. I want you to notify me when that sub is on our tail at two thousand yards. Rico, plot a course directly to that AUV."

Rico acknowledged Williams's order and laid out the course and determined the distance.

At the same time, Ross responded, "Aye, aye, sir. Notify you at two thousand yards."

When the calculations were complete, Rico nodded to Samuels, and both men walked up beside the captain.

Rico said, "Captain, we know what you are going to do, and, with all due respect, we would like to ask you to reconsider."

Williams smiled at Rico and Samuels and in a low voice replied, "I knew both you and Mike would figure it out. I'm sure the XO has as well. We cannot and will not allow a foreign government to hold an axe over our heads due to some advanced weaponry. That weaponry, no matter what phase it was in, is and was ours. That weapon was hacked out of our military intelligence computers and the Chinese government beat us to the punch when they created it."

Williams continued, "We had written orders to follow, and we have done that. Now, I'll tell you what my verbal orders were from CINCPAC himself. My orders were to get the Tarpon out of Chinese waters with those sonar tapes. If any offensive action was taken against the Tarpon or us, we are to respond in kind but I'm not going to do that. There's a better way. Right now, the Chinese lost a boat by going too deep and we lost a boat by that, what I'll call, advanced laser cannon. We are going to teach the Chinese a lesson in tactics that they won't forget, and, in the future, they will think twice about messing with us because of that lesson. Everything we have done to date is recorded here on this boat, and I hope, eventually by satellite. We can't be sure of the latter. We are the greatest country in world with the greatest navy in the history of the world and that will never change in my book, gentlemen. CINCPAC told me that we also now know the how and when they got into our experimental weapons computer system. So back to your stations and let's get to it."

Rico and Samuels returned to their stations as ordered. Both Rico and Samuels took a long look at Doyle. He smiled back at them and gave them a thumbs-up.

36

Two for None

Ross phoned Captain Williams and said, "Captain, we are closing on the AUV awfully fast, and that Chinese sub is two thousand yards behind us. Wait a second, that sub has opened her outer torpedo tube doors and there's also a low-pitch hum in the water."

Lee cut in and said, "Captain, that means they are powering up the AUV, and Captain Wu now knows, for sure, he can't use his towers."

Captain Williams remained perfectly calm and called Sonar. "Sonar, bearing and distance to that AUV?"

Ross responded, "Aye, aye, sir. We are dead on her and the range is four thousand yards and closing awfully fast, sir."

Williams replied, "Very well. Give me a report every time we are five hundred yards closer to the AUV and let me know when we are at two thousand yards."

Ross again replied, "Aye, aye, sir."

Captain Williams called Watson. "Mr. Watson, are all tubes loaded and missile silos ready?"

Watson replied, "Yes, sir, and ready when you want them, Captain."

Williams replied, "Very well. Open the torpedo tube outer doors."

Samuels looked at the panel directly behind Rico, who was still focused on the bottom contour chart. Samuels replied, "Captain, outer doors on all tubes are open, sir."

Captain Williams responded, "Very well. Misters Watson and Samuels, ready tubes one, two, three, and four."

A moment later, Samuels replied, "Tubes one, two, three, and four are ready, Captain."

The captain replied, "Very well. Sonar, range to that AUV?"

Sonar responded, "Range three thousand yards and still closing fast. Captain, torpedoes in the water!"

Williams turned to Samuel and ordered, "All ahead full. Left full rudder. Release torpedo countermeasures."

Samuels was all ready to release the countermeasures and answered, "Countermeasures are in the water, Captain."

There were several explosions. As he heard the explosions, Ross immediately reported that he still heard torpedoes coming at them.

Williams asked, "Sonar, bearing to that AUV?"

Ross, with a raised voice, "Bearing to AUV is two-seven-four, Captain, and there's two torpedoes coming at us."

Williams answered, "Very well," and turned to the helmsman and ordered, "Come right to two-seven-four."

Doyle, checking his stopwatch and calculator, said, "Captain, impact by those torpedoes in thirty-four seconds."

Williams answered both Ross and Doyle with, "Very well."

All personnel in the control room were focused on their jobs. There was complete silence except for Captain Williams barking out his orders. Williams looked around for a quick check of the panels, instruments, and indicators to ensure all were at their ordered points. He looked at Lee as he confirmed the compass repeater located in front of the helmsman. Lee's face was pale white with large beads of sweat rolling downs his cheeks. He caught sight of Captain Williams looking at him and he gave Williams a somewhat sheepish grin and a thumbs-up. It was hard for Williams to keep a straight face. He thought to himself, "Lee has got to be filling his pants by now."

The helmsman reported, "Steady up on two-seven-four."

Williams replied, "Very well. All ahead flank. Rico, do we have deep water to the north of us?"

Rico replied, "All you need, Captain."

Williams responded, "Very well."

At the same time, Doyle started counting down the remaining thirty seconds to torpedo impact and Ross told Williams they were inside two thousand yards of the AUV with the Chinese sub fifteen hundred yards astern of the Cardinalfish.

Williams knew he was now closing the distance to the AUV very quickly and did a mental calculation in his head. He checked the weapons computer to ensure his mental calculations were correct. They were the same. The control room was incredibly quiet as he ordered, "Helm, right full rudder and do it smartly."

Captain Williams responded to the orders repeated back to him with, "Very well."

Lee heard Captain Wu screaming and yelling, and then ordering the AUV to fire the laser cannon as the Cardinalfish rapidly made her turn to the north. At the same time, Lee reported, "Captain, Wu powered up the laser and is firing it."

Williams replied, "Very well."

The low-pitch hum from the AUV became very loud and a "pop" was heard as the cannon fired. The beam missed the fast-turning Cardinalfish but hit the pursuing Chinese submarine.

The Chinese submarine caught the brunt of the beam. The sub took a laser cut on its pressure hull just forward of its sail as it tried to avoid the laser beam. It caught its crew totally by surprise. The water stream, propelled by the immense water pressure, immediately flooded that compartment and the added increase in water weight caused the sub to begin heading towards the ocean floor. She was blowing high pressure air into all her tanks and the boat tried to maintain her depth to no avail. The implosion of her hull at a far greater depth was heard by the Cardinalfish sonar operators, and they reported the same to Captain Williams. Wu heard it as well.

Williams knew by his mental calculations that the torpedoes fired from the Chinese sub, now in pieces and on the ocean floor, would miss the Cardinalfish due to her sudden increased speed and rapid course change to the north.

The two remaining Chinese torpedoes acquired the AUV as their target. Two explosions were subsequently heard as the Cardinalfish helmsman reported, "Steady on course due north."

"Control room, Sonar reporting. We have lost contact with both the Chinese sub and the AUV. They have been destroyed and are no longer on our screen. The two remaining torpedoes from that sub took out the AUV."

Captain Williams, shaking his fist in the air said, "Yes, we got two for none!"

Williams had to quiet down the cheering crew. He called Sonar again and asked, "Sonar, what are the positions and range to the remaining ships?"

Sonar answered, "Captain, the three destroyers appear to be moving away from us at high speed."

Williams responded, "Very well. Let me know when they are outside our sonar range of detection."

Ramirez answered, "Aye, aye, sir. Notify you when they are out of our range."

Captain Williams picked up the phone and dialed in all the ship's compartments. "This is the captain. To all hands, well done, well done! All of you performed your duties in an exemplary manner. Secure from battle stations. We're going home."

The cheering could be heard throughout the boat.

Captain Williams handed the phone to Doyle. "This is the XO. Section three has the watch."

Williams turned to Doyle. "In thirty minutes, I want all officers not on watch in the wardroom to conduct a critique of what we have just gone through."

The XO replied, "Aye, aye, sir. Sonar, do you hold any contacts?"

Sonar replied, "Control room, we hold no contacts at this time. Those Chinese ships are out of range."

Doyle turned to the helmsman and ordered, "All ahead two-thirds and make your course zero-nine-zero. Planesmen, make your depth six hundred feet."

The helmsman replied, "All ahead two-thirds and come to course zero-nine-zero."

The planesmen responded "Make the depth six-hundred feet."

Doyle replied, "Very well. Mr. Petrone, how far is it to international waters?"

Rico answered, "Three hours at this speed, XO. We have open and deep water all the way."

Doyle responded, "Very well. Mr. Samuels, bring us up to periscope depth and raise the radar and radio masts. Report any contacts that appear in our range."

Samuels answered, "Aye, aye, sir. Up to periscope depth and deploy radar and radio masts and report all contacts."

Doyle responded, "Very well."

Thirty minutes later, all the officers not on watch were seated in the wardroom except for the reactor section and those officers on watch. Captain Williams was about to make his opening statement when the phone rang.

"Captain, this is Samuels. We hold three radar contacts, in formation, heading directly for us. The range to those targets is fifteen thousand yards. I think its Captain Wu and his boys coming after us regardless of our position."

Williams asked Samuels, "Do you have their speed yet, Mike?"

Samuels replied, "Yes, sir. They are doing twenty-two knots. It may take them a little longer to catch up to us as the sea state is picking up."

Captain Williams looked at his watch. He turned to Rico and asked, "How soon to international waters?"

Rico, after checking his watch, responded, "We're in international waters in about an hour and thirty-six minutes.

Williams made another mental calculation at the same time Rico was doing the same.

Rico spoke before Williams had a chance to speak. "Captain, at twenty-two knots, and not considering the added increase of the sea state, they can catch us before we get to international waters in forty minutes if we don't increase our speed."

Williams smiled, looked at Rico, and replied, "No they won't. We are increasing our speed to be in international waters before they catch up to us."

Captain Williams, called Samuels in the control room and ordered an increase in speed to all ahead full.

After Samuels acknowledged the order, he turned to Rico and said, "If they attack us in international waters, then shame on them. We'll have them by the short hair! And Mr. Petrone, you're good. My math is the same as yours."

Both men smiled at each other as Rico replied, "I'll take that as a compliment, sir."

International Waters

Captain Williams was correct. The Cardinalfish crossed into international waters minutes before the Chang Ling caught up with them.

It didn't take long before Captain Wu contacted the Cardinalfish via the UQC. Ramirez contacted Samuels in the control room and informed him that Captain Wu wished to speak to the captain.

Samuels called Williams and informed him that he had a call from Wu on the UQC. Williams acknowledged Samuels and left his cabin and entered sonar.

Williams took a breath and said, "This is Captain Garrett speaking."

Captain Wu began, "This is Captain Wu. Captain Garrett, you are a pirate and a killer of my Chinese countrymen. You destroyed Chinese vessels and property. Once I inform President Lin of your actions and he contacts your president, your country will hand you over to us and you will stand trial for murder and be hung."

Captain Williams responded, "Captain Wu, you are the killer of the USS Tarpon, an American submarine on a diplomatic mission at the request of a US-friendly country and ally. You killed one hundred fourteen men and women on that boat. Unfortunately for you, we were successful in rescuing twenty-six of her crew including her captain."

Williams continued, "We also have a record of the sequence of events leading up to your attack on her and onboard internal conversations as she was destroyed. We also have a record of your numerous depth charge runs on my submarine. We have a record of some sort of an attempt to destroy us with an unknown weapon that was stationary on the ocean floor. We were forced to defend ourselves against that stationary weapon. We have a record of one of your submarines firing torpedoes at my boat and much more documented aggressive actions taken by you. Now what do you have to say about that?"

There was no answer from Wu, so Captain Williams went on. "Captain Wu, we are now in international waters and so are you. Any provocation from you will warrant your legitimate and immediate destruction. I will take out all three of your ships if you so much as bat an eye in a manner that I don't like. I am sick and tired of your aggressive behavior. Do you clearly understand me?"

Williams could hear the tension and anger in Wu's voice as he responded, "Captain Garrett, I will have President Lin issue a strong protest on your actions with your president and we will see who hangs first. I repeat to you that you killed two submarines, one research vessel, and a set of navigational stationary towers inside the China Sea."

Now Williams was angry, and he couldn't hold it in anymore and responded, "Wu, you are not ignorant of the truth. You had better check your satellite and vessels recordings. Your first submarine chased us well below her crush depth and she imploded. She was following your verbal orders. We have it on tape. Your second boat was destroyed by your so called "research vessel," which we identified as an automated laser weapon. We turned to avoid the laser beam fired at us and your boat bore the brunt of the beam and was hit by it and was destroyed.

"Additionally, as we turned away, the two remaining torpedoes that were fired at us from that second Chinese sub ran on to its new locked on target, which was the AUV, your so-called research vessel. The towers were destroyed because we determined them to be laser weapons by our remote drone. They were illegally constructed and installed with the fiber optic cable stolen from a Hong Kong cable layer that you destroyed. My guess is that the crew will never be found because you probably murdered them. We have onboard seven Japanese fishermen that you abandoned to the sea after scuttling their fishing boats and murdering one of their captains. I encourage you to have President Lin contact our president and we'll see who remains in command of his vessel, and which one of us dies when the actual truth is brought to the media and to all of the world governments."

Williams continued, "Now I have one more thing to say to you. You can go to hell for all I care. I said this to you once before and I'll say it again, so it is forever locked in your distorted mind. We are now in international waters. You make any move on us and I will blow you out of the water without any hesitation, and with a smile on my face. Captain Garrett out."

Wu responded, "See you in hell first, Garrett. Captain Wu out."

Williams entered the control room and ordered Doyle, "Battle stations and do it loudly so that Chinese dog on the surface can hear it. I want him to know that we'll do exactly what I said I would do if he became aggressive. Open outer torpedo doors and our silo doors and do it loudly."

The XO responded, "Aye, aye, sir. Sound the alarm for battle stations."

When the alarm sounded, the Cardinalfish crew manned their battle stations and were prepared to engage the remnant Chinese fleet.

Captain Wu, hearing that the American submarine was going to battle stations and torpedo doors opening, ordered all three destroyers to reverse course and head back into Chinese territorial waters.

Sonar reported that Wu and the other two destroyers were turning due west and returning to Chinese waters.

Williams was heard saying, "That's what I expected. I cut off his genitals. Poor, crazy, spineless jellyfish! He's dead meat!"

Once the Chang Ling and the other two destroyers were out of the area and sonar held no contacts, Captain Williams ordered the Cardinalfish to periscope depth. The radio antenna was raised above the water surface and a message about the doomed Tarpon and the actions of Captain Wu and their fleet was sent to CINCPACFLEET and COMSUBPAC.

The encrypted message read:

In international waters. Returning to Pearl with twenty-six Tarpon survivors, including Captain Duggan. Have sonar tapes for new carrier. New laser weapon used by Chinese vessels to destroy Tarpon. Have minimal damage from numerous depth charge attacks inside South China Sea by Chinese destroyers. President Mitchell can expect a strong objection from Chinese President Lin on necessary courses of action taken by Cardinalfish for survival. Seven Japanese fisherman taken aboard after Chinese Coast Guard set them adrift for trespassing. Japanese government notification requested. Additional information on our mission is sensitive. Recommend closed door briefing. ETA: five to six days. Tango down. Signed Williams.

After the message was sent, Lee read the message board and turned to Captain Williams and asked, "Captain, in your message you included the words 'Tango Down.'" May I ask what those words mean?"

Williams, smiling and facing Lee, replied, "Tango Down, in nautical terms, is when an enemy has been engaged and defeated in a combat scenario."

Lee, now smiling as well, answered, "I never saw that acronym in the Dictionary of Naval Abbreviations. Is it really included?"

The captain responded, "Obviously, the Naval War College doesn't have the latest edition of the DICNAVAB (Dictionary of Nautical Abbreviations) in its library!"

Lee left the control room laughing and muttering under his breath, "I wonder if there's one for blasted the hell out of them!"

Pearl Harbor

Rather than checking his boat's position on the DRT table, Captain Williams walked into Navigation and asked Senior Chief O'Hara for the current location of the Cardinalfish.

O'Hara pointed to a dot on the bottom contour chart and replied, "Captain, that's our current location taken twenty minutes ago. We are about three miles outside of the entrance to Pearl Harbor."

Williams smiled at O'Hara and said, "Thanks for the info." He walked out of Navigation and into the control room. "Mr. Watson, what is our current depth?"

Watson replied, "Sir, we are at two hundred fifty feet."

Williams replied, "Very well. Surface the boat and set the maneuvering watch."

Watson answered, "Aye, aye, sir. Surface the boat and set the maneuvering watch." Watson called Sonar and asked if there were any sonar contacts within the boat's range. There were none. He turned to the planesmen and ordered ten degrees rise and bring the Cardinalfish up to periscope depth. Once at sixty feet, he raised the periscope and made a complete circle scanning for all surface contacts. There were none. He also sounded the diving alarm three times and announced over the public address system, "Now, surface, surface, surface."

As the boat's bow broke the surface, Mr. Watson, instead of being the dive officer, became the officer of the deck and the conn. He and two lookouts climbed up to the ship's bridge once the lower sail hatch was above the waterline and open. Using their binoculars, they began a three-hundred-sixty-degree scan of the horizon. Both lookouts reported no visible contacts.

Captain Williams walked into the radio room and spoke to the radioman on watch. "I want to send two messages. The first one is to COMSUBPAC and CINCPACFLEET. ETA subbase 1300. We require a medical support team to tend to twenty-six survivors from the Tarpon, including Captain Duggan. Once moored at the pier, I request a meeting with COMSUBPAC, if available, and as soon as possible, for mission debriefing and discussion. Signed, Captain E. Williams, Commanding Officer, SSN Cardinalfish. The second message goes to the Pearl Harbor Navy Harbor Control. Request two ocean going tugs for the USS Cardinalfish at the harbor entrance by 1230 to maneuver to the designated pier assignment at the submarine base. Signed, Captain E. Williams, Commanding Officer, SSN Cardinalfish."

The radioman acknowledged Williams's request and began creating the messages.

Captain Williams walked back into the control room and ordered the radio mast to be raised to send the messages. He also ordered the speed reduced to all ahead one-third. Both messages, when completed, were immediately sent and received after the radio mast was raised.

He returned to his quarters, sat down, and reviewed the ship's logbook entries from the time the Cardinalfish left Pearl until she returned to Pearl. He was satisfied with all information in his chronological entries and wrote the last entry which read, "Entered Pearl Harbor, with assistance from two tugs, for designated subbase pier. Requested medical assistance team for Tarpon survivors. Mission satisfactorily completed with no crew loss of life and two torpedoes used. Thank God." He signed the entry, closed the logbook, and left it on top of his desk.

He sat there for a few minutes thinking about everything that happened during this hazardous patrol. The XO knocked on his door and Williams replied, "Enter."

The XO entered the stateroom and took off his hat and said, "Captain, we've had a successful mission without any loss of life or significant damage to the boat. There are a few minor repairs that need to be made from the depth charge attacks. I think this crew has earned a special privilege. I request your permission to fly the Jolly Roger flag as we enter port with an attached star for our crew and all of Pearl Harbor to see."

Williams smiled and replied, "You know that the Jolly Roger flag signifies we were in a combat scenario and the star signifies we were have a second victory. I'm not sure flying that flag is legitimate for this mission but it's a good sign of our success and to keep up morale."

Doyle added, "Captain, they tried numerous times to sink us or force us to give up and we didn't. They lost two subs, an AUV, and two bottom-sitting laser towers. The Tarpon was lost but we survived. That was just bad luck for them. We came home all in one piece and with no loss of life. That must mean something to the crew. They deserve to see that flag flying as we enter port for their actions and bravery in keeping us all alive and bringing us home."

Williams thought for a moment and then answered Doyle, "Okay, Billy, fly the Jolly Roger flag next to our American flag for the crew."

The XO replied, "Yes, sir, and thank you, Captain." As Doyle stood in the doorway, he asked, "Once we are all secure, how about meeting in the wardroom with the rest of our officers and having one drink before we have to meet with the admiral?"

Williams laughed and replied, "Good idea. Doubles all around. Lord knows we deserve it after this trip!"

The Reminiscent Letter

Rico went to his cabin now that the Cardinalfish was close to the harbor entrance and heading home. He opened his locker and removed the letter he wrote in his moments of free time. It was addressed to his wife and children.

He removed the letter from the envelope and began to read:

My darling Sharon and boys,

My hope is that this letter will eventually reach you. If it does, there are a few things I wish to tell you that I may not be able to tell you in person.

First, my thoughts, prayers, and love will always be with you. I love you all so very much. I know I probably don't show it or say it enough and I'll try to do both more often when and if we get back home. I also know that I really don't deserve you and I realize just how lucky I am to be with you.

Sweetheart, I have never forgotten the first time I saw you. My first thought was, "Wow!" You were at the beach, wading in the surf with a girlfriend. The mild sea breeze was blowing through your hair, and you looked fantastic in that skimpy white and black bikini! You caught sight of me staring at you. You smiled back at me and waved. I waved back never realizing that you were waving to another girlfriend who had just arrived and was standing behind me. You laughed out loud and shook your head "no" and pointed to her standing behind me. How embarrassing that was for me! I turned and started to walk away, and you came running over to me. We shook hands as we exchanged names. I mentioned a dance happening that night and asked you to go with me. You removed your sunglasses and as I stared into those big deep green eyes, you said, "Yes." That answer took my breath away.

Ever since that day, we have never been apart except for my military duties. This life together has meant more to me than you will ever know. We have two wonderful boys who are well-behaved and mannered mostly because of you. I know that they will become terrific men with or without me. I love them so very much. Together, we are all truly blessed.

Please say a prayer for me and the rest of the crew. They are a great bunch of men and women.

I can't wait to be back home and hold you in my arms, kiss you, and tell you how much I love you and missed you.

Hope to see you soon.

All my love always,

Rico

Rico put the letter back in his locker and climbed up into his bunk. He was almost asleep when the order to set the maneuvering watch resounded throughout the boat. He washed and dried his face, and walked to Navigation.

The Briefing

Once the Cardinalfish was moored alongside pier two, the shore power cable, potable water, and secure phone lines were connected. Captain Williams left the bridge and went to his cabin and wrote the appropriate entries in the ship's logbook. The radioman knocked on his door.

Williams responded, "Enter."

The radioman entered the captain's cabin and said, "Captain, we received a message from COMSUBPAC," and handed it to Williams.

The message read, "Captain Williams, I have the rest of the day open and am ready to receive you at the earliest convenience." It was signed Rear Admiral Chad Morgan.

Williams grabbed a shower and dressed in a clean khaki uniform plus a black tic. The ball cap went into the closet and he put on the uniform combination hat. He tucked the Cardinalfish logbook under his arm and then knocked on Commander Doyle's cabin.

Doyle opened the door and saw Williams standing there. He smiled and said, "Well now, the two of us are all dressed up and have somewhere to go!"

Williams smiled and responded, "Billy, I'd rather not go to this dance, if you don't mind, but you and I have no choice on this one."

Doyle smiled back at Williams and replied, "Let's go get it done so we can go home for a little while and be with our families."

The XO followed Williams up the ladder and out through the boat's sail doorway onto the main deck. Both men were surprised to see Captain Duggan laying on a dory and waiting for the next ambulance to the hospital. Captain Duggan held up his hand and motioned for them to come over.

When they did, Duggan calmly said, "Captain Williams, I want to thank you, your XO, and your crew for saving not only my life but the lives of some of my crew. I would like to apologize for my behavior while aboard the Cardinalfish. I think you would have acted in the same manner if it were your boat and crew and what we had to endure. I will never forget what you did for us. Thank you again."

Williams, still holding Duggan's hand replied, "Captain Duggan, I know you would have done the same for us if the roles were reversed. It was an honor having you aboard my boat."

Duggan smiled and asked, "May I ask you to do me a favor?"

Williams responded, "Anything, Captain."

Duggan put his hand under the sheet and pulled out the Tarpon logbook. He handed it to Williams and said, "Everything that happened on our mission to and in the South China Sea for those sonar tapes is written in my logbook. I know that Admiral Morgan will want to read and review what's written. You know where to find me if he has any questions."

Williams tucked the Tarpon's logbook under his arm holding the Cardinalfish's logbook. Both Williams and Doyle shook hands with Duggan and then left for COMSUBPAC headquarters.

They preferred to walk after having spent all that time at sea inside the Cardinalfish. Both men had to show their identification badge to the security desk located inside the entrance to Admiral Morgan's office.

After reviewing their IDs, US Marine Sergeant Morrell said, "Follow me please, sirs, as the admiral is waiting for you."

Both Williams and Doyle glanced at each other and said nothing.

Morgan's chief of staff, Captain Vince Peters, was waiting outside the admiral's office for them.

Both Williams and Doyle shook hands with Peters and said, "Hello, Vince. How have you been?"

"Never mind the chit chat!" Peters replied. "You guys have stirred up one hell of a hornet's nest. The president, the joint chiefs, and the secretaries of the Navy and Defense in Washington are doing damage control on your escapades! Be prepared to get your butts chewed unless you have an excellent defense for your actions. Did you guys really sink two subs, an AUV, and take out twin stationary towers? If you did, you had to be plum crazy! The tension between China and the United States is at an all-time high and China's President Lin is threatening war."

Williams replied, "You'll hear and get everything when we explain, in detail, our decisions and actions while in the South China Sea to Admiral Morgan. We also have the Tarpon's logbook with all of Captain Duggan's entries all the way up until we rescued him and some of his crew. One hundred fourteen good men and women are dead. They were deliberately killed by the Chinese."

Peters shook his head saying, "Are you kidding me?" He knocked on Morgan's door while thinking about all those dead men and women.

Admiral Morgan responded, "Enter."

Morgan stood up and walked around his desk and over to the conference table near the large picture window looking out into the harbor.

One side of the table had two empty chairs. The other side of the table had five chairs with three naval officers seated at the table. All three officers stood up as Morgan, Peters, Williams, and Doyle approached the table.

Morgan said, "Allow me to introduce these gentlemen to you. This is Captain Rizzo, CINCPACFLEET's chief of staff, and this is Commander Rourke from the Judge Advocate General's office, and finally, this is Commander James who will be recording our conversations for as long it takes to sort out all of the details of your mission."

All the introduced officers shook hands with Williams and Doyle. Their faces were without smiles. No cordial greeting was exchanged after the introductions. This was not the kind of welcoming home that Williams and Doyle expected.

Morgan spoke after everyone was seated at the table. "Gentlemen, we are here today to validate and document the legalities of the courses of action Captain Williams took while in the China Sea. We are also here to determine how and why the Tarpon disappeared."

When everyone was ready, Admiral Morgan asked Captain Williams to begin.

Williams stood up and handed the Tarpon's logbook to Admiral Morgan. Morgan looked at Williams with a surprised look on his face.

Williams nodded and said, "Admiral Morgan and gentlemen, that is the logbook of the USS Tarpon. She no longer exists. She rests in small pieces at the bottom of the South China Sea in more than twelve hundred feet of water. As you know, Admiral Morgan ordered my boat, the Cardinalfish, to search and find the Tarpon after she failed to report in at the appropriate time. We found the Tarpon resting on the ledge of a sea mount at a depth of seven hundred fifty feet. We deployed our DSRV several times to rescue the survivors, twenty-six in all. One hundred fourteen Tarpon crew lost their lives."

"Captain Duggan, her skipper, was one of the survivors," Williams continued. "He explained, in detail, what happened to his boat. Although we didn't know all the information at the time, we eventually determined that the Tarpon was sunk by an underwater laser cannon with a maximum range of two thousand yards. Our DSRV operators saw that her stern, aft of the reactor spaces, was missing. The planes, the propeller, and its cowling were nowhere to be found. The port side of the pressure hull, aft of the reactor spaces, was neatly cut while the starboard side was partially cut and torn. I believe the weight of that part of the hull separated due to the excessive weight and was torn off as it fell to the sea bottom. We have a video of the Tarpon."

Captain Rizzo asked Williams, "Do you mean to tell me that the Chinese have a laser cannon with a range of two thousand yards that works underwater, and we didn't know about it?"

Williams replied, "Yes, sir, that is correct. When we figured it out, we also found the fiber optic cable with an attached coupler that activated and operated twin stationary towers, each equipped with a similar laser cannon. Each tower had a rotating turret on top. The towers could be activated from shore, from a surface vessel, aircraft, submarine, and from an AUV. We were required to destroy those two towers or face the same result as the Tarpon. By the way, that cable is the property of Hong Kong. It was stolen from their cable layer about six to eight months ago. In addition, there is no trace of the ship or her crew."

Admiral Morgan responded, "That means they somehow hacked into our military experimental weapons computer system and stole our research and beat us to the punch! Our research has the range for that kind of weapon at about five hundred yards and that's only on the surface. We have no underwater capability at this time."

Williams nodded and continued, "After we got Captain Duggan aboard along with his remaining crew, he described how the Chinese destroyed the Tarpon. It's all written in his logbook for your review and analysis. By the way, he managed to collect the sonar tapes on their new nuclear aircraft carrier. Here's the thumb drive with the data on that carrier."

Admiral Morgan then asked Williams, "The Chinese are claiming that you sunk two of their submarines, and an AUV, and destroyed two underwater communication towers. Can you explain the how and why you did that?"

Captain Williams, trying not to smile, answered, "Admiral and gentlemen, every action and decision we took and made is recorded in our onboard computer and in my ship's logbook. Admiral, here is the Cardinalfish's logbook for you to read, review, and copy if you wish. It's all written down. I'm sure we had a satellite or two positioned over the South China Sea that may have some information and bearing on some of the events as well. It may not have much information as we were pretty deep most of the time."

Williams reached into his pocket. "Admiral Morgan and gentlemen, every verbal order given, every discussion, and every conversation throughout all of our engagements with the Chinese are copied onto this thumb drive. So, in other words, you have all my thoughts, words, decisions, and commands written down in the ship's logbook. Also, you have all the same information as it happened on that thumb drive. The other thumb drive is Captain Duggan's. It contains the sonar tapes on that Chinese nuclear aircraft carrier. Again, it cost us one hundred fourteen lives."

Williams poured himself a glass of water and took a long drink. He looked at Admiral Morgan and Captain Rizzo and replied, "Sirs, the Cardinalfish never, I repeat, never, took any offensive action against the Chinese fleet. We were forced to destroy the two laser towers due to their capability and opportunity to destroy the Cardinalfish. They were destroyed by two of our torpedoes. We took no offensive action against their ships, per your written and verbal orders. We withstood numerous depth charge attacks by Chinese destroyers and submarines and vessels attempting to block our attempts to return to international waters. A Captain Wu wanted our latest weapons and technology intact for China. We destroyed what was left of the Tarpon only after we rescued the survivors. That was to ensure they got none of our weapons or technology. I was prepared to destroy the Cardinalfish, if necessary."

Captain Peters asked, "So, how were their subs and that AUV destroyed if you never fired upon them?"

Williams smiled and replied, "We used good old American dodgeball tactics, so to speak!"

Morgan, surprised, asked, "What in the hell is dodgeball tactics?"

Captain Williams said, "I'll explain it, but you won't believe it until you read it in our logbook or on that thumb drive. True, we destroyed the twin towers, but we did not destroy their vessels. I must tell you in all sincerity and respect that I really wanted to eliminate all of them for what they did to Tarpon and what they tried to do to the Cardinalfish. It took great restraint to follow your orders admiral."

He continued, "Admiral Morgan verbally told me about the fiber optic cable as it was originally passed to us by the Hong Kong government. Lord knows how they knew but more than likely, it was by a spy or mole in the Chinese Communist government. But there may be another possibility. If Hong Kong, or any other country, was transporting that cable by ship, the Chinese Coast Guard probably intercepted her for trespassing. They sunk two Japanese fishing vessels for that reason. Per your orders, Admiral, we picked up seven Japanese survivors in a life raft and got their story. Those are the seven we sent over to the hospital with the remnant Tarpon crew."

Williams turned to Commander Doyle and asked him to speak. Doyle stood up and began to speak. "Gentlemen, a quick change of subject but just for a couple of minutes. Two months ago, the Chinese launched a new destroyer type. They call it a Type 055 destroyer. This destroyer is very technologically advanced. Her name is the Chang Ling. Her commanding officer was a man named Captain Wu. His destroyer was activating those towers we just spoke of as well as the AUV. That is how they destroyed the Tarpon. He is the man who ordered multiple depth charge attacks on both the Tarpon and the Cardinalfish."

Captain Peters asked, "Did you sustain any damage from those attacks?"

Doyle replied, "Yes, sir, we did, but the damage is minimal internally. We'll need to make minor repairs before we go out again. We cannot determine the pressure hull condition until we put her up in drydock for an examination."

Doyle continued, "The Chang Ling, as Captain Williams said, was capable of activating and using the laser cannons from either his destroyer, the AUV, or from the towers. We believe that the laser cannons can also be activated from aircraft. When we destroyed the towers, he became irate and ordered one of the Chinese subs to attack us. She followed us down below her crush depth and imploded. We were above our crush depth limit. We have the occurrence on our onboard sonar computers. After that, Captain Wu ordered the second sub to pursue us, but not below her crush depth, and attack us using torpedoes."

Admiral Morgan asked, "How did you know that?"

Captain Williams answered Morgan's question. "Admiral, your astute idea about putting a Chinese interpreter from the Naval War College aboard the Cardinalfish was pure genius! His help and assistance were invaluable. If I may say so, sir, we might not be here today if it wasn't for Lei Wang Joe Skiboski and his translations and advice."

Captain Peters asked, "Lei Wang Joe who?"

Everyone opposite Williams and Doyle was laughing.

Williams replied, "Just call him Lee when you meet him, as I am sure you'll know how great a help he was."

Doyle continued, "That second Chinese sub fired four torpedoes at us. Two of those torpedoes exploded when they met our countermeasures. We changed course towards the AUV and increased our speed. That was a direct collision course at their AUV. We knew that the AUV was about to fire at us due to the low-pitch hum that it emits through the water just before it fires. Our sonar picked it up and . . ."

Commander Rizzo interrupted Commander Doyle. "How did you know about the hum?"

Captain Williams replied, "Captain Duggan and his lead reactor officer described and heard it just before there was a loud 'pop' and the Tarpon began flooding uncontrollably in her after spaces. Additionally, his rescued sonar tech continually worked with our sonar team to identify that hum. We weren't exactly sure until our drone conducted a close visual inspection of the two stationary towers. The laser cannon's electrical powering up hum has a much lower pitch than the usual Chinese fifty-cycle electrical hum."

Rizzo nodded and replied, "That's very interesting. Thank you for that. I'm sure our experimental weapons group will be very interested in what you have heard and documented."

Commander Doyle continued, "When we heard that low-pitch hum, we increased speed to all ahead flank and turned away to starboard just within one thousand yards of the AUV. Two things happened as we avoided its laser beam. Those Chinese torpedoes locked onto the AUV, instead of us, and took it out. We heard the explosions. Secondly, the laser beam, when fired by the AUV, cut into their Chinese sub behind us that fired those four torpedoes. We could hear water rushing into that sub. Our sonar team told us she was blowing tanks but still going deeper. We heard another explosion and sonar reported that the boat had imploded well below her crush depth."

Captain Williams cut in and said, "After that, we had a conversation with Captain Wu. He was angry, irate, and irrational at the loss of the towers, the two subs, and his AUV. He threatened us with depth charges and ASROCs. He heard us deliberately sounding our general alarm, opening torpedo outer doors, and calling for battle stations. We had been at battle stations ever since we started looking for the Tarpon and later for the twin towers. The alarm was just for effect. I threatened him with the complete destruction of his remaining three ships. He backed off. We changed our course to due east and headed for international waters. He changed his mind and course and pursued us again but didn't catch up with us until we were in international waters. I threatened Wu again, telling him that if he initiated any action against us, I had every right to blow him out of the water as we were now in neutral waters. He backed off, reversed course towards China, and implied the Chinese political hammer."

Admiral Morgan looked at the Cardinalfish's captain and executive officer and replied, "What you just described to us is totally amazing. It's hard to believe that you took out three vessels and two towers by using their own aggressiveness. I have never heard of anything like that in the history of submarine warfare. Plus, you were able to save twenty-six doomed men and women from the destroyed Tarpon. Amazing! Totally amazing!"

Commander Rourke added, "Admiral Morgan, we'll need to make a copy of the logbook and that computer thumb drive. I'll sign for them and leave the copies with you, as we'll need the originals in Washington to deal with President Lin and China. I'd say, from a legal perspective, that everything Wu did can be clearly construed as an act of war. But you know that any kind of combative action by the United States could or would lead to nuclear annihilation of the globe. I can't answer for President Mitchell, the secretary of the Navy, the joint chiefs, or Washington, but I can tell you that a definite harsh course of action is undoubtedly and definitely warranted."

Rourke turned to the present recording officer and told him to stop recording.

Rourke continued off the record, "Gentlemen, I think the best way to handle this whole scenario and situation is to go with the following course of action and statement, provided it is agreed to and approved by our government:

"The Tarpon was ordered into the South China Sea by CINCPAC-FLEET at the request of our Navy Department. The Hong Kong government made a request of our government to investigate their missing fiber optic cable-laying vessel. The Tarpon was used because of her deep diving ability and use of drones. When the Tarpon failed to report in and was presumed missing, CINCPACFLEET ordered COMSUBPAC to initiate a rescue mission to find and assist the Tarpon. The Cardinalfish was deployed to the South China Sea and found the Tarpon disabled in deep water. A daring rescue mission was undertaken and twenty-six of her crew was saved. The Cardinalfish returned to Pearl Harbor with the survivors."

Admiral Morgan smiled and said, "That will more than likely be the story the media gets. But all of you and I know the harsh reality that the Chinese government and Captain Wu will pay dearly for their aggressiveness and the taking of American lives. It is now just a matter of how and when."

Morgan continued, "Additionally, as Captain Williams mentioned, the Hong Kong government lost its cable-laying vessel in the North China Sea some time ago. We can't prove it just yet, but it's obvious that the Chinese probably stole the cable and then destroyed the cable layer. The tension between China and the surrounding countries around the South China Sea is extremely high. Each of them desire control of that area and are declaring it as part of their own individual country. Washington and our Navy Department have deployed a carrier battle group to that area as a deterrent to prevent aggressive actions, including a war, by any of them."

Commander Rourke said, "Now to the matter at hand. This successful mission was a Tango Down mission. Confronting an enemy or enemy force of five ships plus an AUV and coming home victorious is monumental! Admiral, the actions taken by the Cardinalfish and these two officers and their crew are exemplary. None of what happened in the entire China Sea will probably ever be divulged until it's declassified twenty years from now. To get the story straight, if you can call it that, Captain Williams and Commander Doyle will, more than likely, be requested to testify before a congressional committee of some sort. There will be a closed-door session, which will be extremely embarrassing to the Chinese government."

Captain Peters added, "The Cardinalfish will need a partial refit for damage repair. She could be inactive for a month or more."

Admiral Morgan replied, "That refit will be finished in less than a month. Do you read me? Both Captain Williams and Commander Doyle will be detached from the Cardinalfish and at Washington's disposal."

Before Admiral Morgan could continue, Williams stood up and responded, "Admiral, I do not wish to be removed from command of my boat. With all due respect, sir, I deserve to remain as her skipper."

Doyle stood up and added, "Admiral, that goes as well for me, as I am her XO, sir."

Admiral Morgan responded, "My mistake. We'll send you to DC, TAD (temporary assigned duty), if requested." A big smile came across his face as he said, "I meant to say temporarily detached. Is there anything else that needs to be discussed?"

Captain Williams replied to both Morgan and Peters, "Yes, sirs, there is. I would like to recommend that Lieutenant Commander Petrone be considered for command and Lieutenant Commander Samuels as an executive officer. I wish to have Doyle remain with me on the Cardinalfish as XO. The Navy Department may consider him for command. If that happens, it is well deserved. Additionally, I would like to keep a minimal rotational watch section on board my boat while undergoing the refit. Do I have your permission to deal out leave and liberty for my crew? They deserve it after this last mission."

Admiral Morgan replied, "Granted for your request. We'll consider and decide on your Doyle, Petrone, and Samuels requests later. Is there anything else?"

Williams figured he might as well go for broke. "Yes, sir, I would like to request a party at the Royal Hawaiian for my entire crew and their families, and all of you as guests, as a "well done" from CINCPAC-FLEET and COMSUBPAC for what we accomplished."

Morgan smiled and answered, "That's mighty bold of you, Captain!"

Williams replied, "Yes, sir, it is. May I mention that I had you as my teacher and mentor in being bold, Admiral."

Everyone was laughing as Admiral Morgan replied, "Granted. You'll get your party. It has already been paid for by your successful, completed mission."

DC Bound

Captain Williams and his family were lying on Waikiki Beach in Honolulu when he heard his cell phone ring. He looked at the number and knew the call was from Captain Peters from COMSUBPAC.

He answered, "This is Captain Eric Williams. It's fourteen hundred. Come on over and I'll buy you a Mai Tai."

"Eric, hold that drink for some other time. I was just calling to let you know that we are holding two seats on a MAC (military airlift command) flight from here to El Paso, Texas, the day after tomorrow. It goes out on Monday morning at 0800. You'll link up with another MAC flight out of El Paso to Washington, DC. You have two rooms at the BOQ (bachelor officer's quarters) at Langley Air Force Base on the DC beltway for Monday night and thereafter for as long as you and Doyle need them. A representative from Chief of Naval Operations has set up a car and driver for transportation purposes for you, if needed."

Williams replied, "Thanks, MAC."

Peters answered, "The name's Vince not MAC. Oh, I get it, now."

Eric laughed and responded, "Okay, Vince. Do you have any idea where the meeting is going to be and who'll be attending?"

Vince answered, "It's being set up inside the secure conference room at Langley Air Force Base. We know some of the attendees but not all. There'll be representatives from Chief of Naval Operations (CNO), SECNAV (Secretary of the Navy), NJAG (Navy Judge Advocate General's Office), SECDEF (Secretary of Defense), and a member of the House and Senate Armed Forces Committees. Oh, and there'll be no press at this meeting. It will be a closed-door session. Retired Vice Admiral Wilson also agreed to be there to help and support you. Admiral Morgan remembered that you served under him when he was your commanding officer, and you were a junior officer on your first nuclear boat."

Williams replied, "That's right. It will be good to see Marv Wilson again. It's been a long time since I've seen him or talked to him. Vice Admiral, huh? Well, good things happen to good people."

Peters responded, "Anyway, have a good trip and I'll see you when you get back. You can buy me that drink when all this is over. Both Admiral Morgan and I know everything you did was in the best interests of the Navy and the country. Don't sweat it too much. It'll work out fine."

Williams answered, "Yeah, right! You know as well as I do those events can be distorted, turned around, and not supported in the best interests of the country. By the way, have you called Doyle yet?"

Peters said, "He's my next call. I'll see you both when you get back. Good luck to the both of you."

Williams hung up the phone and called to his wife who was now wading in the warm Hawaiian water. He threw her a towel when she stood in front of him.

He smiled and said, "Honey, I just heard from Vince Peters. Billy Doyle and I fly out on a MAC flight for DC on Monday morning. We'll be staying at the BOQ at Langley Air Force Base."

The next two days seemed go by way too fast. Before they realized it, Williams and Doyle were standing in line and boarding the plane to El Paso. The good part of the flight was that the plane was a Boeing 767. The seats were comfortable, and the plane was air conditioned. The bad part of the flight was that their seats were over the wing, and they continually heard the hum of the engines. The second flight was much better. During the flight to DC, they ate a roast beef sandwich with mustard or mayonnaise, limp lettuce, a small bag of chips, a cookie, and some gum. The cold bottled water came from the onboard aircraft refrigerator.

The plane landed at Langley Air Force Base at 2400 (midnight). Doyle looked at his watch and read 0800 (8 a.m.). He commented that there must have been a slight tail wind to get them to DC a little early.

As they were leaving the aircraft, the aircraft copilot pointed and said, "There's a car waiting for you over there by that hangar. It will take you to the BOQ, sirs."

Both Williams and Doyle thanked the copilot and walked towards the car. They were surprised to see who the driver was.

The XO smiled. "Well, well, well, Petty Officer Mahoney, what are you doing here?"

Mahoney saluted and replied, "My parents have a cottage on Chesapeake Bay and I'm here on leave. But a little birdie told me you and the captain were coming here for a meeting, so I volunteered to be your driver. Shipmates stick together, sir."

Williams responded, "Very well, Mahoney. I'm glad you're here."

Mahoney replied, "Captain, I wanted to be here and had to be here just to let you know that the whole crew is behind you and supporting you in any way we can. Also, it's just like standing the watch back aboard Cardinalfish, sir."

Williams answered, "Okay, Petty Officer Mahoney. How about taking us to the BOQ, dropping us off, and then head back home to your parents' place. Do you know what time to pick us up in the morning?"

Mahoney replied, "Captain, the meeting is scheduled to start at 0930 at the base secure conference room. Check in is at 0915. With your approval, sir, I'll pick you up whenever you want me too. However, the breakfast bar is really good here and I recommend having a good meal before the fun and games begin inside that conference room."

Captain Williams looked at Doyle. They both nodded in agreement. He turned back to Mahoney and said, "Mahoney, you talked us into that breakfast. What time do you suggest?"

Mahoney asked, "Captain, may I eat with you and the XO if you are alone?"

Doyle answered her, "Petty Officer Mahoney, we wouldn't have it any other way. It would be a pleasure."

Mahoney, opening the car doors, suggested, "Well, sirs, the conference room is just five minutes from the breakfast grill. So how about I pick you up at 0805, right after morning colors (the raising of the American flag and the national anthem ends)."

Once the bags were in the trunk and Mahoney was behind the wheel, she turned and said, "There's just one thing: I recommend you don't eat the grits here because they are not genuine."

Doyle asked, "What's that?"

Mahoney, smiling, replied, "Grits. They just don't taste like down south grits."

There was a humorous discussion of just what good grits should taste like until Mahoney dropped Captain Williams and Commander Doyle off at the BOQ.

Accountability

Captain Williams, Commander Doyle, and Petty Officer Mahoney enjoyed a quiet breakfast together sitting at a single table away from most everyone else. No one ordered the grits. The conversation became serious as they finished eating. Mahoney asked permission to ask a question concerning their last mission.

Mahoney asked, "Captain, if you went through all of this with an admiral, a few captains, and other senior officers in Hawaii, why do you both have to do it again here in DC?"

Both Williams and Doyle laughed.

Mahoney replied to the laughter, "What's so funny? This isn't funny at all. This could be extremely dangerous for both of you. You both could lose the Cardinalfish."

Williams stared at Mahoney for a moment and then responded, "Mahoney, there are two games being played concerning our mission. The first game is what I will call the 'hands-on' game and the second one is called the 'political' game. Both are important. The first one is important because of what happened to the Tarpon and almost to us. We defended ourselves in the best way possible without us becoming an offensive weapon and taking Chinese lives. The lives lost on both sides belong to the Chinese captain of their battle group. The Chinese government likely sanctioned and gave Captain Wu permission to kill one hundred fourteen Americans.

"When we entered the picture, they tried to kill us as well. We were smarter than they were. For every move they made, we countered with a better one. Captain Wu became a madman and was way too aggressive with his men and his ships. He lost both when he tried to destroy the Cardinalfish. Someone must pay for those losses. The Chinese government is attempting to make us the scapegoat by saying that we killed Chinese sailors and destroyed their ships. They may throw him to the wolves to prevent a military confrontation by calling him either a rogue commander or by saying that he was insane. We'll see how and when which one plays out."

Mahoney sat quietly and listened to what Williams had to say. She looked at her captain and replied, "I understand that one, but what about this one?"

Williams took a deep breath and answered, "The political game is a nebulous game because only those in control of the game know what the outcome will be. There are a lot of things to consider in this game. First, who is at fault? Can the fault be substantiated and factually proven? Can the fault be shifted to the one who is not at fault? Each side will attempt to prove the other side is at fault. But in this case, I think the US government has the upper hand and the American fist will hit hard. Why do I say that? Because all the while we were in the South China Sea, we recorded and documented every conversation, made every correct decision, and took every right deliberate action."

Williams continued, "Our government will have records and documentation from any US or ally satellite that was stationary over the

China Sea while we were there. Additionally, we had a former natural-
ized Chinese citizen aboard our boat during our mission who teaches
and consults both foreign and American line officers at the Naval War
College in Newport. We also have the official logbooks from both the
Tarpon and the Cardinalfish of everything that took place. Finally, if
necessary, they can obtain Captain Duggan's testimony and the survivors of his crew to prove the Chinese deliberately used and tested a
new laser weapon on an American submarine, the Tarpon. They went
out of their way to destroy her and kill Americans."

Mahoney looked at both Captain Williams and the XO and said,
"So, it's a piece of cake then, right?"

Doyle answered this time. "No, because we took one action
without Chinese notification or our Navy's permission, and we may
end up making some form of restitution for it."

Mahoney then asked, "Which action was that?"

Doyle responded, "We destroyed those two towers containing
their laser cannons. They will claim the cable was theirs, but Hong
Kong is missing their cable plus their cable-laying vessel is missing and
presumed sunk. We may have to answer for destroying the towers."

Mahoney only had one thing to say. "Sirs, having been there with
you and the rest of the crew and knowing what I know and what you
just explained, this closed-door session could really suck for us!"

Williams answered, "Yes, but we just have to go and play their
game but tell the truth and substantiate it. Speaking of the game, it's
time to go."

The three picked up their trays and placed them in the cart for
the kitchen help. On the way out Williams paid for all three breakfasts.
As they all got in the car, Mahoney turned to Captain Williams and
thanked him for the breakfast, the casual conversation, and the expla-
nation and then wished them good luck.

Captain Williams and Commander Doyle checked in at the secure conference room at 0910 (9:10 a.m.). A sergeant at arms escorted them to a vacant table with two microphones and three empty chairs. On the table was a pitcher of water, two glasses, and some note paper and pens.

Under his breath, Doyle commented, "What no ice, scotch, and hors d'oeuvres? Who's running this place?"

Williams told Doyle to sit down and be quiet and replied, "No fooling around here, buddy."

Lee was sitting directly behind Williams and Doyle and replied, "After all this is over, it's on me, gentlemen."

Both men smiled at Lee and said, "You're on!"

At the table to the right of Williams was Commander Rourke from the JAG office at Pearl Harbor. To the left and across from Williams and Doyle sat the Chinese delegation, which included a naval officer. Lee leaned forward and whispered to Williams and Doyle that the Chinese naval officer was Captain Wu. Also seated at the table was a Chinese diplomat, who resided in DC, plus a senior member of the Chinese Communist Party.

Doyle asked Lee, "Yeah, but can they speak American?"

Lee answered, "All of them speak English, but more than likely, they will speak only in Chinese for effect."

Williams, Doyle, and Lee all chuckled at the remark.

The gavel came down at exactly 0930. The senior member overseeing and conducting the investigation was Senator Alex Fenwick. He introduced himself as the senior member of the Senate Armed Services Committee. The two other men sitting on the dais were also introduced to the foreign and American attendees.

Each attendee stood up and gave their name, position, and relevance to the hearing.

Senator Fenwick began by saying, "Good morning, gentlemen. Now that you all have introduced yourselves, I am going to explain how this session will proceed and how it will be conducted. First, I want to make it perfectly clear that there will be no unannounced outbursts by anyone in this room. Secondly, all testimony given today, and any necessary subsequent days, will all be recorded. Both sides will automatically be given a complete and unabridged copy of the testimony given today. You can do with it what you want after the proceedings are over. Lastly, I will remind all parties that I will not stand for perjury, blasphemy, or colorful metaphors during these proceedings. Do I make myself perfectly clear?"

Both the American side and the Chinese side answered with, "Yes, we understand."

Senator Fenwick asked Captain Williams to stand up and raise his right hand. After being sworn in, Williams sat down and turned on his microphone.

Fenwick said, "For the record, please state your name and position."

Williams answered, "My name is Eric Williams. I am a United States Navy captain, and I am the commanding officer of the nuclear submarine Cardinalfish."

Doyle looked at Captain Wu who looked totally confused and surprised. Wu whispered in the diplomat's ear that the captain he spoke to during the events in the South China Sea was a Captain Leroy Garrett.

The diplomat raised his hand and stood up without being recognized, saying, "Senator Gavin, this man is not the commanding officer of the submarine we encountered in the China Sea. This man is an imposter!"

Fenwick responded, "Sir, please sit down and be quiet. You will have your turn to speak after we are finished with the American officers involved in these proceedings. However, Captain, would you care to answer his comment at this time?"

Williams, looking at the Chinese delegation, answered, "Yes, sir, it would be my pleasure. During the episodes in the China Sea, I gave a fictious name. My reasoning was simple. If I gave my real name, the Chinese could, I'll use the term, 'investigate me,' and possibly use it against me or our government as the commander of a nuclear submarine."

The Chinese delegation was beginning to become unsettled at Williams's remarks.

Fenwick then replied, "Captain Williams, my sergeant at arms is going to give you a copy of your testimony taken at Pearl Harbor several days ago. Do you recognize it and is it your exact words taken down by a legal recorder present with you at that time?"

Captain Williams reviewed the document and answered, "Senator Fenwick, those are my exact words given at that time, except for several parts that were classified material and statements. I presume they were excluded due to the sensitivity of the statements and for national security."

Senator Fenwick had the sergeant at arms give a copy of Captain Williams's statement to the Chinese delegation seated at the table. Fenwick said, "Mr. Diplomat and Captain Wu, I am providing you with a copy of Captain Williams's statement to conserve time for other matters at hand. If you wish, we can take a fifteen-minute break to allow you to review and read it if you so desire."

Captain Wu answered, "Yes, sir, we will need time to read it before going forward with these proceedings."

Fenwick said, "Very well. We'll take a fifteen-minute break."

The session was called back into order after fifteen minutes and the questioning of Williams continued. But before Fenwick could ask his question, Captain Wu raised his hand and asked that he be recognized to make several comments on Williams's Hawaiian statement of facts.

Fenwick replied, "Again, Captain Wu, you and your delegation will have your turn after we are finished with Captain Williams and not before. Please hold your comments for then."

Fenwick continued, "Captain Williams, I'm going to show you a logbook of the SSN Tarpon. Would you examine it please?"

Williams reviewed the logbook entries and then answered Fenwick, "Senator, this is the official logbook of the Tarpon. It was given to me by Captain Duggan, the commanding officer of the Tarpon. He gave it to me when we arrived in Hawaii before he was taken to the hospital for medical treatment for injuries sustained when the Tarpon was attacked and destroyed by a, then, unknown Chinese weapon."

The Chinese diplomat stood and strongly objected to Williams's comments. He began, "Senator, there is no specific and documented evidence to indicate that any Chinese vessel is to blame in the unfortunate incident leading up to the Tarpon's demise. But there is supportive evidence that Captain Williams deliberately went out of his way to destroy Chinese ships and kill Chinese seamen."

Fenwick looked at Williams and asked, "Is there anyone else in this room that knows about that logbook?"

Williams replied, "Yes, sir. Commander Doyle, my executive officer on the Cardinalfish, was with me when Captain Duggan handed it to me on the pier when we left the boat for COMSUBPAC's office."

Fenwick asked, "Commander Doyle, will you please stand up and be sworn in?"

After being sworn in, Doyle was asked by Fenwick, "Commander, will you please tell us about the logbook?"

Doyle answered, "Senator, we were leaving the pier at the subbase in Pearl Harbor when Captain Duggan waved us over. He reached under his bedsheet and pulled out the Tarpon's logbook. I saw him hand it to Captain Williams. We took both that logbook and the Cardinalfish logbook to COMSUBPAC's office where we all reviewed the log entries made by Captain Duggan before, during, and after the destruction of the Tarpon."

Fenwick asked, "Who is we?"

Doyle replied, "A representative from CINCPACFLEET, COM-SUBPAC himself, Captain Peters, Captain Williams, and I all reviewed and read the logbook."

Fenwick asked, "What did the logbook say?"

Doyle answered, "Captain Duggan made an entry stating that he was attacked first by a destroyer called the Chang Ling with depth charges and then by an unknown, to him, weapon that projected a low-pitch hum, lower than the typical Chinese fifty-cycle electrical hum, and then a 'pop.' After that 'pop,' the logbook states that immense flooding took place on the Tarpon, aft of the reactor spaces. The boat could not be saved or conduct an emergency surface due to the added extra weight of the seawater. She had no propulsion. She settled on the shelf of an underwater mountain. In navy terms, it's called a sea mount."

Fenwick then asked, "Other than the logbook, were you able to substantiate that occurrence?"

The XO answered, "Yes, sir, we were. We, the Cardinalfish, were sent into the China Sea to find Tarpon when she failed to report to COMSUBPAC headquarters at Pearl Harbor. We found her sitting on the shelf, at seven hundred fifty feet, and sent over our deep submersible rescue vehicle. They heard tapping emanating from inside what was left of the boat. They made several trips and managed to save twenty-six men and women including Captain Duggan, Tarpon's commanding officer.

"On the last trip, the DSRV operator took a video of the Tarpon aft end. The stern planes, the rudders, the propeller, and its propulsor were missing. For informational purposes, it's the ring around the propeller of a submarine that decreases cavitation. The port side, aft of the reactor spaces of the sub, looked like it had been cut by a knife cutting through butter. It was a smooth cut with no jagged ends. The starboard side aft of those spaces was partially cut and then appeared to be torn off due to the weight of the piece that was cut away from the stern of the Tarpon. We gave the film to COMSUBPAC, sir."

Commander Rourke raised his hand and was recognized by Fenwick. After being sworn in, Rourke stated, "Senator, we are prepared to show you the video the DSRV took on her last return trip from the Tarpon to the Cardinalfish."

Fenwick agreed to see the video. A portable screen was set up along with a computer. Rourke identified a computer thumb drive with a written date and a Cardinalfish label on it and plugged it into the computer. The first thing everyone saw was the hull numbers blacked out but slightly readable. They were identified as belonging to the Tarpon. The video showed exactly what Commander Doyle had described.

Again, the Chinese diplomat stood up and objected that the video could be of any submarine and that there wasn't evidence to support it being the Tarpon or that it was destroyed by Chinese warships.

Fenwick immediately ordered the diplomat to sit down and wait his turn.

Commander Rourke raised his hand and was recognized. Rourke replied to the diplomat's statement by answering, "Senator Fenwick and sir, we are prepared to get the testimony of Captain Duggan via satellite from the Hawaiian hospital. He was in the DSRV when this video was taken. He will tell us all that these films are of his boat, the Tarpon, and are legitimate. We have twenty-five of the Tarpon crew that can be called to substantiate the events leading up to, during, and after Tarpon's demise."

Fenwick then made a statement to Captain Williams. "Captain, President Lin of the Chinese Republic of China has lodged a serious complaint against you, the Navy, and your ship, the Cardinalfish. They claim that you took aggressive actions numerous times and eventually destroyed the twin towers used for sonar and bottom navigation, two of their nuclear submarines, and what they call an AUV. And then, in international waters, you threatened them with the destruction of three additional ships, all being destroyers. Would you care to respond to these accusations?"

William smiled and stood up and replied, "Senator, first, for informational purposes, our government was requested by Hong Kong to assist them in determining what happened to their cable ship laying fiber optic cable in the South China Sea. It totally disappeared and has not been found or heard from since its disappearance. COMSUBPAC ordered us to prepare to assist Hong Kong. In preparing for the search mission, we received additional orders from PAC to also search for the Tarpon. It was a twofold mission for us."

Williams stopped and poured a glass of water. His intention was to let that sink in to all who were in the room.

He continued, "We received a message from COMSUBPAC that a satellite sighted some debris on North Reef in the Paracel Islands. We diverted to the area and used our two-man mini sub to enter the lagoon. They found debris as evidence that the Tarpon was either crippled or destroyed. We didn't know how or why at the time of the debris discovery."

Lee pulled a photograph of the piece of cabinet with the signed Playboy picture from his briefcase and passed it to Doyle.

Williams took it and held it up, saying, "Senator, this is what was on the North Reef beach. There were also official Tarpon documents held together by a metal fastener. Would you care to examine the picture that has the Tarpon name written on it?"

Senator Fenwick responded, "That is not necessary. Please continue with your statement. If necessary, I'll ask for one of those divers to come and testify."

Williams sat back down in front of the microphone and continued, "By reading my log entries for my boat and Commander Doyle's testimony, you know we found the Tarpon on that sea mount shelf in the South China Sea. After seeing her stern, we knew she had been attacked but we didn't know how or why. I immediately ordered heightened watch and surveillance activities to prevent a similar occurrence to my boat. Our sonar picked up the convoy of three destroyers, two subs, and an unknown vessel at the time. That unknown vessel was the AUV. I was contacted by the convoy commander, a Captain, who boasted and bragged about sinking us like the Tarpon. He spoke perfect English as he told us he had a four-year tour here in DC as a diplomatic emissary. He demanded our surrender for trespassing in Chinese waters. I tried to reason with him but to no avail. He became aggressive and started making depth charge runs on my boat. They were unsuccessful, but he kept trying.

"I will deviate from my continuing comments for a moment to inform you that one of the survivors from the Tarpon was their leading sonar tech. He volunteered to work with my sonar team to try and identify the low-pitch hum below the Chinese fifty-cycle electrical hum and the 'pop' that was heard on the Tarpon before the flooding took place. They were successful in identifying both. That's how we determined the hum was from a laser weapon of some sort and the pop was the discharging laser beam of destruction.

"We used an automated drone to look for the Hong Kong fiber optic cable and found it connected to twin towers two thousand yards apart. There was a coupling device attached to it. That device could receive signals or orders of operation from a ship, and, in this case, the Chang Ling, a plane, a submarine, or an AUV. To prevent their use against the Cardinalfish, we destroyed the towers. Captain Wu became angry and overly aggressive and sent one of his subs to destroy us. Well, their crush depth was above ours and she exceeded her crush depth and imploded.

"Next, Captain Wu ordered the second sub to attack us using torpedoes. They fired four torpedoes at us. We deployed our countermeasures and destroyed two of those torpedoes. The other two were still pursuing us. I ordered an increase in speed and set a collision course for the AUV. When we got inside two thousand yards, the maximum firing range of the laser, we heard the AUV's low-pitch hum which meant it was powering up. At the last moment, we altered course away from the AUV just in time as the laser cannon fired. The beam struck the second Chinese sub, and she began to take on water. She couldn't hold her depth and she went below her crush depth and imploded. We heard and documented both implosions on our sonar recorder.

"Lastly, because we had turned away from the AUV, the last two torpedoes from that second doomed sub locked onto the AUV as its target and destroyed it. Captain Wu became a crazy man and came after us again. He had no idea that he had destroyed his own vessels by his over-aggressiveness, stupidity, and poor decision-making."

At this point, Captain Wu couldn't take it anymore and stood up and started screaming and yelling at Williams. He threatened everyone in the room with death. He swore revenge on the United States through his government using nuclear weapons. He yelled that everything that was said was lies, unmitigated lies.

Senator Fenwick used the sergeant at arms to contain Wu. At the same time, the Chinese diplomat was trying to calm him down and shut him up.

Lee, sitting behind the American table, translated everything Wu was yelling.

Finally, Captain Wu was restrained and removed from the room in the custody of the Chinese Communist Party member.

Fenwick asked Captain Williams, "Is there anything you would like to add?"

Williams answered, "Yes, sir, there is. Upon our return to the submarine base at Pearl Harbor, my weapons officer verified the serial numbers of all torpedoes and missiles we loaded before leaving on this mission. He also confirmed all the serial numbers on all those weapons upon completion of the mission. That is our protocol, normal routine, and part of his duties and responsibilities as the weapons officer. The number and type before we left for the China Sea and the number and type of all those weapons exactly matched when we returned from the China Sea, except for the two torpedoes used on the stationary laser cannon towers. In other words, Senator, we took no aggressive action on Wu, his ships, his subs, or that AUV. Those were also my orders from COMSUBPAC. He did it to himself. We merely out-maneuvered Wu and his fleet."

Fenwick then asked Commander Doyle, "Commander, is there anything you would like to add?"

Doyle replied, "Yes, there is, Senator. Everything that took place is documented and recorded. You have the complete sequence of events as they happened except for one piece. Senator, the Chinese got their hands on our technology for that weapon and improved upon it without our knowing it and without our approval to take it and use it. They hacked into our classified military experimental weapons computer system. In my humble opinion, sir, they should be held accountable for their actions not only in the South China Sea but also for stealing US classified weapons materials that they used against us.

"Their reason for destroying the Tarpon is simple. Their technology is well behind ours. There is documentation for my statement. Now I know that we, in the Navy, are far below your level of responsibility and accountability as a senator, but I am positive that the President of the United States, with your help, needs to go and kick them in the ass! I apologize for using that word, but Senator, that word is appropriate in this case. Thank you for allowing me to speak my mind, sir."

Fenwick was red in the face when he said, "Thank you both for being here today and presenting your side of the events."

He then turned to the Chinese diplomat and asked, "Sir, do you have anything you would like to say at this time?"

He stood up and replied, "Senator Fenwick, these proceedings have been nothing more than a kangaroo court against the Chinese government and its people. Captain Wu assures me that your submarine destroyed three of our vessels and threatened Captain Wu and two other ships while in international waters. We cannot and do not agree with Captain Williams's and Commander Doyle's testimony and comments. I will communicate with our President Lin, and I am sure he will be talking to your president. You deliberately wasted our time here today and that, I assure you, will not go unnoticed. The information, data, and records, you and I both know, can be artificially fabricated. Today's evidence that you have is certainly false, inaccurate, and fictitious.

"There are only two people in the hearing that can be verified with true information. That is your submarine captain and our Captain Wu. Based on Captain Wu's reaction to your lies, accusations, and innuendos, I will be reporting to President Lin that he demands satisfaction and retribution from your government and from Williams, if he is truly the Cardinalfish commanding officer."

Fenwick looked at the Chinese diplomat and replied, "Sir, your country has and is attempting to annex all the adjacent countries and territories on or adjacent to the South China Sea to its empire. That does not go unnoticed. The United States will deploy any battle group or groups it deems necessary to prevent your taking command of that sea and countries who disagree with being annexed to China. The facts here today are a clear and a definite indication that you don't care nor wish to remain peaceful with all other countries on or in that sea. You do not have the United States over a barrel, so to speak.

"These events that occurred in the South China Sea between Wu and the Cardinalfish are a clear and definite example of who is the superior nation, regardless of your stolen laser cannon. Our president is most anxious to come face to face with President Lin about your terrible losses between Wu and Williams. In fact, he is chomping at the bit to hold you accountable for the loss of one hundred fourteen Americans that you killed for no reason."

"I have one other item to mention," Fenwick continued. "The United States now has an additional three military bases in the Philippine Islands. They are for defense against any aggression you initiate against those countries that are adjacent to the China Sea against their wishes. I strongly recommend and urge that you and your country proceed with due caution. You can rattle your saber, but if you do, we will take that saber away from you and throw it away. You may think you have us economically, but you don't have us militarily. The day is coming when that economic burden will be removed. I bid you good day and may your God help you, sir, because we, the United States, will not much longer."

Supportive Evidence

Captain Williams and Doyle headed for the Langley Officers' Club after the closed-door session ended. Joining them was Lieutenant Commanders Samuels and Petrone. They had to ask for a larger table as Lee and Commander Rourke also joined them. Captain Peters appeared out of nowhere and was asked to join them as well. All of them were glad to see him in Washington to attend the hearing.

Williams asked, "Excuse me, but what the heck are all of you doing here?"

Rico was the first to answer. "Captain, we were sent here to bring you up to speed on the latest developments concerning the Tarpon and that Hong Kong cable layer. At the request of the Hong Kong government, the Navy Department contracted a deep diving submersible from a commercial outfit in Cape Cod. It was flown to Hong Kong and then deployed in the South China Sea. They found and then dove on what's left of the Tarpon. They created a video of what she now looks like after we destroyed her. She is in pieces, but the stern is intact and so is the reactor. So, we now have pictures of her, before and after we found her. But there is more to the story."

Samuels added, "Sir, the Hong Kong cable layer, the Liberator, has also been found in the South China Sea. She was found by using side scan sonar. She rests in over three thousand feet of water. There were and are no survivors after conducting a search and rescue mission assisted by the Japanese government. Once found, the deep submersible photographed and made a video of the wreck. Rico and I were asked to review the photos of the cable layer to compare them to the photos of the Tarpon. The Liberator was literally cut in half. When you look at the two halves of the ship, where they were once together, you'll see two exceptionally smooth elongated 'cuts,' which caused her to sink. When she went down, she split open like you would open an egg over a skillet. There are jagged edges on both sides of the hull three feet below the main decking."

Williams thought for a moment and asked, "You are telling me that the Chinese used that laser cannon on the cable layer?"

Rico answered, "Yes, sir, Captain. Evidently, they hooked onto the cable as she was laying it. Once they were hooked on, they fired the laser from, more than likely, the AUV and sunk the ship. Then all they had to do was pull it off its drum and tow the cable close to shore, rewind it, connect it to those two built towers, and they have control of three laser cannons. Hong Kong has lodged a formal complaint against the Chinese Communist Government through the United Nations. They are also preparing a case for submittal to the World Court. Tensions are high.

Williams responded, "Wow! The AUV was operational and took out the cable layer. How big was the Liberator?"

Captain Peters replied, "The Liberator was five hundred fourteen feet long. It had to take some time to cut through from one side to the other. The crew had to know what was happening and abandoned the vessel. Again, there are or were no survivors. You can guess what happened to them and their lifeboats and rafts. I'm guessing here, but they, more than likely, will pursue this as a murder, hijacking, and sinking case through the World Court. Lord only knows what the ramifications will be as the Chinese will never admit what they did."

Lee replied, "They'll lose all rights and arguments for annexing the South China Sea. Don't forget, gentlemen, that we have them right where we want them. They are still accountable for sinking the Tarpon and killing Americans. Add to that the sinking of two Japanese fishing boats and killing a captain. Then add the cable layer incident. The only way they will now be able to annex those adjacent countries on the China Sea is by an armed conflict. You know what that means."

While all the discussion was going on, Senator Fenwick appeared and said, "I'm sorry to interrupt your lunch, but all of you have been immediately ordered to the Pentagon, including me. Something big is about to go down."

As they all got up, Senator Fenwick paid the check and replied, "It's the least I can do for a bunch of, what did the Chinese call you? Oh yes, you are a bunch of murdering pirates."

They all were smiling and said "Aargh" as they left for the Pentagon.

Requiring
Substantiation

Captains Williams and Peters, Commanders Doyle and Rourke, Lieutenant Commanders Petrone and Samuels, along with Senator Fenwick and Lee Skiboski submitted their identification cards to the Pentagon security desk. After they were cleared to enter, a US Marine sergeant major appeared in dress uniform and asked all of them to follow him. The elevator took them down to the lower floor of the Pentagon. Waiting for all of them was another security desk. When security approved their entry, the sergeant major led them to an unmarked door and closed it behind them after they were in the room. He remained at parade rest outside the door.

Sitting at the head of the long table was the National Security Advisor (NSA) to the President of the United States. Also seated at the table was a member of the Joint Chiefs of Staff, the Assistant Secretary of the Navy, and representatives from the Department of Homeland Security, and the US Defense Intelligence Agency. Also sitting at the table were two other men in civilian clothes who did not identify themselves. They were presumed to be from the FBI and CIA.

The man at the head of the table stood up and said, "Good afternoon, gentlemen. Please take any seat at the table."

After everyone was seated, he began, "My name is Sam Whittaker. As you probably already know, I am the national security advisor to President Mitchell. We are all here today because you created one hell of a hornet's nest in the China Sea. Senator Fenwick is the exception. Based on the information you have, the scenarios you encountered, and other events you experienced, we need to decide how we, the United States, are going to proceed with China. Before we start, may I ask each of you to stand up and give your name? We'll start on the left side of the table but the two men at the end are exempt."

After each introduced themselves, Whittaker opened his brief case and put on the table the Tarpon's logbook, the Cardinalfish's logbook, several computer thumb drives, a video disk, and numerous photographs taken on North Reef in the Paracel Islands in the South China Sea.

Whittaker said, "I need to inform you that those of us who weren't with you in the China Sea have reviewed all of the information and data that sits on this table. Your CINCPACFLEET and COMSUBPAC were gracious enough to send over the documentation material to us while you spent time with Senator Fenwick behind closed doors."

Whittaker continued, "I must tell you that Captain Duggan was not fit enough to join us, but we got his side of the story as he presented his thoughts, comments, and explanations. I need to talk to you all to ensure that we have the whole picture, so to speak. So, let's begin. Captain Williams is there anything you would like to tell us that is not part of the official record from your submarine, North Reef, or from the numerous engagements you had against Chinese forces?"

Captain Williams stood up, but he was motioned to remain seated. "Mr. Whittaker," he replied, "I can tell you, without any hesitation, that those of us from the Cardinalfish are lucky to be alive. Both the Tarpon and the Cardinalfish faced an unknown extremely powerful weapon. We, of the Cardinalfish, owe our lives to Captain Duggan and his surviving crew for giving us a lead to determine exactly what happened to the Tarpon, and almost to us. Based on their information and working with us, we were able to determine what the unknown weapon was and how and when to avoid it. That weapon had a definite identifiable signature. Additionally, Captain Wu of the Chinese Navy was extremely aggressive and uncooperative once he knew we were searching for the Tarpon. It didn't matter to him that we were there also looking for the Liberator, a cable layer, at Hong Kong's request. He flat out didn't want us to know that he used laser cannons on an American submarine. But I believe there is more to this story that we don't know, and we may never know."

Rico was looking down at the table, doodling, and slightly shaking his head.

Whittaker caught sight of him and asked, "Mr. Petrone, do you have something to add, or do you disagree with what was just said by your captain?"

Rico stood up and was motioned to take his seat. He replied, "Mr. Whittaker, I have a thought about all of this, but I have not spoken to Captain Williams yet and it just occurred to me. I would like to talk to Mr. Skiboski as well, both in private."

Whittaker looked at Williams and asked, "Does Mr. Petrone have your permission to air his thoughts on this matter with the rest of us?"

Williams replied, "Yes, sir, he has my permission."

Whittaker responded to Rico, "Please proceed, Mr. Petrone."

Rico asked, "Mr. Whittaker, may I ask for a moment to talk to Lee?"

Whittaker replied, "You have it, sir."

Rico turned towards Lee and asked a couple of questions. Lee smiled and answered them while Captain Williams listened to their conversation. He nodded in agreement.

Rico answered Whittaker, "Sir, you already know that the Cardinalfish did not take any offensive action against those six Chinese vessels. We were purely defensive. Three of those six vessels were sunk due to orders given by Captain Wu. There are only two ways that we can determine the truth about all of this. One is to question Captain Wu and we already know that the Chinese government isn't going to let that happen for whatever reasons. Secondly, we may be able to search the wrecks of the two submarines and the AUV for evidence."

Whittaker asked, "What do you mean by that, mister?"

Rico responded, "Sir, the two Chinese subs both imploded. They will be spread out all over the sea bottom, and so will the AUV, from torpedo hits. We need to dive on those wrecks just to see what we can find. I asked Lee if he remembers saying to us in the control room that the first sub that followed us below her crush depth mentioned that the orders to follow us deeper was outside of the written sanctions issued by an admiral named Chen Blejong. I believe and think that the written sanctions were issued and amended orders from the head of their navy, Admiral Blejong, and that Captain Wu followed them and is trying to protect his government. China wants to have the countries and territories adjacent to the South China Sea annexed to their country, as well as any other country close to that body of water."

Senator Fenwick asked, "Why didn't you mention any of this while at Pearl or at the hearing earlier today?"

Rico replied, "Honestly, sir, I didn't think of it then. If I did, I still would not have mentioned it with the Chinese present. If I did, they would be out there destroying or collecting it before we had a chance to find it. We don't need additional tension added to the already aggravated international relations between our two countries."

Whittaker, smiling, responded, "Mr. Petrone, have you ever considered joining our National Security Agency after retiring from the Navy?"

Rico replied, "With all due respect, sir, I am Navy all the way! When I retire, I intend to sit on a beach somewhere, listen to rock and roll, drink strawberry margaritas, and write my memoirs for future generations of my family."

Whittaker cleared his throat and asked if there were any other issues that needed to be addressed.

Captain Peters stood up and said, "Mr. Whittaker, we can and will dive on those Chinese wrecks using our DSRV, with the approval of our government and with the Chinese government's approval. She is a deep diving rescue vessel, but she can obtain or pick up anything we find of interest all the way down to the size of a dime. May I ask that you to go directly to President Lin and then go through our Navy Department should you decide to search those wrecks. Instead of just a rogue captain, there may also be a rogue admiral."

Whittaker responded, "Captains and gentlemen, we'll take the ball from here. I think your DSRV may not be able to go to the bottom of the China Sea. China would never agree after what has happened. We may be able to contract Woods Hole Oceanographic to dive in those waters. Thank you all for coming at a moment's notice. Captain Williams, I envy you as you have a brilliant crew and an officer that thinks outside of the box. Too bad he's not interested in becoming a member of our security team!"

Rico asked to speak again. "Gentlemen, if you intend to obtain or even have permission from the Chinese government, you'll need to create what I'll call a 'camouflage' excuse. If Woods Hole agrees to the mission, you'll need to call it a research expedition searching for a special plant or animal."

Whittaker, now smiling, asked, "Mr. Petrone, are you sure you are not interested in joining our group of special thinkers? You'll fit in very nicely."

Rico, displaying a slight grin, replied, "Mr. Whittaker, with all due respect, the only way I would consider joining your organization would be if you gave me my own submarine to command and have Albert Einstein as my executive officer. We both know that such a case will never happen!"

While all others were laughing Whittaker's last comment was, "Mr. Petrone, you underestimate what your government can do if we need you! I'll have Miss Jones, my administrative assistant, write a note to the Archangel Gabriel and see if Albert is interested in agreeing to Mr. Petrone's proposal."

The laughter was loud and long.

Volunteering?

Rico, along with Captains Williams and Peters, Commanders Doyle and Rourke, Lieutenant Commander Samuels, Lee Skiboski, and Petty Officer Mahoney, flew in a chartered government plane back to Pearl Harbor. The plane was spacious, had a bar, and featured movies, none about submarines. The men talked about the proceedings in DC as well as what the possibilities were following the conversations with Sam Whittaker, the president's National Security Advisor.

During the flight, Captain Williams asked to speak to Rico in private. They sat in the back of the plane.

Williams started the conversation. "Rico, I am surprised at your comments with Sam Whittaker. He's right about the fact that you constantly think outside of the box. I have no problem with what you suggested or said, but you must realize that you may have tagged yourself for making numerous trips down to the bottom of the China Sea. Even if you find those wrecks, what do you expect to find that will help substantiate your premise about Wu and Blejong keeping it from President Lin?"

Rico looked at Williams and replied, "Captain, you and I both know that it's a crapshoot at best. But there is a possibility that one or both subs may have written sanctions in the safe located in the captain's cabin. Every boat captain, regardless of country, has a safe in their cabin for money and sensitive and classified information. If we find one or both of those safes, maybe the documents will be inside and still readable. That's what I was thinking about and alluding to when we were with Whittaker. It didn't occur to me when we were dodging the Chang Ling and those other five vessels. It popped into my head as Whittaker was asking questions and we were all answering him."

Williams looked at him and asked, "Rico, are you checked out in deep diving submersibles?"

Rico answered, "No, sir. Someone else will be riding to the bottom. It could be Mr. Watson and Petty Officer Taylor, but not me."

Williams smiled and responded, "Mister if they ask me for a volunteer, you're it! It was your thought and your idea so you will bring it to fruition. Consider yourself volunteering. Report to Mr. Samuels once we get back to Pearl and get yourself checked out for the numerous joy rides that the Woods Hole submersible will be making. Besides, you'll be the senior man aboard, so consider it your first command, Captain!"

Rico replied, "Yes, sir. Me and my big mouth!"

Mix and Match

Rico knew something was up as soon as the plane taxied to the terminal ramp. Senior Chief O'Hara was waiting for him with a large package wrapped in brown paper. It was stamped "FOUO" (For Official Use Only). The senior chief was smiling but Rico was not.

O'Hara handed Rico the package as Rico was leaving the terminal for his car and home, with his baggage in hand. The flight had been a long one and none of the passengers had much sleep.

Rico forced a smile and asked, "What's this?"

The senior chief replied, "I was asked to meet you when you landed and give this to you by COMSUBPAC's Operations Department head. I'm guessing here, but I think it has to do with another mission to the South China Sea. You didn't volunteer, did you? You know what they say about volunteering. If you did, you'll be sorry."

Rico tucked the package under his arm, picked up his bags, and replied, "Sorry isn't exactly the correct word. I didn't volunteer. I was shanghaied by Captain Williams. I'll give COMSUBPAC's ops boss a call and tell him I got the package. Anything else I need to know?"

O'Hara responded, "Petty Officer Mahoney gave me a call from DC after she took herself off leave status to drive all of you around. She said what she heard and saw was remarkably interesting. Of course, she didn't, nor wouldn't, divulge any of it. What's going on, sir?"

Rico smiled and replied, "If I tell you then you get to come along, and I don't think you would like it. So, mum is the word of the day."

Samuels joined them as they were talking and cut in. "Excuse me, but I have some especially important news for Mr. Petrone. Will you excuse us, Senior Chief?"

O'Hara nodded, saluted, and responded, "Aye, sir. I was leaving anyway. Good luck to you, Mr. Petrone."

Rico looked at Samuels and asked, "What's the latest news?"

Samuels replied, "Surprise, surprise, surprise, your wife and boys are here in your new quarters. They know you're here."

Rico smiled and answered, "Thanks, I'll see you later," as he began walking faster to get to his car.

Samuels laughed and asked, "Hey, don't you need the address to find them?"

Rico laughed and replied, "Oh, yeah, thanks."

After getting the address from Samuels, he threw his luggage in the back seat of the car after lowering the convertible top into the trunk. The small home was only ten minutes away. When seeing the home, he smiled and thought, "What a quaint place." He left the bags in the car and stood there watching his sons roughhouse with each other in the front yard.

The boys, seeing their father, ran to him with big smiles, yelling, "Daddy, Daddy!"

Sharon, hearing the commotion, stopped washing the dishes and took off her apron. She smiled at her reflection in the dish cabinet glass door as she straightened her hair. Rico, now carrying the boys, walked through the front door.

Seeing Sharon standing in the kitchen doorway, he put the boys down, saying, "Boys, how about going back outside and help Daddy by bringing in his luggage and packages? One of them has a surprise for you. You can have them when you bring them in from the car."

Sharon and Rico held out their arms as they walked towards each other. They gave each other a warm and gentle hug and Rico gently kissed her and held her close for a long time without saying a word. Holding his hands on her face and looking into her eyes, he said, "Gosh, I missed you so much. You have no idea of how many times during this trip that I thought about this moment. I love you, Sharon."

She answered him, "I love you, and missed you too."

The boys came back into the house with Rico's bags. After dropping the bags, they gave Rico more hugs. It felt great to receive all those hugs and kisses from the boys and his wife. He really missed giving, receiving, and sharing his love and affection with his family. After answering each other's questions over dinner, Rico put the kids to bed and headed for the bedroom to shower, be with his wife, and to get some long-anticipated sleep.

Sharon joined him in the shower. After showering, they dried each other, still kissing, and caressing each other. Rico picked Sharon up and carried her to the bed. He rolled over and faced her after their long and torrid lovemaking and softly kissed her closed eyes. She smiled, saying, "Darling, I really love these homecomings. I missed you so much. I'm hoping you'll be home for a while."

He didn't have the heart to tell her about leaving again so soon. Smiling, he kissed her again without saying anything, rolled over, and fell asleep.

It was 0630 (6:30 a.m.) when he woke up. He rolled over and saw his wife was still asleep. He decided to let her sleep and walked into the kitchen to start a pot of coffee and filled a bowl with yogurt and fresh blueberries. Once he had the coffee, he sat at his desk eating his breakfast. He stared at the unopened package in front of him from COMSUBPAC. He sighed a deep breath as he tore open the package.

The documents inside detailed the trip to the South China Sea to search for the two Chinese subs. He was required to meet with the representatives from the oceanographic company from Cape Cod in a few hours. Rico was not happy about this trip, as he wanted to stay home for a while and be with his family. But duty was duty. He showered once more, shaved, and put on a clean uniform. Both boys and his wife were about to have breakfast as he kissed them and said goodbye to them. He smiled at his wife and said, "I'll call you later."

She smiled and replied, "Honey, don't be unhappy. It's okay, we'll be here. I'll make your and the boys' favorite for dinner if you're coming home. It'll be sloppy joes, French fries, and coleslaw, with ice cream sundaes for dessert."

Rico smiled back and said, "That's great." He thought to himself, "Just like what we eat aboard the Cardinalfish!"

Rico checked in with the security desk at COMSUBPAC's headquarters. The meeting was being held in secure conference room number two. He attached a visitor's badge to his pocket and proceeded to the conference room. Captains Williams and Peters, along with representatives from the oceanographic company, were seated and waiting for him.

Rico asked, "Am I late?"

Williams replied, "No, we were early and going over the Cardinalfish's logbook and the charts used from our mission. We have a fairly good idea where to look for those two Chinese subs. The water is deep there, and it is quite a bit closed in with a valley right in the middle of the search area. It shouldn't be a problem for these guys and their deep diving vessel."

Rico inquired, "We're going with their submersible?"

Captain Williams responded, "It's a bathyscaphe named Emily. It's kind of like a miniature submarine and comes with all the usual attachments. She's equipped with a hydraulic arm, acetylene cutting torch, sonar, a UQC, and video equipment. The reason is simple. We're hoping they won't attempt to attack or investigate a civilian vessel and our diplomatic corps in cooperation with Taiwan, Hong Kong, Japan, and Vietnam have asked and obtained permission to dive in that area for oceanographic research purposes. They think the dives will be to improve the fishing grounds. They have no idea that we are looking for the imploded subs."

Rico responded, "Has she got visual heavy reinforced viewing ports?"

Peters replied, "Yes, she does, and she has high intensity lighting which I forgot to mention earlier."

Rico smiled and said, "Very clever, very clever, indeed. When do we start?"

Peters replied, "Yes, clever is the word. Speaking of word, when and if we find the safe and the documents, the code words are, 'We found the plants.'"

Rico, making a funny face, asked, "Plants? Marine biologists don't use the word 'plants.' They identify everything by genus and species."

Peters laughed and replied, "Remember, we're a sort of chameleon. We're matching deep diving with a civilian company with military and civilians aboard her and mixing business with pleasure as this company has no data or information about the marine life on the bottom of the China Sea. You and the deep diving vessel with the designated crew fly out of here in four hours."

Rico went home, packed a bag with mostly civilian clothes and one uniform, kissed his wife and kids goodbye, and drove to the airport. He began reading and going through the operating systems and vessel equipment as he waited to board the plane along with the rest of the group.

Truth Seeking

Rico was studying the operating manual for the deep diving submersible when a man with gray curly hair and a salt and pepper beard walked over to him and held out his hand.

Smiling, he said, "Hi, I'm Jake Thompson. I work for the oceanographic company out on Cape Cod, and you must be Rico Petrone."

Rico stood up and shook Jake's hand, saying, "Yes, I am, and nice to meet you. May I call you Jake?"

Jake replied, "Jake is just fine, if I can call you Rico."

Jake sat down next to Rico and said, "That stuff is kind of boring, isn't it? Once we get to Japan, I'll take you over to Emily, and we'll have hands-on training before we go out and make those dives."

Rico closed the book and was surprised at the plane's destination. He asked, "Japan? We're going to Japan? Why Japan?"

Jake laughed, "Now you sound just like Mike Samuels from your submarine. He doesn't wait for answers either."

Rico responded, "How do you know Mike?"

Jake answered, "We were ocean engineering majors at Florida Atlantic University in Boca Raton, with minors in marine biology. We've been friends for quite a few years. He went subs and I went civilian."

The public address system announced that the MAC flight was ready for boarding and the group of men lined up to get aboard.

The pilot in the cockpit made an announcement once everyone was seated. "May I have your attention please? For your information we are stopping at Guam to refuel before going on to Kyushu, Japan. You'll have about thirty minutes in Guam to stretch your legs. There isn't much there except for military. So don't stray too far from the plane. Thank you for your attention."

The stopover in Guam was uneventful as well as the rest of the flight into Kyushu. A van met the men at the airport and drove them to the research vessel carrying the bathyscaphe, Emily.

Once aboard the ship, they got under way for the designated search areas in the South China Sea. It took the ship ten days to arrive at the search area due to a low-pressure area over the China Sea causing high winds and heavy sea. During that time, Jake taught and showed Rico how to operate the deep submersible. Jake drew a schematic of the submarine compartmentation to bring Rico and Lee up to speed on how to correct any leaking problems. Lee's position on Emily was on the front padding looking out the forward view port. The ship's video system was above Lee so he could see out the view port and read the Chinese written on the sub's bulkheads.

Jake surprised Rico when he told him that Emily's maximum diving depth was fifteen thousand feet. Rico looked at him and replied, "Why would anyone want to go that deep? There's nothing down there."

Jake replied, "Rico, down there is a lot of different kinds of plants and animals that we have never seen or yet discovered. You will be amazed at what you will see but also at what you hear."

Rico answered, "I can't wait for that. It will be great!"

The mini sub carried a maximum of three people. That would be Jake, Rico, and Lee. Their expertise covered Emily's operations, submarines, and Chinese writing. Jake was five-feet-six inches tall and built like a football player. Rico was five inches taller. Lee was the same height as Jake with a skinny build. Each dive was a tight fit for the three men.

Arriving at the first search area, Jake, Rico, and Lee climbed aboard the bathyscaphe and prepared for launch. The ship's crane picked up and lowered the mini sub into the water. All systems were checked out once more just to make sure all were properly operating. The three men were told when and if they discovered the Chinese safe, they were told to say that they found a brand new and unusual plant species. Additionally, that they are collecting a sample for research and examination, just in case anyone might be close by and listening.

Jake called to the ship when the diving checklist was completed and requested release from the crane cable. The request was relayed to the divers in the water and the mini sub was released from the crane. The vents were opened, and the ballast tanks filled with seawater and the vessel headed down for the bottom. The first two days were boring, although both Rico and Lee marveled at the new and different kinds of marine life swimming around down there.

It was well into the third day of searching when Emily's sonar finally detected something metallic on the sea bottom. As the sub got closer, portions of a Chinese submarine hull came into view. The Chinese submarine's sail was separate from the imploded pressure hull. The national Chinese flag floated gently in the slow-moving current at the top of the sail.

A near catastrophe occurred as Emily became entangled in some loose cabling floating in the water column while moving over the wreckage. The cabling blended into the dark surroundings. The three men saw the cabling too late, and it became fouled in one of the bathy-scaphe's two propellers.

"Topside, this is Jake. One of our props has become fouled in some cabling floating in the water. We are attempting to remove it. Stand by."

The increased tension and anxiety were very evident in topside's response. "Jake, you know you have to get free on your own. We have no way of helping you. What is the status of all your systems including air supply?"

Jake replied, "All systems are in the green. Air level is reading forty-five percent. We will attempt to free ourselves with the hydraulic arm. We have time to work this out. We'll keep you posted."

Once they were entangled and unable to get free, Rico thought of his family. There was no way they could get to the surface from thirteen thousand feet. He began praying to himself as did both Jake and Lee. All three men could see the fear etched in each other's faces. If they couldn't get free, that fear would change into despair combined with acceptance.

Luckily, the hydraulic arm cut the cabling and freed Emily. There was enough oxygen left in the supply tank to get back to the surface. Topside, just to be prepared, readied the decompression chamber which could comfortably hold all three men at one time. The three men would remember this dive for a long time.

On the next day's dive, Rico sent a message topside to the research vessel, "This is Emily. We have found an area of marine growth. We do not see any of the plant life we are looking for. We are ascending to the surface. We'll call you again as we get close to the surface. What are the existing weather conditions? Over."

A transmission came from the research vessel on the surface. "Emily, roger your last. Weather conditions are good. Seas are two to three feet and winds are out of the west at five to six knots. Over and out."

Once the mini sub was safely aboard the research vessel, Jake, Lee, and Rico left it and headed for the mess deck with a DVD disk. Commander Doyle and representatives from the oceanographic company reviewed the disk. There was no doubt that this Chinese boat exceeded her crush depth and imploded. There was no evidence of a safe anywhere within the wreckage area.

Finding the second Chinese submarine was more difficult. The search area was much larger. They found the second Chinese boat on the fourth day of searching. She was strewn all over the sea bottom and in pieces at three thousand two hundred fifteen feet. Rico confirmed, based on the size of the debris field, that this sub was hit by the remaining two torpedoes fired at the Cardinalfish when being attacked by the Chang Ling and Captain Wu.

They turned on a video camera and sent continued movies of the wreckage up to the research vessel to additionally read and translate the Chinese writing on bulkheads, compartmentation, hatches, and doors. The search of the area continued for an hour and twenty minutes before they came upon a portion of the upper compartmentation of the sub. Rico, referencing a schematic of a typical Chinese nuclear sub, guided Jake through the wreckage that were areas of interest.

Lee suddenly yelled, "Come to all stop. Come a little left and point the camera down a little. Over more. Just a little more left."

Jake followed Lee's instructions.

Lee, now calling the research vessel, "Topside, we are now stationed above the possible plant life we have been looking for. Do you see the dark green area located just left? Over."

Topside responded, "Yes, we see it. Over."

Lee answered, "Great! This is where we want to look. Searching around the area, over."

The research vessel again replied, "Roger that. Status check shows you have four hours of power and air left. Over."

Jake used the hydraulic hand and arm to sift through the submarine wreckage. Thirty-five minutes later, both Rico and Lee spotted the sub's safe at the same time. They had to use the acetylene torch to cut through some of the surrounding twisted metal bulkhead and cabinetry. After twenty minutes more, the hydraulic arm picked up the sub's safe and Emily began the upward rise to the surface.

Rico radioed the research vessel. "Research vessel this is Emily. We found the unusual species of plant life. We have a sample and are bringing it to the surface. Over."

Topside responded, "Roger that. Congratulations. See you soon. Over and out."

A Chinese destroyer was floating very close to the research vessel as the mini sub surfaced. The safe remained under the water's surface and out of sight. Rico noticed that the Chinese were aboard the research vessel and concluding a search of the ship. The Chinese boarded their launch and returned to the destroyer. The destroyer got under way once the launch was in its davits and headed in a westerly direction.

When the destroyer was well out of sight, Emily was hoisted up and returned to her cradle.

Once again, the three men went to the mess deck with a DVD of the search area as the safe was lowered onto the aft main deck. It was rinsed off with fresh water and cleaned up.

Lee, Rico, Jake, and the Cardinalfish XO went to the after deck and inspected the safe. Lee read the Chinese writing on it and verified it was from the Chinese captain's cabin. They were unable to open the safe, so a welder used an acetylene torch to cut the lock out and it was opened. Amazingly enough, the safe had maintained its watertight integrity. Lee went through and read the various papers that were stored in the safe.

Lee stood up as he read the next document in his hands. He looked at the others and said, "Oh holy cow, this is it. This is a signed document authorizing Captain Wu to prevent any foreign country to interfere with China annexing the China Sea or even trespassing into it."

The XO asked, "Who signed it? Was it Admiral Blejong or was it President Lin?"

Lee went through reading the various papers that were part of the entire document he was holding. Lee smiled and replied, "It is signed by Admiral Blejong. He left specific orders for Captain Wu to never divulge these orders to anyone."

Rico looked at the rest of the group and said, "Now the fun really begins. Our government now has the reasons why the Tarpon was destroyed and why Captain Wu attacked the Tarpon and the Cardinalfish. Now, President Mitchell can present these papers to President Lin, and we get to see what he is going to do about them."

Admiral's Briefing

Once the research vessel docked in Kyushu, Rico, Lee, Commander Doyle, and Jake headed for the US Navy aircraft carrier Ronald Reagan. The admiral's barge picked them up at the dock and took them to the carrier, which was anchored outside the harbor in anchorage alpha. Lieutenant McElroy, the admiral's aide, was waiting for them. Once aboard the carrier, he escorted them to the admiral's quarters.

Admiral Joe Leonardo stood up as they entered the stateroom. He held out his hand and said, "Welcome aboard the Reagan."

Rico, Commander Doyle, Lee, and Jake all stood at attention while shaking hands with the admiral.

Leonardo smiled and said, "At ease gentlemen, and have a seat. Would you care for a drink before we begin?"

The group response was, "Yes, sir, please."

Admiral Leonardo asked, "Hot or cold coffee, tea, ice water, or a cold beer?"

All four men asked for water with ice. Rico asked that his have a twist of lemon, which brought a raised eyebrow from Doyle.

Once the drinks were served, Leonardo asked, "May I have your names please for my visitor's log?"

After receiving the names of the four men, Leonardo asked Doyle, "I believe you are the executive officer of the Cardinalfish. Is that correct?"

Doyle responded, "Yes, sir, that's correct. May I introduce the Cardinalfish's navigator, Lieutenant Commander Rico Petrone."

Admiral Leonardo smiled and replied, "Nice to see you again, Rico."

Rico answered, "Good to see you as well, admiral."

Doyle was a little surprised that the admiral and Rico knew each other.

Doyle asked, "How do you know each other, admiral?"

Leonardo replied, "Rico and I sort of played softball together. I was the pitcher for my team and Rico was on the other team. He put one over the centerfield fence to beat us by one run. That ball was hit so hard and long that I believe it is still going around the earth in orbit."

Rico couldn't help himself and burst out laughing.

He looked at Leonardo and replied, "I'm sorry, Admiral. I was just doing my job. That pitch was in the middle of my power zone. I just got lucky and nailed it."

Leonardo smiled and responded, "Bull hockey! We knew your reputation for hitting homers and the fact that you had a chance to play in the major leagues and turned it down for the Navy and submarines. Considering what I know about you, the Navy is happy that you made the right choice."

Rico replied, "I am too, sir. I have a good career as a member of the Navy."

Leonardo chuckled and said, "Now, let's get down to business. Did you find what you were looking for?"

Doyle responded, "Yes, Admiral, we did. Lee Wang Joe Skiboski interpreted the papers after we found and retrieved them from the Chinese submarine captain's safe. We have them with us. Lee can translate them for you if you wish."

Leonardo answered, "Lei Wang Joe who?"

Lee, with a deep sigh, responded, "Admiral, my name is not important. Just call me Lee.

Leonardo replied, "Very well, Lee. No need to translate them. Just give me a quick synopsis of them."

Lee began, "An Admiral Blejong wrote orders for a Captain Wu to keep all foreign vessels, military or otherwise, out of the China Sea. Captain Wu used three destroyers, two submarines, and an AUV to do so. We know about a cable layer and our submarine, the Tarpon, being destroyed. We also know about two Japanese fishing boats. We don't know how many others have been destroyed. The orders forbade Captain Wu from divulging all information concerning Blejong's orders. By the way, we believe President Lin has no idea what has been happening in the China Sea. But he may have told Blejong to do it and not to mention his name.

"The Chinese military hacked into our military classified experimental weapons project files and collected data for an underwater laser cannon. The range for our prototype was only five hundred yards. They perfected it out to two thousand yards. They also stole a fiber optic cable from the cable-laying vessel that Wu destroyed and connected it to a pair of underwater towers on the sea bottom. Those towers, connected to the fiber optic cable and the coupler, became fully operational laser weapons. They also produced an AUV that could be controlled by Chinese ships, aircraft, or submarines. That AUV also carried a laser cannon."

Lee continued, "The Cardinalfish destroyed the laser cannons in the two towers by using two torpedoes. Captain Wu went ballistic and ordered the two subs and the AUV to attack and destroy the Cardinalfish."

Doyle interrupted and said, "Admiral, Wu made numerous depth charge attacks on the Cardinalfish to either destroy her or prevent us from getting back into international waters. Captain Williams, our skipper, was brilliant in never taking any offensive action on the Chinese vessels. The two submarines and the AUV were destroyed by Wu's own orders. One sub chased us below her crush depth and imploded. The second Chinese sub was destroyed by a laser burst from the AUV. The AUV was destroyed by two runaway torpedoes meant for the Cardinalfish. Captain Wu turned tail and ran after we managed to return to international waters."

Admiral Leonardo was totally shocked and amazed at the report he just heard. He looked at Rico, Lee, Jake, and Doyle and replied, "Wow! That's quite phenomenal! You took out three vessels using none of your offensive weapons."

Rico answered, "Yes, admiral. It was Tango Down to crush depth. We used Wu's anger, impatience, and intolerance against him. We had and used our exceptionally accurate bottom contour navigational charts to keep us out of harm's way."

Leonardo asked, "Who was your navigator on the Cardinalfish during all of this?"

Rico replied, "I was, Admiral. I was transferred there, from DC, for that specific job."

Leonardo smiled and said, "Well, now, that figures. So, I presume that you are here to use my communications system to send coded messages to whom?"

Doyle responded, "Admiral, we need to send the message that we have what I'll call 'pirate orders' from Admiral Blejong to Captain Wu. They will be enroute to Pearl and eventually to DC and ultimately given to the President and his NSA secretary for a response to China's President Lin."

Leonardo picked up his phone and called for a messenger with blank message forms. The messenger knocked on Admiral Leonardo's door ten minutes later.

Commander Doyle filled in the blank message forms and wrote "TOP SECRET" on each form. He verbally requested that the message be encrypted to prevent any dissemination to other agencies and outside countries. Admiral Leonardo concurred.

Leonardo turned to the four men after the messenger left for the secure traffic radio room and asked, "Well, gentlemen, what's next? Is there anything I can do to support you?"

Doyle replied, "Admiral, we will take a charter flight from here, with a stop in Guam to refuel, and then it's on to Pearl. What happens next depends on what CINCPACFLEET and COMSUBPAC have in store for us."

Jake interrupted and said, "Admiral, with your permission, I'm going with them. I was trained and signed paperwork stating that I know how to handle, divulge, and destroy classified material. I know all of this is classified and I can never divulge it, but I really would like to go home and try and forget about all of this!"

Leonardo answered Jake, "Sir, you are going with them. Why? Because questions that may arise concerning your diving operations in the China Sea can and will be substantiated by you as Emily's operator. Have a nice trip, Jake."

The four men shook hands with Leonardo and thanked him for the drinks and for his willingness to assist them.

Confrontation

The flight from Japan to Pearl Harbor was uneventful. All four men were anxious to get home and relax for a while, but it was not to be for the three men from the Cardinalfish. Commander Doyle, Rico, and Lee shook hands with Jake and said goodbye to him as they all collected their luggage.

Captain Williams, along with Samuels, were waiting for Doyle, Rico, and Lee outside of the terminal.

All three men simultaneously asked, "How are the repairs going on the boat, sir?"

Williams answered them with a frown on his face, "Gentlemen, the repairs are going well but right now, that doesn't concern you or me. We've been ordered back to DC as soon as possible. A military chartered plane is waiting for all of us right now. I know you all have been away from your families for quite a while. I'm going to go against the grain here and tell you to report back here in three hours. That will give you some time at home and to grab some clean clothes and uniforms. Spend some time with your families if you can because I think we'll be in DC for a while."

Rico asked, "Well, if all of us are going to DC, who is in command of the Cardinalfish while we are away as she continues to be repaired?"

Williams smiled and answered, "Captain Blood Watson, our weapons officer, is in command, and he is in high heaven right now!"

All of them, except Williams, were laughing.

Williams, Doyle, Rico, Samuels, and Lee all jumped into Williams's brand new seven-passenger Subaru. They remarked about the new car smell and asked for the radio to be turned on. The luggage was put in the back, and they each took a seat and buckled in. Lee wanted country and western music, Doyle asked for Frank Sinatra music, Samuels wanted sixties rock and roll, and Rico enjoyed classical music. Williams had the final say as it was his vehicle, so he chose the news station. Listening to the news nearly put all of them to sleep, except for Williams who was doing the driving.

Rico was the first to be dropped off at home. He grabbed his bag and eagerly walked to the front door. It was close to lunch time, and he could smell hamburgers cooking on the stove. He thought to himself with a smile on his face, "Oh no, not more burgers!" He snuck in through the front door, tip-toed into the kitchen, and grabbed Sharon by her waist.

She screamed and jumped, turned around, thinking it was one of the boys and was surprised to see Rico. She dropped the spatula and hugged and kissed her husband.

Rico said, "Hey honey, those burgers smell good. Do you have one for me?"

She replied, "You don't have time for more than one. Now go grab a shower and repack your bag, as you don't have much time before you have to leave."

Rico inquired, "Sharon, how do you know that?"

Sharon smiled and said, "Don't you know the military wives club knows all before you do?"

Rico laughed and replied, "Okay, I'm following your orders, ma'am."

Both boys excitedly ran into their parents' bedroom when they were told that Dad was home.

They excitedly asked, "Did you bring us anything from Japan, Dad?"

Rico smiled and produced two plastic samurai swords for them. They headed outside to play with them, but Sharon told them to sit and have lunch with their father, as he was going away again in a couple of hours. Rico stared at his family while eating.

The burgers and the swords also made it to the lunch table. It was a fun time for the whole family.

After lunch, the boys went outside to play. Rico and Sharon sat on the couch together and enjoyed some time alone. They discussed plans for when all of this would be over. Sharon suggested that Rico make out a leave request to ensure he had some quality time with the boys before going out to sea again. Rico thought about how much he missed Sharon and the boys when he was away or at sea, but he knew the importance of the upcoming meeting. He hugged and kissed Sharon and the boys as he heard Williams honk the horn to take him to the airport.

The five men boarded the plane for DC. They arrived in DC around midnight and checked into the Holiday Inn directly across the street from the airport. The next morning, a limousine picked them up in front of the hotel at exactly 0845 (8:45 a.m.) and took them to the Pentagon.

Waiting for them in a secure conference room one level down from the main floor of the Pentagon were President Mitchell, National

Security Advisor Sam Whittaker, the Deputy Secretary of the Navy, the Navy admiral on the Joint Chiefs of Staff, several men from other defense and security agencies, and Captain Peters from COMSUBPAC.

Mr. Whittaker stood up and said, "Good morning, gentlemen. Help yourself to the hot or cold drinks, have a seat, and we'll get started."

When the introductions were over, Whittaker asked Captain Williams to brief President Mitchell and all the others present on the China Sea mission. There was one question after finishing his brief. It was from the President of the United States.

President Mitchell asked Captain Williams to please define "Tango Down" and the meaning of flying a Jolly Roger flag when entering port.

Williams replied, "'Tango Down' announces that an enemy has been defeated in a combat scenario. Flying the Jolly Roger flag with skull, swords, crossbones, and stars implies that a US Navy submarine, capable of carrying out top-secret undersea missions, recently returned home from a successful mission. Each star is for a successful mission. It is also flown to enhance crew morale when entering port."

Mitchell smiled and replied, "Thank you very much, Captain Williams."

Lee was next. He briefed everyone on his responsibilities and actions during the China Sea mission and the subsequent search mission for the two Chinese submarines. When he was finished with his brief, he produced the "pirate papers" (the warrants) taken from the Chinese submarine safe and handed them to Mr. Whittaker. Included with the warrants was a Chinese-to-English translation. After reviewing them, Whittaker passed them to President Mitchell.

Mitchell looked at the papers and asked, "Are we sure these are genuine, and that Lin created them and passed them on down his chain of command?"

Lee answered, "Mr. President, in my opinion, they are genuine. I have used some of Lin's documents when teaching at the Naval War College."

Mitchell thanked the men for their briefs, turned to Whittaker, and asked, "Are we ready to connect to Beijing and President Lin?"

Whittaker had the projection screen turned on at the far end of the table.

Captain Williams asked, "Mr. Whittaker, is the projection screen set up for both audio and visual?"

Whittaker responded, "Yes, we have both audio and visual set up at both ends. President Lin already knows that President Mitchell wishes to speak to him. President Lin has interpreters on hand. Lee will translate for us."

Mitchell picked up the receiver of the "red phone" positioned next to him at the end of the table and pushed a button on the phone. All heard the phone ringing and the visual of President Lin appeared on the screen.

President Lin began. "Good day, President Mitchell. How are you?"

Mitchell responded, "Good day, President Lin. I'm fine and I hope all is well with you and your family."

Lin replied, "Thank you. All is well here. I think I know why you are calling me at this hour?"

Mitchell answered, "Mr. President, I am calling because I am genuinely concerned about what has been happening in the China Sea and all of the surrounding countries trying to annex it as their own. I must tell you, sir, that certain events have been brought to my attention that require your immediate attention and action."

Lin, pretending to know nothing, asked, "What is the problem, Mr. President?'

Mitchell answered, "President Lin, I am sure you aware that a Hong Kong cable layer was attacked and destroyed by vessels of your Chinese Coast Guard or Navy? I am positive that your diplomat here in Washington, DC, has already briefed you and you already know about this."

President Lin looked surprised. He said something to his chief naval officer seated next to him at his table.

Lin's expression turned to anger. He replied, "Mr. President, I know nothing about that. My Navy secretary knows nothing about it either. If it's true, I assure you I will handle it in the most appropriate way."

Mitchell continued, "There's more, Mr. President. Our nuclear submarine, the USS Tarpon, was attacked and sunk in the South China Sea by a Captain Wu. She was sent there at the request of the Hong Kong government because their cable layer was missing, and the Tarpon was asked to search for survivors and there were none. One hundred fourteen men and women of the Tarpon lost their lives.

"A second submarine, the Cardinalfish, was sent to find her. They found her in time to rescue twenty-six of her crew, including her captain. When she tried to return to international waters, she was attacked by this Captain Wu, using three destroyers, an automated underwater vessel, and two of your nuclear submarines. In trying to destroy the Cardinalfish, your Captain Wu lost the AUV, and both nuclear submarines and their crews. When the Cardinalfish managed to return to international waters, Captain Wu turned around and headed back to his homeport somewhere along the Chinese coast. The Cardinalfish safely returned to Pearl Harbor, but in a damaged condition."

Lin interrupted Mitchell. His face turned beet red, and he responded, "Sir, I know nothing about any of this. I assure you I will investigate it and get back to you. If it is true, I will deal out the appropriate punishment to whoever is responsible."

Mitchell continued, "I am not finished, Mr. President. My Cardinalfish, to protect itself, had to disable those twin towers both equipped with offensive laser cannons capable of firing out to a range of two thousand yards or one nautical mile. That AUV, also armed with a similar laser cannon, was also destroyed. All of them can and could be controlled by any of your ships, planes, submarines, or an AUV. My nuclear submarine, Tarpon, was destroyed by one or more of your laser cannons. How do we know that? My deep submersible rescue vehicle took a video as she rescued the twenty-six survivors. That video shows evidence that the stern was cut off by a laser weapon. The Cardinalfish was able to identify the type of weapon used by its sound signature projected through the seawater."

President Lin was now considerably upset. It showed on his face, and it was projected in his voice.

Lin replied, "Mr. President, are you deliberately accusing me of starting a war against you and your country? Considering the social and economic conditions that are currently between us, do you really think I would go out of my way to throw all of that away?"

Mitchell responded, "If it wasn't deliberate, why the hell am I missing one submarine and one hundred fourteen of its crew? There's more, Mr. President. I have in my possession certain documents, signed by you, that detail orders by one of your admirals to have this Captain Wu take offensive action against all foreign flag vessels, including those from the United States, Taiwan, Hong Kong, Vietnam, and Japan. Ironically, they are all countries trying to either obtain sole and complete possession of the China Sea, or they desire to remain independent from China. So why in God's name did you destroy my submarine and murder its crew?"

President Lin didn't know what to say. He was screaming and yelling at his Secretary of the Navy. His secretary was yelling back at Lin.

President Mitchell held up his hands to get Lin's attention.

He spoke to Lin in a calm voice, "Mr. President, may I make a suggestion to you? To get to the bottom of this, I suggest a meeting between you, me, and the nations that have an interest in the China Sea at a totally neutral location. Neither you nor I want a nuclear war. We both know that such a war would wipe out our countries, not to mention the human race. I shall expect an answer in twenty-four hours."

President Lin nodded and responded, "President Mitchell, I do not want a war with you and your country. There is a lot more at stake. I am thinking about the economic aspects of what you owe China. I agree to contact you within twenty-four hours, but I am not sure if I will have all of the answers in that short timeframe."

Mitchell responded, "President Lin, you have twenty-four hours. Goodbye."

Mitchell hung up the phone and turned towards everyone in the room. He wasn't smiling.

Whittaker asked, "Mr. President, you never showed nor mentioned the Chinese warrants that we have in our possession. Why not, sir?"

President Mitchell responded, "Because those papers are my ace in the hole. I refer to the game of poker. You must know when to bluff and when to raise. Right now, I am holding the winning hand!"

Before leaving the room, President Mitchell thanked everyone for attending and providing support for such an important meeting.

The crew of the Cardinalfish and the other attendees were now wondering, with the stakes being so high, if President Mitchell really knew the strategy and winning ways of playing the game of poker.

Cards on the Table

President Lin contacted President Mitchell at the White House within the twenty-four-hour time limit set by the US president concerning the alleged attacks on two American submarines in the China Sea by the Chinese Navy.

Mitchell's phone rang. He answered, "President Mitchell."

President Lin responded, "Good morning, President Mitchell. I trust you are well. I have done as you requested and spoke to Admiral Blejong, our Peoples Liberation Navy head, and to Captain Wu, the commanding officer of our destroyer, the Chang Ling. They both claim that they have no knowledge of such incidents regarding your two submarines, the Tarpon, and the Cardinalfish. They also tell me that they were aware of the cable layer in our waters and that the vessel had our permission to install fiber optic cable across the China Sea. As you know, and can verify, we had a typhoon here and after it passed, the cable layer had disappeared and was nowhere to be found. Our Coast Guard conducted a search from the cable layer's last known position and found no evidence of the ship or its crew."

President Mitchell interrupted President Lin and asked, "President Lin, did you have the opportunity to read and review the Chang Ling's logbook? Entries in that logbook are solely made by its commanding officer. In this case, I presume that it was Captain Wu."

Lin replied, "Yes, sir, I did. There weren't any written entries in the logbook concerning your submarines. The logbook does stipulate numerous entries about practice maneuvers in the South China Sea area using depth charges, but nothing about offensive actions on or against US warships. There are also entries made by Wu while searching for the cable layer."

Mitchell responded, "I see. So, you're claiming that you have no evidence about one hundred fourteen men and women of the United States submarine Tarpon being killed by your laser cannons. Is that correct?"

Lin replied, "Mr. President, how many times do I have to tell you that there aren't any? I am saying that there is no evidence supporting your claims anywhere. Admiral Blejong informed me that if you lost one submarine and had another damaged, it must have been from the typhoon. I'm sorry but that is what I was able to determine."

Mitchell was now very perturbed. He put the phone on speaker, ended the visual, and began pacing the room. Whittaker, sitting in the room with Mitchell, was trying to calm him down.

Mitchell took a deep breath and let it out. He tried not to let his anger appear in his voice as he replied to President Lin. "President Lin, I have videos, pictures, and official logbooks from both of my submarines. I have a video of the Tarpon resting on the shelf of a sea mount after being destroyed by either the Chang Ling, your AUV, or towers. I have recorded threatening underwater conversations between the captain of the Cardinalfish and your Captain Wu. I have official recorded sonar trackings of two of your submarines, which, by the way, were destroyed by Captain Wu's own intolerance, impatience, and incompetence. I also have recordings of your laser cannon, or cannons, being fired at the Cardinalfish and destroying your own AUV."

Lin interrupted Mitchell and answered, "President Mitchell, if you have what you are claiming you have, I would like to read and review them. Would you be willing to share them with me?"

Mitchell thought to himself, "He took the bait!"

He replied to President Lin, "Of course, I would. That's why we have been talking to each other these last few days. I propose that we meet in Geneva, Switzerland, at the Geneva International Meetings Center in three days. I also intend to invite the Secretary General of the United Nations plus members of that organization from the countries of Vietnam, Taiwan, Hong Kong, Japan, Malaysia, Indonesia, and the Philippines. The captains of the Tarpon and the Cardinalfish, plus several of their officers, will also be attending.

"I strongly suggest and recommend that you invite and bring along Admiral Blejong and Captain Wu with all the information and official records that are pertinent to the discussed and identified events between your ships and mine. That facility has secure conference rooms. I'll have the room reserved and scanned before we start the meeting. I recommend using the Four Seasons Hotel des Bergues Geneva for lodging. That is where my staff and I will be staying. I suggest that this meeting be without any media or press present. This is just between you and I and our countries."

President Lin replied, "Very well. I will see you in Geneva in three days. Goodbye, sir."

Mitchell answered, "Thank you for your call, President Lin. I look forward to our meeting and rectifying all conflicting information between us. Goodbye."

Mitchell looked at Whittaker and said, "Ever been to Geneva, Whit?"

Whittaker replied, "No sir, but I guess I'm going with you and not to take in the sites."

A Special Request

Two days later, President Mitchell, National Security Advisor Whittaker, Captains Duggan and Williams, as well as Commander Doyle, Rico, Samuels, and Lee all arrived in Geneva and checked into the hotel.

While checking in, they were met by representatives from several of the countries and territories adjacent to the China Sea.

"President Mitchell, it is nice to see you again. You may not remember me, but my name is Sana Fujiwana. I am the Prime Minister for Japan and her emperor. I, and others from the surrounding countries and territories, wish to have a closed-door meeting with you before we all meet President Lin and his military people. May I ask you to honor that request?"

Mitchell bowed to Fujiwana and then, shaking his hand, replied, "Mr. Prime Minister, may I ask you for the subject for such a meeting?"

Fujiwana replied, "Mr. President, the subject is the China Sea and China's aggressiveness. We do not wish to discuss it out in the open but in private quarters. Our reasons for such a request are to ensure that President Lin does not become aware of our intentions before your meeting. I checked into this hotel a day before you and have a private room for later this afternoon. With your consent, shall we say in two hours in the secondary conference on the second floor? Please bring all of your associates with you."

President Mitchell took a moment to think about what was requested and agreed to the meeting in two hours.

The vice presidents of the Philippines, Indonesia, and Taiwan, as well as the Chief Secretary of Hong Kong, the General Secretary of Vietnam, and the Prime Ministers of Japan and Malaysia all rose as President Mitchell and his group entered the conference room. These leaders all in one room surprised Mitchell and the rest of his group. He wondered what was about to be discussed.

Fujiwana requested all to please take a seat as he began to speak, "President Mitchell, I am going to speak for all members in this room except for Vietnam. Although Vietnam is present, they are a Communist country and wish to remain so for the time being. However, because they are adjacent to the China Sea, they agreed to be here today. They want the China Sea open to all countries, as do the rest of us. That is the reason we asked for this meeting."

Fujiwana stopped for a moment and took a drink of tea, then continued, "We are here today because of the current situation between your country and China. I assure you, all of us, and I mean all of us, have no intention of annexing the China Sea as our own. We merely stated that idea with the hope of stalling Chinese aggression towards all our countries. Alone, none of us can hold back China from taking over our countries. Together, with the help of the United States and the United Nations, we have a chance of retaining our governmental philosophies and our countries."

Mitchell said, "Thank you all so very much for having this meeting with me. I am pleased and honored that you wanted to speak to me concerning this matter. However, we are not here to debate or decide the ownership and openness of the China Sea. May I respectfully request holding that subject in abeyance until the current meeting with China is concluded?"

Vice President Alonto of the Philippines interrupted Mitchell asking, "If your meeting is not about the China Sea, may I ask what your meeting is about?"

Mr. Whittaker stood up to answer, "Mr. Vice President Alonto, we are here today due to the loss of one hundred fourteen crew members of an American submarine who recently lost their lives in the China Sea by Chinese aggression. President Lin needs to answer certain questions and issues concerning this matter. That is why we are here."

Mitchell added, "Gentlemen, I understand your fears and frustrations and realize that they need to be addressed. I cannot and will not talk to you regarding this annexation issue until we, the United States, have finished with President Lin regarding the loss of American lives. You know that it is my responsibility to the American people. My recommendation for all of you, with my support and approval, is to go before the United Nations and present your case. I will communicate with my UN representative and have him reach out to all of you to support and help you retain your goals and objectives on this matter. That's the best I can do at this time. If you do not receive satisfaction through the UN, I am more than willing to meet with all of you again immediately after the next UN meeting and we'll work together for a satisfactory solution."

Fujiwana answered, "Thank you, President Mitchell. We are a little embarrassed about not knowing of your real intentions of your Geneva meeting with China. It is obviously more important and significant than our use of the China Sea. We all agree to wait and see. Thank you so very much for your time."

President Mitchell shook hands with all the foreign nationals present in the room. He made a mental note of talking to his Secretary of State concerning the China Sea annexation or lack thereof.

The next day the American contingent met with President Lin, Admiral Blejong, and Captain Wu.

52

Truth or Consequences

President Lin, along with Admiral Blejong, Captain Wu, and an interpreter, were the only ones representing the Chinese government.

The US Secret Service worked with the Geneva International Meetings Center to ensure the conference room was a classified room and completely secure. President Lin's security staff did the same as well. There weren't any conflicts of interest concerning the conference room and its associated equipment.

Representatives from Vietnam, Hong Kong, Taiwan, Japan, Indonesia, Malaysia, and the Philippines were in attendance for the meeting, along with their interpreters.

The meeting started the morning of the third day with coffee, tea, water, or juice. The meeting center provided some traditional Swiss treats of Meitschibei (hazelnut-filled pastry), Spanish Brotli (hazelnut and apricot jam-filled pastry), Birnbrot (pear, candied fruit, and nut pastry) and Carac (a miniature pie filled with chocolate and covered with a tasty sweet green icing).

The morning coffee session was the last time of the day that everyone was smiling. The Secretary General of the United Nations sat at the head of the table. The Chinese delegation and the United States delegation sat on opposite sides of the table preparing for the inevitable confrontation. The security clearances for each attending member were inspected and confirmed. All was in order from a security perspective.

"Good morning, as you all know, my name is Michael Flynn. I was born in Dublin, Ireland, and I am Secretary General of the United Nations. I will not explain the rules that will be followed at this meeting as you, no doubt, know them. We will follow, just for the record, Roberts Rules of Order. However, I will not tolerate screaming, yelling, swearing, or blasphemy. You will all remain seated at this table, regardless of how heated the conversation gets. I want to make that perfectly clear. Anyone who does not follow these instructions will be removed from the conference room."

Flynn continued, "We are here this morning for two reasons. The first is to try and determine whether the Chinese government took offensive actions against the United States and whether the United States did the same against China. A second reason for consideration, at the request of the countries on the China Sea, is that all countries bordering it are all mutually satisfied with how it will used by their country and other surrounding and adjacent countries and territories."

"I call upon the United States President Mitchell to begin, since he requested this meeting."

"Thank you, Mr. Secretary," Mitchell began. "I and representatives from the United States Navy are here this morning to substantiate and confirm the aggressive actions taken by the Chinese Navy in the China Sea by Captain Wu and his group of three destroyers, two submarines, and an AUV. By having automated control of three underwater laser cannons, he destroyed, without provocation, a US Navy nuclear submarine, the USS Tarpon. One hundred fourteen men and women were killed in that attack. When the Tarpon failed to report in, another nuclear submarine, the USS Cardinalfish, was deployed to investigate her status.

"Once the Tarpon was found, a deep submersible rescue vessel discovered survivors trapped inside what was left of that submarine, unknown to Captain Wu. The DSRV rescued twenty-six men and women. One of them was Captain Duggan, seated on my left. When he was rescued, he had in his possession two items. One was the Tarpon's official logboopok, and the other was a recorded sonar tape, emanating a very low-pitched hum through the water. The logbook details Captain Duggan having a conversation with Captain Wu via the underwater telephone. I submit to you the logbook, the sonar recording of the hum, and the conversation for the official record. I will not leave the logbook with you. That is United States property. However, I'll have copies made of the pertinent entries for your review and, if you desire, for your records."

Mitchell stopped for a moment and took a drink of cold water. He waited a few minutes as Secretary Flynn and all the attendees reviewed the logbook and watched the video of the DSRV rescuing survivors on the room's large projection screen. The Chinese group appeared to be upset, including President Lin. There was a lot of muttering and whispering going on.

Flynn remarked, "Please continue, President Mitchell."

Mitchell answered, "Thank you Mr. Secretary. I submit similar information concerning the Cardinalfish. Here is her official logbook, underwater UQC conversations, sonar recordings, and some videos as they occurred at the time of the incident. There is a large time difference between the Tarpon being attacked and the Cardinalfish being attacked by Captain Wu. He was unsuccessful in destroying the Cardinalfish because a sonar technician who was rescued from the Tarpon recorded that low-pitch hum and a 'pop' the instant before she took on water and sank. He worked with Captain Williams's chief sonar technician, Petty Officer Harry Ross, and they were able to identify that low-pitch hum and 'pop' as being an underwater laser cannon.

"Captain Williams was contacted by Captain Wu, who asked for him to surrender. When he learned that there were survivors from the Tarpon aboard the Cardinalfish, Wu decided to try and destroy her. A Chinese nuclear sub was ordered by Wu to pursue and destroy her. Our sub could go deeper than the Chinese sub. Their sub imploded when she exceeded her own crush depth. You will hear that on the official sonar recording. When Wu knew what had happened, he deployed the second sub to go after the Cardinalfish and she launched four torpedoes to destroy her.

"The first two torpedoes exploded upon reaching Cardinalfish's defensive countermeasure devices. The second two torpedoes continued pursuing our submarine. Captain Williams changed course, increased speed, and headed directly at the AUV. He turned the sub at the very last moment and was able to get out of the way of those two torpedoes. Because of their homing ability, they locked onto the AUV and headed directly at her. Right before they exploded and destroyed the AUV, the AUV fired her laser cannon and took out the pursuing second Chinese submarine. We have submitted all the information concerning these events to you for documentation purposes. Additionally, I have the sonar tapes from the Cardinalfish for these two events as well for your review. But we are not finished yet."

Secretary Flynn interrupted Mitchell. "President Mitchell, can you prove without a doubt that your submarine, the Cardinalfish, didn't launch her own torpedoes at the Chinese fleet?"

President Mitchell asked Captain Williams to answer that question.

Williams answered, "Mr. Secretary, before we depart on any mission, we document by serial numbers all, and I mean all, of the weapons being carried on board. They are verified again when we return to port by the very same procedure. Two of the onboard torpedoes were used to destroy two stationary laser towers on the sea bottom being powered up to destroy the Cardinalfish. I am submitting to you a certified, as authentic, and correct copy of the serial numbers when we left and when we returned to Pearl Harbor. Please note that the serial numbers are the same in both cases, except for the two used torpedoes. The names and types of missiles are blacked out as they are classified information. The Cardinalfish, under my command, took no offensive action against Captain Wu and his fleet of destroyers, subs, and the AUV. This documentation proves that."

Flynn thanked Captain Williams and, while passing the documentation around the table, asked President Mitchell to continue.

Mitchell responded, "Yes, sir. Once the Cardinalfish returned to Pearl Harbor, I authorized, with the permission from our military Joint Chiefs of Staff and the official Chinese government, sending an oceanographic research vessel to the China Sea on a research mission. We told the Chinese government, and the surrounding countries adjacent to that that sea, that we were looking for a specific form of plant life not yet discovered. The oceanographic company, while looking for that plant life, was using a bathyscaphe that happened upon a sunken submarine. That wreck was identified as a Chinese submarine. It was a recent wreck, as there wasn't any evidence of marine growth on the wreckage. A pair of marine biologists found the sub's locked safe quite by accident. It was brought to the surface and opened."

Before Mitchell had the chance to continue, Admiral Blejong and Captain Wu began arguing with Flynn that the research vessel operated under false pretenses and that the information collected was inadmissible. President Lin had no idea what was going on. He was totally shocked at the behavior of both of his subordinates. Flynn managed to quiet things down and had both Blejong and Wu removed from the proceedings to a separate room along with two security people.

Mitchell was allowed to continue. "The contents of the safe were totally intact. The safe remained watertight until the time it was opened on the after deck of the research vessel. The marine biologists found documents written in Chinese, along with money and other papers that were returned to the Chinese government.

"At this point, I would like to ask President Lin a question. What answers did you receive from Admiral Blejong and Captain Wu when I spoke to you earlier in the week? I'm asking if they told you anything about all that I have described to you during today's meeting."

President Lin was obviously upset. He regained his composure and said, "President Mitchell, I had no knowledge about Admiral Blejong, Captain Wu, their activities, and what you just described. I do not condone the loss of American lives. I do not need nor require taking any kind of position that is a precursor to a low-intensity conflict or an outright war with the United States. Our philosophy regarding your country is that we do not need to have a war to bring you to your knees. We can and will do it through simple economics. I will tell you that it is working by the amount of your own country's deficit. I am sure you know it by the many examples of imports and exports you have had to deal with over the last two decades along with the associated costs and fees."

Now it was Lin's turn to take a drink of cold water and continue. "You have come here and presented information that may or may not be true. But you do not have any of the official written Chinese documents, nor the official logbook of the Chang Ling, documenting the suggested actions taken by Captain Wu. As far as I am concerned, he is a naval officer of utmost integrity, that is, until I discover otherwise. If he exceeded current Chinese policies concerning the China Sea, it was not at the direction of the formal Chinese government. That is all I have to say on this matter."

As Lin took his seat, Mitchell opened his briefcase. He pulled out several Chinese documents, closed his briefcase, and asked President Lin, "Well then, sir, how do you explain these? And sir, I have additional original copies of these documents."

Mitchell slid the documents across the table to Lin. Lin picked them up and read them. His face turned beet red as he continued to read.

He looked at President Mitchell and responded, "President Mitchell, I have never seen these before, nor do I have any knowledge of them. I tell you this on the graves of my ancestors. I do not and did not authorize these warrants that allow armed confrontations with other countries."

Mitchell replied, "President Lin, I believe you wrote these documents, and they were amended by Blejong. But in all countries and in all military services, regardless of country, the man or woman in charge is always solely responsible for the actions of their subordinates. I know it and so do you. I also know that you will deal with Blejong and Wu in your own traditional Chinese way. However, sir, I suspect that you did write and authorize your Coast Guard to keep trespassers out of the China Sea. As the top official of your country, you are totally responsible for what happened in the China Sea. Your country, being represented by Admiral Blejong and Captain Wu, took American lives. Blejong and Wu are your direct representatives. They follow your orders. As such, you, as the President of China, are responsible for these deaths."

Avoiding Mitchell's last statement, Lin answered with a raised voice, "Mr. President, you do not have, nor is there any proof of, your insinuations or accusations. I take exception to your remarks."

Mitchell, now smiling, said, "President Lin, yes, I do. Your signature is at the bottom of each of those documents. But more than that, you have a golden opportunity to prove to the world and to the Chinese people that you have their best interests at heart. The opportunity is seated right here before you. Are you willing to sit here with representatives of Vietnam, Hong Kong, Taiwan, Japan, Indonesia, Malaysia, and the Philippines, and work out a satisfactory oceanographic treaty for all of you? The goal is to share responsibilities for negotiating and implementing international fishing, including fishing limits, research, travel, and transportation shipping agreements for all involved countries adjacent to the China Sea. The United States has had, for a century, similar agreements with all countries that are adjacent to both the Atlantic and Pacific oceans, including China. And you don't even have to change the name of that body of water."

President Lin paused and thought for a moment while looking at each representative from the countries of interest. He smiled and said, "President Mitchell, I will consider it. This petty fighting about who it really belongs to is waste of time, effort, money, and resources. I will remain here with these representatives to discuss it and, if agreeable to all present, see if we can come to a workable agreement."

Mitchell responded, "President Lin, there is one more item that needs to be addressed. If we were face to face in the World Court, or in any other courtroom for that matter, you would be guilty as charged for crimes against Japan, Hong Kong, and the United States. There will be no argument nor disagreement with what I am about to say to you. You, as the President of China, allowed your military to kill Americans and destroy American property. That is undeniably an overt act of war. I not only want, but demand, that Blejong and Wu stand trial for murder. Furthermore, your government will pay the United States, or deduct the cost from our debt to you, the cost of building a replacement submarine for the Tarpon. You will also pay for the deaths of the one hundred fourteen crew members who lost their lives in the amount of one hundred thousand dollars per crew member. The American government will pay four hundred thousand dollars for their deaths through a life insurance policy that is held by all military members. I will present this last statement, as a referendum, at the next United Nations assembly. If you disagree, then I will initiate embargoes against your country and halt all imports and exports to and from your country until you agree. I will cease all payments on American financial notes until you agree. If you still refuse or deny responsibility and accountability, I will see you at the World Court.

"Such American actions, as you just said to me, will bring you to your knees. Also, any kind of armed confrontation against the United States, or any other country, by China will bring serious consequences and repercussions from not only the United States, but from the rest of the world. The entire free world will support the United States against you. Why? Because if this atrocity were to happen to them, we would stand behind them and support them. They know it and believe it."

Hearing what Mitchell had to say brought an immediate and deep hate and anger and it showed on Lin's face. He looked at Mitchell and said, "President Mitchell, you demand? How dare you demand!

If Blejong and Wu did exceed their orders and responsibilities, I will apologize for them and I will deal with them when I return home to Beijing. I will call that day 'Reckoning Day.' We do not want nor desire to fight the free world for control and domination. We will continue to do it just the way we are doing it now until the entire globe is Communist and under our control, no matter how long it takes."

Mitchell, looking at Lin, replied, "President Lin, that will be a cold day in hell!"

53

Reckoning Day

President Lin contacted President Mitchell three days after China and the representatives from the countries adjacent to the China Sea agreed to and signed a tentative cooperative agreement over the China Sea in Geneva. In the Oval Office of the White House, Mitchell, along with his security advisor, Whittaker, his press secretary, and the speech writer, were going over a speech to the American people concerning peace coming to the countries and territories adjacent to the China Sea and the loss of American lives in that body of water.

Mitchell pushed the speaker button on the red phone after he was informed that President Lin was calling. "Good day, President Lin."

President Lin replied, "Good day to you, Mr. President. May I ask you to open your video link as I would like you to view live events as we speak to each other?"

Mitchell replaced the phone receiver and selected the video link on the red phone. President Lin appeared wearing a red silk Chinese tang suit with a decorative bright yellow dragon on the front of the jacket. The collarless top was open rather than buttoned.

Mitchell smiled. "Why, President Lin, I see you are going casual today. Nice tang suit! I especially like the dragon."

It was now President Lin smiling as he replied, "Yes, President Mitchell, there are times when I need to be casual and today is one of those times. However, I see you are wearing an old navy-blue sweat-shirt with the sleeves cut off with the words, 'Oh, yes I can!' Why do you wear those words, Mr. President?"

President Mitchell, smiling again, answered, "My wife gave me this sweatshirt a while ago. She says those words to me all the time. It's a wife thing."

Mitchell changed the subject. "And what can I do for you, today, President Lin?"

President Lin's facial expression changed to one of frustration. "Mr. President, Admiral Blejong and Captain Wu have escaped. I have people looking for them. I have been able to account for all my ships and planes, so I know they must still be in China. I am continuing to search for them. I assure you I will find them and deal harshly with them for what they did without my knowledge and authority. I must also tell you that I am somewhat concerned about my own security. I believe Blejong will attempt to create a military controlling regime here in China."

Mitchell nodded and replied, "I am sure you discovered and sub-stantiated the truth about them and what their intentions were." Mitch-ell was remembering the coup that brought Lin to power in China.

President Lin continued, "Yes, I have. I will contact you when I have found them."

Mitchell, said "Thank you, President Lin. I appreciate your call, knowing how close they brought our countries to an open war. The families of the lost Tarpon crew members are still crying out for justice and retribution. Both of us need to go forward with clear and open minds to continue to maintain peace. We also need to do it courteously and expeditiously, if possible."

President Lin nodded and replied, "I agree. Good day to you, sir. I'll be getting back to you when I have them in custody."

Mitchell answered Lin, "Good day to you as well."

National Security Advisor Whittaker looked at President Mitchell and said, "Mr. President, I have been thinking about this whole situation, and I honestly don't like it."

Mitchell replied, "What do you mean, Sam?"

Whittaker answered, "It's quite possible that Lin initiated this whole thing and passed the buck to Blejong and Wu. That way, he's in the clear and those two guys bear the blunt of the blame."

Mitchell responded, "Do you know what, Sam? I have been thinking the very same thing since hanging up the phone. But I don't see any way of altering the situation in finding those two guys or holding China accountable. The only way we would know the truth is to be able to talk to them and I don't think we'll ever get that chance. It's like that old child's game, button, button, who's got the button?"

Whittaker said, "Well, sir, I am willing to bet that both Blejong and Wu have close allies that support them in high places inside their navy. If they were ordered to keep quiet by Lin in writing those warrants, their navy buddies may go after Lin. That premise is based on what we know about all three of those guys and the regular trend of deaths occurring in the high echelons of the Chinese government."

Mitchell replied, "That's what Lin said as well. It just might happen and then our relationship with China will get a lot tougher. We'll just have to wait and see what happens."

Four days later President Lin telephoned President Mitchell.

"Good morning, President Mitchell. I am calling you today with some particularly good news. We found and captured both Blejong and Wu at the Russian/Chinese border near the town of Khabarovsk. They were handed over to us by the local FSB, the Russian Security Service. As you already know, the FSB used to be named the KGB."

President Mitchell asked, "Were they alive when you found them?"

Lin responded, "Yes, Mr. President, they were alive, but had been tortured by the FSB. They were severely beaten and had their tongues cut out. They will never speak again but they can still write. May I please ask you to turn on the video screen on your phone?"

President Mitchell turned on his video screen. The courtyard of the famous Suzhou Gardens appeared on Mitchell's screen. Facing each other were Admiral Blejong and Captain Wu with hoods over their heads, their hands tied behind their backs, and kneeling on the ground.

President Lin asked, "Mr. President, can you see both men kneeling in our beautiful gardens?"

Mitchell responded, I see two men but how do I know that they are Blejong and Wu?"

Lin answered, "Because I say they are. One moment please."

Mitchell could hear Lin giving orders to someone who was not in the video area. Several minutes later, two men removed the hoods of the two kneeling men. A close view of the two men's beaten faces showed them to be Blejong and Wu. Mitchell recognized them from sitting at the conference table in Geneva.

Mitchell answered Lin, "President Lin, I do recognize both men as Blejong and Wu."

Lin responded, "That is good. Now I will continue."

Lin gave orders and the hoods were replaced over the heads of the two men. Two swordsmen stepped beside Blejong and Wu. Lin uttered an order and both men were beheaded.

President Lin replied to President Mitchell, "Mr. President, I am now very sure that justice and America's desire for retribution are now appeased. Other than the monetary aspects, is there anything else I can do for you?"

Mitchell replied, "No and goodbye." Mitchell, Whittaker, and the press secretary were in shock as to what they had witnessed. It was horrific!

Whittaker looked at Mitchell and said, "Would you care to bet how long Lin lives before someone else takes his place?"

Mitchell replied, "No bets on that one, Sam. Let's keep working on what I need to say to the American people to finally settle this matter. We also need to write one hundred fourteen letters to the families of the Tarpon crew. Please ask our Secretary of the Navy to follow up on that issue. I will sign all those letters as their Commander-in-Chief. I also want a memorial service for them here at Arlington National Cemetery. A military medal is appropriate as well. Also, please ensure the families of the deceased members of the Cardinalfish crew receive the insurance money in a timely manner."

Whittaker replied, "Yes, sir. I'll pass along your wishes to the Navy and the military insurance company. The media will also be informed of the memorial ceremony at Arlington Cemetery."

Diplomatic Changes

Secretary of State Susan Nardi was in a meeting with David Ridings, the US diplomat for China. They were discussing the assassinations of Admiral Blejong and Captain Wu. The elimination of these two men brought serious concerns to China's President Lin remaining in power. Admiral Blejong was their top military officer, advisor, and he oversaw the entire Chinese fleet.

Susan's secretary buzzed her phone. "Madam Secretary, there is a Chinese diplomat named Liang Jiayi calling. He wishes to speak to you and Mr. Ridings. Something unpleasant is evident in his voice and I can tell he is upset. I have him on hold on line two."

Nardi looked at Ridings and pushed the number two button on the phone. "Good afternoon, Mr. Jiayi. How are you today and how may I help you?"

Jiayi responded with a shaking voice, "Madam Secretary, I am concerned about the events currently happening in Beijing. May I request an immediate meeting with both you and Mr. Ridings if he is available? It is in both of our countries' best interests that I speak to both of you immediately. I can be at your office in ten minutes."

She told Jiayi to hold a moment and, looking at Ridings, asked, "You heard his comments. Can you stick around and meet with him right now?"

David replied, "Yes, I have no problem with now."

Twelve minutes later, Nardi's secretary escorted Jiayi into the office.

Both Nardi and Ridings stood up to greet him.

After the usual courteous greetings were exchanged, Jiayi accepted a scotch on the rocks, which was highly unusual for him. He took a drink and a deep breath, then began, "Madam Secretary and Mr. Ridings, I asked to meet with you because President Lin is in jeopardy. He asked me to meet with you so that the United States has an opportunity to prepare."

David replied, "Mr. Jiayi, please explain your last comments."

Jiayi continued, "There has been rioting in Beijing and in some of the surrounding provinces. Admiral Blejong was greatly admired and loved by not only our Navy, but by the common people of our country. They are extremely angry about his death and the way it was advertised, shall I say? My government is leaning toward a replacement for not only our Navy, but for our entire armed forces. The potential replacement is General Aiguo Anguo. In English, his name means lover and protector of country. He has advertised his intentions to annex the countries and territories adjacent to the China Sea no matter what the cost. Not only does it include Japan, Indonesia, Vietnam, Taiwan, and Hong Kong, but it also includes Malaysia and the Philippines. He doesn't care that some of those countries are allies with the United States."

Nardi asked, "Isn't that the general who killed hundreds of peaceful protestors in Wuhan Province about three years ago?"

"You are correct, Madam Secretary. He is the very same. If he is brought to power, I am convinced that the tensions between our two countries would be greatly increased to the point of a possible armed conflict. He is ruthless, murderous, and merciless. There are factions, in all walks of life, that support him and believe in what he says and does.

Ridings asked, "How and why could your country allow this to happen?"

"Mr. Ridings, I am sure you know that we are over-populated. We do not have adequate natural resources and food. We provide all types of services, including imports and exports, to sustain life and country. The money that the world provides is predominantly spent on those necessities as well as keeping up our armed forces. Our China Sea is one of the world's best fishing grounds and we heavily rely on what it provides us. This is an attempt to block out all others for our long-term survival.

"I love my country and the job I perform for her. I am not a politician nor a military participant. If General Anguo comes to power, it will be by the assassination of President Lin. When and if that happens, I will ask you and your country to allow me to remain here as a legal immigrant, doing everything in my power to help and assist you in dealing with the new China. I have no relatives in China nor anywhere else in the world. Many of my friends are here and their friendship and support are important to me. There is nothing for me in China. I'm sorry to bring you sad tidings, but it is important that you know and have the time to prepare."

Nardi, now seated next to Jiayi, shook his hand while replying, "Mr. Jiayi, your tenure here these last few years has demonstrated to us that you are an honest man who is and has been open and honest with our diplomatic corps and our country. Mr. Ridings and I will do everything we can to help you remain here in the United States when and if this general comes to power and you still wish to remain here."

With tears in his eyes, Jiayi replied, "Thank you so very much for your kindness and support in my personal matter. But I have one question for you. How will you and your country deal with General Anguo?"

Nardi answered, "Mr. Jiayi, at this time I have no idea. But I can tell you we will try our best to keep the peace between our two countries because none of us here in Washington, or any other place in this country, or the world for that matter, wants another war."

After Jiayi left, Nardi immediately called the President and the NSA to inform them of this last conversation with China's diplomat to the United States. President Mitchell called for a special meeting with all security agencies within the government to discuss courses of change and alternatives about policy and security with China if Lin was to be eliminated. The meeting included the vice president and the secretary of state. The focus was on China's aggressiveness to annex all countries adjacent to the China Sea, her illegal expansion of territorial boundaries, and her threatening interaction with military forces of other foreign countries.

Two weeks after their meeting, President Lin, just as Jiayi had predicted, was assassinated by General Anguo and his army. Jiayi was recalled to China by the military government. He was to be replaced by a former military attaché affiliated with the new President Anguo. After receiving the news of President Lin, Jiayi immediately requested to remain in the United States as a legal immigrant. He cried when they told him he was welcome to stay.

Policy and Security

President Mitchell introduced Susan Nardi and asked her to brief the press conference on Mr. Jiayi's approved asylum request.

Following Nardi's brief, Mitchell stood up at the podium and began to speak to the American people watching the televised State of the Union address. "Ladies and gentlemen, we are here today to decide how to deal with the new regime in China. As you know, the last few administrations of our government have taken a firmer stance concerning her aggressiveness in attempting to annex adjacent countries and territories along the China Sea. She is now attempting to retain her expanded water boundaries up to and including the Philippines, Malaysia, and beyond Japan to Russian territorial waters. We cannot allow this issue to remain unaddressed. Additionally, under President Lin, she created three new bases in the Spratly Islands. We have countered that move by adding three new bases to the two we already have in the Philippines.

"We have permanently stationed and homeported, with Japan's approval, an aircraft carrier battle group in Tokyo Bay. Our reason for doing so is to communicate to the Chinese government, whoever is the president, that we will not tolerate aggressive behavior towards any of the countries and territories adjacent to that sea. Many of those countries are our allies and do not wish to become a part of Mainland China. We will continue to provide a military presence as long as they want us to and with their approval."

After being handed a message from the NSA, the president nodded to him and continued speaking. "Mr. Whittaker just handed me an important message. We now know that China hacked into our experimental weapons computer system using the Supercomputing Center of the China Academy of Sciences, known to us as the SCCAS. They claim they developed their laser cannon all on their own. We know that their technology is way behind ours. So, this official statement of theirs couldn't be any further from the truth. You all know that our submarine Tarpon was lost in the China Sea with the deaths of one hundred fourteen men and women. Twenty-six of her crew survived. Based on the video taken by a rescue vehicle, we know it was no accident.

"In addition, when we met in Geneva, I gave President Lin copies of warrants he signed and disseminated to his Coast Guard to board and escort out all foreign flag vessels trespassing in that sea. Those warrants were amended by Admiral Blejong allowing Chinese ships, led by a Captain Wu, to be aggressive towards any of those trespassers. The new President Anguo has told me that Admiral Blejong and Captain Wu became rogue pirates and were acting on their own initiatives. They were not following the orders of their head of state. I don't believe that either. All the parties involved or included in the Tarpon incident have been eliminated."

After the murmuring died down, Mitchell had more to say. "Ladies and gentlemen, I mention all of these statements to keep you informed and up to speed. We, the United States, and the free countries and territories of the world, will not stand for or tolerate aggressive and offensive actions by any country against us. In Geneva, President Lin agreed upon certain reparations. This new President Anguo has denied and ceased adhering to that agreement. I have lodged a formal complaint to the secretary general of the United Nations. I have also initiated legal actions, through the World Court, against China to reinstate President Lin's agreement for restitution.

"You and I all realize that any offensive action against China, with a man like Anguo in power, would more than likely end in a global nuclear war, and the annihilation of humanity. Quite honestly, I am not willing to chance such a possibility. Working together, here at home and with the free nations of the world, we can and must deter or eliminate all offensive aspirations towards world dominance by any country on this planet. We all have a right to our credence of life, liberty, and the pursuit of happiness. The task at hand is not insurmountable if all the countries in this world are willing to work together without political affiliations. Thank you for your continued help and support in this endeavor."

China Sea Again

Williams, Doyle, Samuels, Rico, Watson, and the rest of the Cardinalfish officers and crew heard President Mitchell's speech. It was worded well but none of the battle information was mentioned. Mitchell did recognize the USS Cardinalfish and its entire crew for a job well done. It ended with Mitchell liking and agreeing to the China Sea mutual agreement and its accomplishing a reasonable semblance of peace within that region of the globe. He specifically emphasized all countries working together for world peace.

The Cardinalfish was still undergoing repairs but was close to being ready for sea trials and her next mission. Most of the officers and crew were on the naval base and undergoing refresher training for their jobs aboard the sub.

At the end of each day, Rico returned to his quarters on the base and spent most of his early evening hours being with his wife and sons. The last weekend before the sub headed for open waters and sea trials, they rented a beach cottage on a nearby island for some quiet, private time. Captain Williams's teenage daughter babysat the boys while they were away.

All the officers and crew accepted Captain Williams's invitation to dinner at the Royal Hawaiian Hotel on Saturday night. He had some words to pass along to them once the main course was over and dessert was served.

He stood up and tapped his glass with his teaspoon and began, "Ladies and gentlemen, our pseudo-captain has a few words of wisdom to pass along to you. Captain Watson if you please! You have the floor."

Everyone laughed and teased Watson about his being in command of the boat while most of the department heads were away in China and DC because of the Tarpon incident.

Watson stood up, laughing as well, and replied, "Ladies and gentlemen, you don't have to worry about a thing concerning going out for sea trials. We are shipshape! My teacher and mentor, Captain Williams, thought it best that I, being the qualified officer here at Pearl, take command of the Cardinalfish while he was away."

Rico interrupted and said, "Are you sure it wasn't because you were the only qualified deck officer left here?"

Everyone started laughing again.

Watson continued, "Mr. Petrone, to address your comment, you are correct! But now I know what it's like to be responsible for a multibillion-dollar nuclear submarine, even while she is out of the water and in drydock. With all due respect to Captain Williams, I would like you all to know that I worked with Lieutenant Martin Wilson, our supply officer, while most of our senior officers were away. It is my privilege and pleasure to inform you that while we are at sea conducting sea trials, all of us will be eating beanie weenies and drinking red Kool-Aid for two weeks! Our fearless leader and friend, Captain Williams, told me to handle everything as if it was my submarine and so I did. By the way, I love beanie weenies!"

Watson received a multitude of flying dinner napkins as everyone laughed at the humor flying around the room. Each person knew that it would be all business and no fooling around following the next twenty-four hours.

Monday morning brought most of the officers and crew back to the Cardinalfish, inspecting, checking out, and testing most, if not all, of the sub's gear and equipment. The drydock began her flooding down at 1300 (1 p.m.). Once the Cardinalfish was free floating, she was moved back to pier two at the submarine base. The crew worked together with shoreside loading parties taking aboard torpedoes, missiles, food, and all other necessary equipment and supplies. Section one had the topside and below decks watches during the evening hours.

The Tuesday morning sun shined on the entire crew as Captain Williams addressed the whole crew on the pier before getting under way for sea trials. He was all business.

After morning quarters, Captain Williams asked the crew to gather around him. He began, "Good morning, all, and welcome aboard to our new crew members. For the benefit of all, I will go over what my expectations are for sea trials. You are to continually listen for new and unusual noises. You are to continue to check and recheck the operations of all the equipment you are responsible for and let your leading department head know about all items that do not seem right. No item is too small or unimportant. Keep a keen eye out for leaks, whether it be drops or a small stream, or worse."

He continued, "Verbally repeat all orders directly as given to you. That way, both you and the person giving you the order or orders know and completely understand them. Do not hesitate to ask questions. If you are asked a question and you don't know the answer, say so. I am proud and honored to be your captain as well as proud to have all of you as crew members of this submarine. Now, let's get to work and get her where she belongs, out at sea. All hands set the maneuvering watch and let's get under way."

The tugs were brought alongside the Cardinalfish. Shoreside power and other cables were disconnected and taken back onto the pier. She was ready to head out to sea.

With morning colors and quarters being over, the maneuvering watch was set, and the tugs took positions forward on the port side and aft on the starboard side to control the Cardinalfish as she moved away from the pier. Together they headed out to the outer marker of the harbor entrance.

The tugs turned the Cardinalfish loose after passing the outer harbor marker and returned to the submarine base. The boat was submerged to periscope depth once the water depth below the keel was at least six hundred feet.

The first thirty-six hours into the sea trials went perfectly. All systems were satisfactory. The reactor was functioning as it should. The oxygen regeneration system and the potable water system were operating without any issues. All electrical systems were carrying the load with no issues. Sonar, radar, and navigational systems were operating normally. The Cardinalfish was battle-ready.

The radio watch contacted Lieutenant Commander Samuels and asked him to report to the radio shack. Samuels thought there was an issue with a piece of the radio equipment, but that was not the case. The watch handed the message clipboard to Samuels as he entered the radio room. He ordered a copy of the message and all messages related to the message subject be sent to Captain Williams at once.

Captain Williams was in the officer's wardroom having lunch with the Doyle, the XO, and Rico. The radioman handed the message board to the captain. After reading the message traffic, Williams passed it to the XO. After reading all the messages, he passed it to Rico.

Rico looked at Captain Williams and said, "This is what President Mitchell and National Security Advisor Whittaker were worried about. They figured it was coming. It was just a question of when."

Captain Williams, standing up, addressed the entire crew on the public address system.

"Now hear this. This is the captain speaking. We have been ordered back to Pearl as quickly as possible. We still have some deeper dives to do, and we'll do them as we proceed back to Pearl. Stay sharp and keep your mind, ears, and eyes on your work and your equipment. We received message traffic coming from COMSUBPAC today that President Lin of the Chinese government was assassinated. He has been replaced by a senior Chinese Army General. China is now governed by a military coup. That is all."

Sea trials were completed satisfactorily, and the Cardinalfish returned to pier two at the Pearl subbase. After arriving and tying up to the pier, Captain Williams, Doyle, Samuels, and Rico were summoned to COMSUBPAC's office. Captain Peters, the COMSUBPAC chief of staff, was waiting for them.

Peters looked at Captain Williams and said, "Here we go again. It's interesting to note that Lin only lasted two weeks and a day before they got to him. We're removing your exercise torpedoes and missiles and replacing them with war shots. You're going back to the China Sea. We'll send your encrypted orders to the Cardinalfish after they are completely written. Mr. Petrone, do you have all of the necessary bottom contour charts aboard?"

Rico responded, "Yes, sir, we do."

Peters replied, "Very well. I'm sorry you and your crew don't have time to see your families before you leave but that's the way it is. These orders come down from the Secretary of the Navy and from the Joint Chiefs. It seems the Cardinalfish has a reputation that she must live up to and the boys in DC have complete trust and confidence in you and your ability to even think outside of the box to get the job done without loss of life or extensive damage to the Cardinalfish. Good luck, get going, and fair winds and fair seas."

Once Captain Williams, Doyle, Samuels, and Rico were back aboard the Cardinalfish, she headed back out to sea. Watson talked to the three officers and informed them that he had managed to get a short note off to their families but nothing about the job or the location.

Once the outer harbor marker was cleared the Cardinalfish prepared to dive to periscope depth and head towards the China Sea.

Rico was momentarily on the bridge with Captain Williams and the two lookouts catching a last breath of fresh air. Rico looking at Williams said, "What was it that Admiral Bull Halsey once said? Oh yeah, I remember now."

Halsey said, "There aren't any great men. There are simply great challenges that ordinary men like you and me are forced by circumstances to meet."

Williams replied with a smile, "Well, shipmate, what do you say we go and meet them?"

CPSIA information can be obtained
at www.ICGtesting.com
Printed in the USA
LVHW081517150922
728474LV00020B/615/J

9 781662 922305